ASTA IN THE WINGS

ASTA

IN THE WINGS

JAN ELIZABETH WATSON

TinHouseBooks

Published by Tin House Books, Portland, Oregon, and New York, New York
Distributed to the trade by Publishers Group West, 1700 Fourth St., Berkeley,
CA 94710, www.pgw.com

Library of Congress Cataloging-in-Publication Data

Watson, Jan Elizabeth, 1972-
 Asta in the wings / Jan Elizabeth Watson. -- 1st U.S. ed.
     p. cm.
 ISBN-13: 978-0-9802436-1-1
 ISBN-10: 0-9802436-1-0
 1. Girls--Fiction. 2. Mothers and daughters--Fiction. 3. Brothers and sisters--
Fiction. 4. Social isolation--Fiction. 5. Maine--Fiction. 6. Psychological fiction. 7.
Domestic fiction. I. Title.
 PS3623.A87245A9 2009
 813'.6--dc22   2008040525

First U.S. edition 2009
Printed in the United States of America
Interior design by Laura Shaw Design, Inc.

www.tinhouse.com

This book is for Aoife.

Contents

Hands, do what you're bid:
Bring the balloon of the mind
That bellies and drags in the wind
Into its narrow shed.

—W. B. Yeats, "The Balloon of the Mind"

BOOK ONE

THE THEORY OF MOVIES

ON THE LAST DAY, the day before everything changed, my mother told me her theory about the movies. It could have been a theory about anything else . . . Mother was always bursting with ideas. A few weeks earlier, she had expressed her thoughts on evolution, which included her conjecture that the towering dinosaur remains in the Museum of Natural History were not dinosaurs at all, but a hoax—a man-made likeness built from human bones.

On this day, however, the subject was movies. I was guilty, I think, of not listening closely enough; I was only seven years old, and greater things beckoned to me. I was busy awaiting the arrival of an insect, concentrating on the sodden strip of bathroom tile—the one just alongside the tub's foremost claw-foot—from which earwigs or silverfish might emerge. Balanced on my haunches, head lowered till my face grazed the floor, I whispered this urgent enticement into the cracks:

"Come out, you big bug."

Above my head but below the lip of the tub, my mother's hand agitated the water. She had a habit of spreading her fingers and raking through the bubbles as if they were in her way.

"Turn the page for me, Asta," my mother said. "I'm about to reach the 'All the world's a stage' speech. Try saying it with me."

I hopped up to stretch my arm over the rim, to reach over the white crop of bubbles that foamed to my mother's shoulders. She kept a tea tray perched on her knees and had positioned her book (a compact Shakespeare that morning—it had been compact Shakespeares for more mornings than I could count) atop the tray with one dry hand.

As was customary, I'd been enlisted to provide the second hand. This task was not bothersome to me. I liked to be in the bathroom at that hour, for the bugs most often emerged just after dawn; I also liked the simmering sound of the bubbles, the sticky presence of steam and vapor in that enclosed space. I even had a fondness for the pages of *As You Like It*, yellowed and softened to the exact texture of muslin. I knew that my touch—my turning—had contributed to that.

"Smooth it down, I can't quite read it," Mother instructed once I'd flipped the page in question. I smoothed it, and she shifted in the water, placed her limbs in better alignment—better to PROJECT THE VOICE, she'd often told me—and began to read aloud.

"'All the world's a stage, and all the men and women merely players,'" she quoted with a piquant trilling of *r*'s. "Go ahead, Pork Chop, try saying it with me."

I didn't respond. Instead, I lowered myself till I lay flat on my stomach and peered aggressively into the rotted tile; I poked at one corner and found it pliable, claylike.

"Is it just me, Asta, or does that line contain a falsehood? Something a little bit off? What word in this line sounds phony-baloney to you? 'All the world's a stage, and all the men and women merely players?'"

That got my attention. I turned my head in her direction, liking a challenge, as well as the word *baloney* (I was hungry), and found myself wishing I had a smart-sounding answer to give.

"Stage?" I hazarded.

"No, *merely*," she said. "Do you know what *merely* means, Asta? It means *nothing more than*. You are merely seven years old, and that is one way of looking at it, a correct way to use it in a sentence. But in this context, doesn't it seem fallacious? It is no mere thing to be a player in these hard times. I know that Mr. Shakespeare had no good reason to anticipate the coming of movies, but still, it seems awfully shortsighted, writing a thing like that."

From the corner of my eye I saw something stirring under the crack: first two pincers and then a long and shining body. Something resembling a shell.

Something resembling an *earwig*.

I laid my finger before it and hoped that this creature would take to me, as I'd once seen a caterpillar take to a stalk—on TV.

"Wiggy!" I hissed between my teeth.

"What's that?" My mother's head surged over the edge of the tub; within a split second she spotted my visitor, dipped her fingers into the suds, and sprayed him in one efficient wrist flick. He twitched once, twice, before scuttling back into the tile.

"Foolish things crawl in your ears and eat the insides of your head," Mother said. "You don't want to be courting those."

I considered her words. "They eat *heads*?" I asked.

"They're not as bad as termites, but still pretty darned pesky," she went on meditatively, as if I hadn't spoken. "What use are earwigs to anyone? It'd be more useful to be a—a fly. Not to *court* flies, mind you, but actually be a fly! A fly on the cellular wall of somebody's brain! The pest, and not the one to whom the pestilence comes! Now wouldn't that be a switch?"

She placed the book flat on the tray, raised both tremulous hands above the water, and clasped them enthusiastically at her bosom. "It is exactly the thing I wish for you to understand about the movies. This is something my own mother used to tell me. Of course, the world's concerns are different than they were during her time—the Silent Era—but our overriding choices remain the same. And there are only two choices—there have never been more than two.

"Are you listening, Asta? You can conduct yourself as if you are watching a movie—with darkness closing in on all sides—or, choice number two, you can conduct yourself as if you are acting in a movie, with your inner light guiding you all the way. Given those two choices, and knowing that these are the only two you will ever, ever have, which would you deem the better one?"

"Acting in a movie?"

"Yes! The better one. We can't afford to reduce ourselves to being mere witnesses. There are times when we must take actions that are entirely of our own making." My mother's eyes fixed on the overhead light above the bathtub. The light wasn't on, but she seemed pleased by whatever she saw up there—as if that dull glass circle had nodded its assent.

"Time flies, but I cannot," my mother murmured, staring at the light. She let both arms slump below the fading bubbles, and the tea tray toppled dangerously to one side. I steadied it, and that seemed to revive her a bit.

The wall-eyed look that sometimes overtook her was replaced by a penetrating one.

"Take that away, would you? And hand me my towel, yes, there's a good girl," she said. "Remind me to take a look at you this morning. Your face is almost as peaked as your brother's. I don't like seeing my children looking so *pinched*." She pressed the drain lever with her foot, and the pipes gave a great belch as the water hurtled toward the eye of the drain. I leaned forward to watch it disappear.

"For heaven's sake, don't let that water touch you," Mother scolded, prodding at my chest with a dripping toe.

* * * * * * * * *

Once Mother had toweled off and slipped into her robe, she took me downstairs to the kitchen, and the daily business commenced.

"Really, Asta," my mother said, giving the skirt of my dress a yank. "Your dress. Would it kill you to pull it up?"

Though I didn't protest, I always disliked the way her fingers went from the lymph nodes under my jaw and armpits to the even more tender ones around my pelvic bones. I'd developed the practice of avoiding her gaze during such probes; I usually stared at the windows, studying the black drapes that were parted to reveal the tar paper on the opposite side of the glass.

The fingers traced and retraced the same circle around my hip bone. "What?" I asked once their motion stopped. "What is it?"

"A lump. You've got a lump here."

Her eyes shone with something like satisfaction. Or was it

impudence? It made me think of the nature show my brother, Orion, and I had watched the week before. The show had featured seagulls, and the plummy-voiced narrator had said that gulls sometimes liked to pluck the eyes *right out* of dead things, as if extracting pearls from oysters.

Mother touched my cheek with her silky, sallow hand.

"I knew you looked peaked. What did I tell you? This time I *knew* it."

I released the hem of my dress. The wool fabric swatted my ankles with the force of an indictment.

"Can you imagine how such a sickness comes into my house when I've done everything in my power to keep you safe? It isn't right." Her voice had a musing quality, an aggrieved softness. She stood and disappeared for a moment into the pantry, returning with her fingers looped in the handles of pinking shears. "I guess I should take care of your hair before work, if nothing else."

I looked at her uncomprehendingly. True, I was used to Mother's brushing my hair in the morning before she left for work; she raked over tangles until my loosened hair fattened the brush and my head jerked backward with the vigor of her strokes. Pain aside, I rather enjoyed this. With my neck so angled, I could study the ceiling and the cumulous cloud shapes (which sometimes transformed into man shapes or tree shapes, as clouds often will) that had collected where the paint had peeled away.

But the scissors were unfamiliar.

I felt something cold and solid against the nape of my neck—a crisp snip. My hair fell free, tumbling over my dress front and around my feet; I blinked as wisps caught in my eyelashes, then shut my eyes completely as the scissors edged closer and closer toward my scalp.

My mother stepped back. "There, that's a help," she said. "Hair is the worst hive of germ activity."

I felt my affronted hair, or what was left; it had become spare and bristly in a matter of minutes. I wanted to ask if she'd hold me up to the mirror so I could see the results but thought better of it. *Don't be vain, Asta—this is hygiene, not beautification,* my mother would be inclined to say. *Besides, you had scraggly little-witch's hair. Now you're a pixie, neat and trim.*

My mother turned her back to me and crossed the kitchen floor, trailing bits of my hair behind her, bits that clung to the soles of her feet. She stroked her own hair—dark, lank hair that hung to the small of her back—until the touch became an absent caress.

As soon as she was gone I pulled a chair out from the kitchen table and clambered up on it. There, in the dusty mirror framed by silver embossed roses, a truculent little boy—my brother's face—looked back at me. Although I was a skinny child, my cheeks had remained obstinately moonchild-round, exactly as his were. And now I had his short hair to boot. I watched my expression change from truculent to grave to amused, till at last a small smile ghosted the corners of my mouth.

I could hear them—Mother and Orion—going through their usual Morning Recitation.

"Anne Bradstreet, 'The Flesh and the Spirit.' 'Dost dream of things beyond the Moon . . . and dost thou hope to dwell there soon?'"

And then Orion's echo, weak but obedient: "'Dost dream of things beyond the Moon . . . and dost thou hope . . . to dwell there soon?'"

And Mother, prodding: "Vachel Lindsay, 'Abraham Lincoln Walks at Midnight.' 'And who will bring . . . '"

"'And who will bring . . .'" Orion began. He coughed then. My expression in the mirror faltered. Unconsciously, my hand went to the hollow in my throat.

"PROJECT THE VOICE," Mother warned.

"'And who will bring white peace,'" I whispered, for this line was my favorite.

"'And who will bring white peace, that he may sleep upon his hill again?'" my brother asked. There was silence. I suppose she kissed him in that silence. I smiled again, greatly relieved, and moved my hand from my throat to the nape of my neck, to feel the new stubble there.

By the time Mother returned to the kitchen, I'd hopped down and tucked myself into the table. She now wore a blue cleaning-woman's smock over a pale-green dirndl skirt. And work shoes, of course. "Asta," she said. "I have to be at work in fifteen minutes so I'll only say this once. You're not to do any homework today. Well—" she amended, seeing my disappointment, "you can do your Bible readings, but there's no need to bother with any of the other books."

"Not even the primer?" I asked.

The primer was the same one my mother had used in her girlhood, with *The Assumption Girls' School* stamped on the flyleaf and her first name, Loretta, indelibly lettered in ink. I could read from it only a little, but I liked the pictures of children who wore proper-looking hats and were always giving tips on how to avoid unpardonable breaches of manners, such as never to take the largest slice of cake off a platter. To do so would be greedy.

"No primer," my mother said. "You need to focus on getting well. I'd prefer you stay in bed and rest."

"Orion and me both," I said after a thoughtful pause.

"Yes, Orion and you both, in your own little beds."

She put on her fox-collar coat and her red rubber zip-up boots (I loved those boots, loved their unabashed cherry-red-ness) and stuffed a pair of rubber gloves into her coat pocket. While she was distracted, I groped under my dress to feel this accursed lump. I felt a tender pang by the jut of the pelvic bone and then the swollen gland responsible for the pang. A mere kernel of a thing!

"Mother," I said, "what would you say are my chances of getting better? Would you say they're not very high?"

She paused at the front door, one slim hand on the knob. "Silly," she scoffed. Her serpentine neck craned against the fox collar. "Come here."

I pushed away from the table and stood before her, in the shadow of her breasts.

"Give me your cheek, Pork Chop," she said, and I did. Her lips brushed my face; they were chapped, dry from the aridity of the house, but her breath was moist. I wanted nothing more than to burrow into that moist warmth and live there like an earwig hidden under the tile. I put my arms around her waist and buried my head against her rib cage, but she extricated me, gently.

"Have a healthy lunch. Orion can help you make it. I'll bring you both something nice for supper later on, all right?"

"And who will bring white peace?" I said, expecting a smile. None came. Mother reached around and adjusted the clip in her hair—an unnecessary gesture, for the clip was already dead-centered as far as I could tell—and with that she was out the door, closing it before I could get so much as a whiff of air.

I must have waited for the rattle of the dead bolts she'd put on the outside of the door. When the rattling stopped, I probably jiggled the knob. I feared a day might come when Mother would fail to lock us in properly.

FORMIDABLE LIVELY

My mother named me Asta after the *Thin Man* movies—after Nick and Nora Charles's dog, to be specific. I'd never seen the film—it was years before I even knew that Asta was supposed to be a *boy* dog—but my mother spoke with great relish about the films she'd seen. Her heart belonged to the actors and actresses of the Silent Era, and I'd seen stills of a younger Myrna Loy, pre-Nora Charles, in the Big Movie Book my mother owned. Pre-Nora Myrna had a naughty Kewpie face and was dressed to look (in my mother's words) "like a Chinawoman."

Mother's vested interest in silent films was a direct result of her mother's influence; my late grandmother, Lucia Lively, formerly Eula Brown, had had a couple of bit studio parts in the mid-1920s, when she was still a teenager. A natural brunette, Lucia bleached her hair gold to attract the cameras, which "had no love for darkness," as my mother put it. For the most part, Miss Lively (as the press sometimes called her) supported the main cast by playing mugging, animated charwomen; she once had three lines of titled dialogue in the role of a U.S. Senator's pretty yet ditzy daughter. But these minor films of my grandmother's had been destroyed. The celluloid had gone up in flames of poisonous and pernicious nitrate, which could burn underwater if one troubled to take it there.

"You should have seen the silent pictures, Asta. So *expressive*," my mother would say, turning page after yellowed page in her Big Movie Book. She would anchor me on her lap and point out each player in turn. "The actresses' eyes . . . sweet Mary and Joseph, look at that eyeliner they gobbed on. Can you imagine having eyes as big and expressive as that?" And I looked at them all, those still, white faces, their bodies in such strange attitudes (all coyly ducked chins and big batting eyelashes, or with eyes that bulged out while their necks were clutched by the hands of villains). "That one, I know *all* about her. She was famous for taking baths in the finest champagne. It left a smell on her like you would not believe. That one liked sticking needles into her arms," Mother would tell me, jabbing a finger to illustrate, "and that one got eaten by her dachshund after she up and died in her apartment and the poor dog was left to go hungry. Died from drinking too much, of course. Weren't those girls pampered!"

I knew my mother thought that she could have been equally pampered, had things gone differently for her; she'd had some stage training in high school and would sometimes wax sentimental about her early acting experiences. "Being someone else allows you to see the whole of things. You have to look at things upside down or inside out or sideways. I could've been bigger if I'd wanted to be . . . I must have been too shy, not formidable enough. But, oh, I remember how exciting it was, standing there in the wings, waiting for my turn to go onstage."

At times Mother's monologues were over my head, but they

could sustain my interest if the words were lovely enough: *for-midable*, for one, was about the prettiest I had ever heard. It was pretty enough to make me decide, there and then, that I should try to look at things sideways. Pretty enough to make me wonder why my grandmother, whom I had never met, had not chosen this as a stage name: Formidable Lively.

It was a pity, my mother's shyness. I would have liked her to have been an actress like my grandmother, albeit longer-lived (poor Lucia Lively was killed in a traffic accident just after her forty-sixth birthday, long after her film career had ended). I would have liked to see pictures of Mother in a Big Movie Book, wearing a drop-waisted gown and a feathered headdress—or perhaps something more smart and contemporary, like a pant-suit. There were countless nights when I lulled myself to sleep with images of my mother onscreen. I would dream of her caught in that conflict between light and shadow, of her flicker-ing image played at the wrong speed—a speed that somehow seemed exactly right.

* * * * * * * * *

The year was 1978. We lived in an isolated Cape Cod–style house in Maine, in the town of Bond Brook, population 849. The next town over was a touristy beach town; its shoreline was infamous, Mother had told me, for having coughed up the body of what was presumed to be the Loch Ness monster but was later identified as a badly decomposed shark. "Such misunder-standings are enough to get newspapermen in a tizzy," Mother sniffed. Admittedly, this all happened in my infancy, and ought not to have had much of an impact. But its legend, or the cor-ruption of legend, was still a part of my consciousness.

We had lived in the house for as long as I could remember. My brother claimed it had not been forever; he had memories of sand beneath his feet, of an airplane overhead, of someone playfully chasing him along a pier—or so he said. His earliest house memories included a babysitter named Rhonda who stayed with us during the day—a girl who couldn't have been much more than a teenager, though she seemed perfectly ancient to Orion. Rhonda spent most of her time filling out magazine questionnaires, every now and then deigning to slap together some peanut butter sandwiches for us, though only upon request. By the time I was two or so, Rhonda didn't come anymore. No one did, except Mother, who came and went, to and fro, from home to work and back again.

My own understanding of the outside world came piecemeal, gleaned from my mother's stories and the ones on the rabbit-eared TV in Orion's room, which played three or four stations (depending on the weather). The television was the God's eye—the jewel of the house.

The TV rarely played movies. It sometimes played community announcements (a fact that pleased my brother to no end, for there was nothing he liked better than hearing about an upcoming baked-bean supper at the Methodist church, even though he had no experience with such events). And an indefatigable cast of TV people paraded across the screen during regular programming hours. I loved watching these TV people, who were always involved in clever occupations (sanding down tabletops, infusing small cakes with honey and wine) and spoke directly to me, as if I could respond. My favorites, though, were the experts on the science and medical shows. From them I learned of the wonders of cellular meiosis and mitosis. I was fascinated by the ghostly looking cells; though confined in their walls, they still had the ability to float, to swim, to butt heads with kindred cells and jauntily sail away. Somehow these ghosts were alive. Somehow they continued to multiply and divide.

A few nights before my mother found the lump, one of the medical programs showed a doctor performing an autopsy—a sight that would have caused Mother to clamp a hand over my eyes. The dead man on the table—the autopsee?—was fat. His belly bulged below his chest, and his features were not unlike Orion's soft-kid paratrooper doll after it had burned in a fire.

The doctor hefted the dead man's upper torso off the mortuary slab. "It helps to think of him as a regular guy," said the doctor, sounding reedy and enervated by the presence of the camera crew. "As someone who had a life once, not so long ago."

* * * * * * * * *

Orion would tell me the story of the black plague whenever I asked him winsomely enough. This was a story my mother had told him more than once; it was a tale trotted out with as much frequency as that of Noah and his ark, or Aphrodite and the golden apples, or the woman with toads that sprang from her lips every time she spoke. While the aforementioned were favorites of mine, the plague story had a special distinction: it had, for me, a ring of truth.

I remember the last time he told me all that he knew. We were in his bedroom having our lunch—creamed corn and Vienna sausages. Had Mother been around, we probably would have had plates and utensils and maybe some napkins to mop up the liquidy corn, but when alone we preferred less formality. We ate with our fingers, in small rations. Mother told us that food weighed the body down, making it less resistant to infection.

While being thin did have its inconveniences—it hurt my bottom to sit on unpadded chairs, and I had to sleep with a pillow between my legs because my knees jabbed into each other—these served as daily reminders of our virtuousness and discipline, two traits that God Himself would surely approve of, we thought. And I must admit to having had a curiosity about all the bones that arose in me, bones most people don't even know they have, bones cropping up with the immediacy of spring crocuses. Sometimes I was a whole bed of crocuses, and sometimes I was a clock with a transparent backing, its tiny gears apparent.

One of the greater inconveniences of our diet was that Orion and I had to pee more often than Mother thought appropriate. Our bladders must have shrunk right along with the rest of us, for our insides clamored to be emptied as soon as we'd drunk anything. Mother was vigilant about the toilet. She wanted to conserve water, she said, but we imagined other reasons: maybe germs or even dismembered body parts—toes and fingers and tongues—would be sent up with each new swirl of water. So Orion and I stood straddling the bowl together, which made the duty companionable, at least. It didn't occur to us that we could have relieved ourselves one at a time without flushing in between! We watched in consternation as the water sloshed around the toilet bowl, and sometimes I held my brother's hand, terrified that a body part would come bobbing up. Orion often said that he half hoped a finger or toe *would* appear, just to enliven things—but just how enlivening that would be, we never discovered.

* * * * * * * * *

Orion was nine years old, and the two years' difference in our ages created an undeniable disparity: he was bigger than I in every sense. Or at least he had been, before his sickness took hold. Each symptom brought singular changes—a purplish, malnourished look in the eyes, a general shortness of breath, and a swelling in his legs that sometimes limited his movements. When bedridden, he looked as helpless and bereft of a kingdom as a felled giant.

But no matter how sick he became, Orion kept certain irrefutable memories for both of us, and this was something I depended upon. He remembered a brief stint in public school before Mother had opted for homeschooling, and he seemed to have retained some knowledge of the skills he had learned. Mother, for her part, attributed his memory to the fact that he was a genius. But what was a *genius*? I didn't know. I viewed him mostly as a boy who told fantastical stories and built model airplanes, piecing the parts together with an architect's passion for structure . . . a boy who played himself at chess and sat furrow-browed over the board for hours. This was the old Orion, the one who stayed with me, and glimmers of *him* came through even when he was at his weakest.

The last time he told me the plague story, the day I am speaking of now, was not atypical. With the TV noise in the background, the two of us sat on Orion's cot and pulled a crocheted afghan over our heads, making a house within a house. "Hear ye, hear ye," we whispered in unison, imitating something we'd seen on some late show or another, but after that we always trailed off, having forgotten what came next. We usually contented ourselves with pushing a can lid back and forth for a while. I pushed it to him, then he to me.

"This meeting should come to order," Orion said out of nowhere, looking startled, then pleased, at having dredged up that lost late-show line. "What will we buy with our dues?"

"Creamed corn and sausages!" I said.

"We already have creamed corn and sausages."

"But soon we won't have them here, we will have them inside us," I said. "And for all we know, the corn and the sausages might be very lonely in our stomachs. They might feel afraid, like Jonah in the whale. If we buy more creamed corn and sausages, there will be enough to keep them company."

That settled, we went about the more pressing business of eating our lunch.

Orion sat with his knees drawn up to his chest, eating the thumb-size sausages directly from the tin and washing them down with the briny sausage water. Bending his fingers into a scoop, he turned his attention to the creamed corn while I kept one eye trained—sideways—on the TV set.

"Orion," I said. "The people on the TV. How come none of them seem as sick as you?"

His eyes flashed on me, irate. "Those shows might have been filmed a long time ago," he said. "For all you know, everyone that you see on TV could be dead now. Or dying."

"Do you think they got an autopsy?" I asked, trying on my new word for size.

"Nah—they get taken to the side of the road, most of them, and are put in a heap. If we went outside right now, I bet we'd still find them, piled as high as my waist—no, my neck." He scowled and reached for another fistful of corn. "I think there might be places where the bodies have been cleaned out so that cars can get through. They get put in dump trucks, stacked on people's doorsteps or in front of churches, maybe."

"Tell me how the plague started."

"I've told you enough times."

"Tell me about the nosebleeds," I persisted. "Tell me all of it, just like Mother tells you."

For a moment I thought he wasn't going to tell me. For a moment there was only the TV voice, buzzing like a fly. Then Orion swallowed, drew his knees closer to his chest, and began to speak—precisely capturing my mother's intonations, her hint of tremolo.

"The plague started some years ago . . . in a faraway land . . . not long after our father died from walking straight into the ocean."

"Like Fredric March in *A Star Is Born*," I added, for I knew Mother's wording almost as well as he.

"At first no one knew it was anything more dangerous than a cold or flu. Then came a swelling in the groin or neck. Livid spots on the body."

"Livered spots, yes," I whispered fervently.

"Glands the size of an egg, or even as big as an apple. Throwing up. Feeling tired. But the surest sign you're a goner is a bad nosebleed. Once that first nosebleed comes, there's no hope for you. You can get a nosebleed just from being dirty, or from putting saliva on someone, or from looking at someone the wrong way . . . the livid spots will spread like hundreds of devil's eyes. Like potato eyes, only uglier." He held up his hands, pinching his fingers into two exaggerated claws. "They grow from the inside out and spread farther in, covering your kidneys and lungs and heart until everything is completely . . ."

"Eaten," I supplied.

Orion tilted his head to swill the last of the sausage water. He set the can down and I took that unguarded instant to reach for him—for the front of his undershirt, which I grabbed in my fists.

"Cut that out!" he said, recoiling.

"I want to see your chest. I want to see if there are devil's eyes on it. Sometimes I can see mine, you know." I hiked up the folds of my dress until my concave chest was in full display; I pointed below my breastbone. "See? There's something moving in there. It *must* be the extra-ugly potato eyes."

"Your dress," he said, disgusted. "Pull it down."

I obliged him. "Tell me about the animals," I said. "How they run wild all over the hillsides. How their owners open their gates wide and let the pigs and cows and horses go wherever they please."

"You just told it."

"Tell me the rest of it, like Mother does."

Orion sighed, but I could tell he was enjoying this authority. He sat up straighter and composed his face until it was convincingly impassive—except for a brittle mirth in his eyes. "The owners push the dogs out and let the cats go free, and the animals walk wherever they please, eating what's left of the dry, dead grass. Sometimes you can see strange creatures feeding off the bodies on the side of the road . . . and these hungry beasts have six wings about them and are full of eyes within. And they rest neither night nor day, saying, 'Holy, holy, holy, Lord God Almighty, what was and is to come.'"

"Amen," I said.

We sat in a respectful hush.

"The beasts really say that?" I ventured, when it seemed all right to do so.

"Yes."

"If they have six wings about them, why don't they fly away?"

"Because," he said. "Because of what was and is to come. That's the answer."

We sat quietly for a while longer; the show with the Chef Man was on, Orion's favorite, and we watched the chef tenderly remove the soft underbellies—the aprons, he called them—of Dungeness crab. Then—more magic—he produced a plate of crabs that had already been sautéed and placed in parsley beds. "A dash of color, see how it adds life to the plate?" appealed the Chef Man, which made me shiver with delight. Orion only snorted.

"The plate doesn't love darkness," Orion said, this time mimicking Mother's voice in a manner that seemed mean-spirited.

There was more to the plague story than Orion had disclosed, and my mother's voice seemed to overlap with the Chef Man's voice until I succumbed to the persuasive force of hers: she spoke of people behind closed doors, in houses I couldn't see. Of half-vacant offices that she was still expected to clean. Of families who enjoyed their last days as valiantly as they could, sealing themselves off from the world to drink wine and cavort around a piano. Of others who said their prayers and did their chores and kept their souls clean to the last. I imagined houses that had become, or were steadily in the process of becoming, entombed. The sound of far-off trucks clanking over bridges meant nothing; there were fewer and fewer drivers, fewer and fewer places left to go.

I wiggled closer to Orion, resting my head against his chest. This time he didn't push me away. "Your heart," I said. "I can feel it going *ker-thunk, ker-thunk, ker-thunk*. It's working so hard."

He shrugged. I listened to the ker-thunking for quite some time, since he seemed not to mind, and I was fascinated by its irregularity: it was like a shy man standing on the stoop of a stranger's house, knocking and waiting for what seemed impossible—an open door. I might have fallen asleep listening to it—this had been known to happen, but I'd also been known to stay awake for hours, tuned in to its staggered beats, its fortissimo, and its *mancando*, its fading away.

Why do I remember these last days in particular? It was, as I said, the last time I heard the story of the black plague in full. Shortly after this night, my mother found the lump in me, and the narrative changed. I'd graduated to *being the story*. What need did I have to hear it told?

THE ART OF COOKING

As a rule, my brother slept for an hour or so after Mother went to work. Each morning, I was left alone with the sound of the humming refrigerator, the cricketlike chirp of the clock, and whatever sounds filtered in from the outside: rain purling down the gutters, whispers that I thought might be falling snow. The last day—the day when my mother shared her theory about the movies—was one of those falling-snow days.

I liked being alone, provided I had books to occupy me. My lessons were something I looked forward to and savored. I would have been in first or second grade that year, had I been permitted to attend the public school in the next town over. But Mother hadn't been impressed with Orion's short-lived public-school experience: "Always got the flu or the measles, or head lice, whatever those kids had," Mother said. "What's the sense of sending you amid all that?" By keeping us at home, she said, she was giving us a fighting chance. (I liked the sound of those words: *fighting chance.* They sounded important—noble, even, in their retaliatory desperation.)

When reading from the primer each day, I liked to situate myself before the living room fireplace. Above its mantel hung a framed portrait of my mother in a bridal gown. Beside this portrait were original paintings of Mother's own making, a display that changed from week to week.

Mother had a manic zeal for seemingly idle pursuits. This zeal manifested itself not only in the act of painting but also in knitting and sewing and the drying of flowers. I don't know where the flowers came from, but there they were, their crying petal-mouths turned upside down from the living room ceiling. Mother also liked decoupage. She'd collect old calendars and advertisements—especially anything that depicted rosy Victorian children or child stars of the Silent Era—and would decapitate the paper tots, pasting their heads to tabletops or any dark surface she could find.

The decoupaged tables and the fainting couch were the objects I loved best in the room. One of the couch's scalloped ends arched upward so that a supine invalid could prop her head up and receive oxygen to the brain. I often wished I could fall into a humdinger of a faint just for the sake of putting the couch to its proper use. Failing that, I sometimes stacked pillows on the flat end of the couch until I had a structure level with the scalloped end and draped a blanket from point to point, making a tent into which I would crawl with a book. In the tent's makeshift darkness, the book's pages glittered and winked.

* * * * * * * * *

On that last morning, while Orion still slept, I sat under the tent and tried to read a promising story in the primer. It was about a girl named Sally Ann who was having a birthday party—that much I gathered from the opening sentence and the accompanying illustration—but when I tried to read further I found I was encumbered by words like *velocipede*. What on earth was a velocipede? I searched the illustration for clues, eliminating the Scottie dog, the ridiculous ribbon in Sally Ann's hair, the picnic basket with its abundance of what looked like small cakes or loaves. I lingered for a while over this picnic basket—its contents spilling out indecently like doubloons in a pirate's chest—and began to feel hungry, so I shut the book and decided to concentrate on the Bible instead. It was sure to be easier reading; I'd heard so many of the stories before, and the saints in its illustrations had a gauntness with which I could empathize.

I suppose I was fortunate in that I could read a little. It came to me rather instinctively, reading did, but even the words I could not decipher had a shapeliness—a *suggestiveness*, in the true sense of the term. I opened the Bible and read a passage near the back of the book: "The Spirit and the Bride say, Come." I flipped through the book's bright plates, looking for a picture of the Bride: Who was she, and why would she beckon to me, of all people? Was she dressed like my mother in her wedding picture—my pearl-bodiced mother with her pearly teeth all glinting?

I poked my head out from under the tent to locate Mother's portrait. She didn't appear to be saying, "Come." She didn't appear to be saying much of anything. Whoever had photographed my mother had allowed her to put a shocking amount of blush on her cheeks, and I was distrustful of such robust color; it seemed eerie and elfish compared with her natural pristine complexion and Orion's and my round, pale, anemic faces.

Was Mother the Bride in question? It occurred to me that maybe the Bride was Mary, but I hoped it wasn't so. While I accepted Mary as the most romantic figure in the Bible and sometimes hoped I'd be next in line to give a virgin birth, I much preferred imperious Jezebel, who'd been tossed from a tower and gobbled up by village dogs who left her remains to rot on the cobblestones. That, I thought, was a whopping good story. Perhaps Jezebel had been wearing a long white wedding veil when shoved from the tower? How spectacular it must have been when it billowed out behind her like a sail!

"Come yourself, Jezebel," I whispered. I put the Bible down to reach for the pencil and notepad that Mother kept handy on the side table. Pressing firmly, I copied the letters—THE SPIRIT AND THE BRIDE—for my mother to review and critique when she got home. My hand moved practically of its own accord, as if it were a planchette. SAY COME JEZEBEL, I printed. I shot a look at Mother's portrait again. She smiled a reassuringly false smile above the mantel, and her firm chin tilted at me as though encouraging me to press on, so I made up a tuneless sort of song that fit the rhythm of my moving hand:

The Spirit and the Bride say, Come, Jezebel,
Right before she fell,
Right before she fell.
The Spirit and the Bride say, Come, Jezebel.
But she said a magic spell
So she wouldn't go to hell
and ended up in a dog's belly . . .

I was pleased with this song and drew out the first vowel sound in "belly" till it rang against the top of my head. My voice always acquired such power when I sang under the tent! I drew a deep breath to sing the song once more, and then heard something—a terrific clatter—up above the ceiling tiles.

God?

I turned my face upward in anticipation.

Orion. It took me a second to realize. He had a knack for falling out of bed, particularly first thing in the morning, and had incurred countless bruises from rolling smack out of a dream and onto the hardwood floor. Mother joked that this was nature's way of curbing his slothfulness; it could not be denied that he required more rest than a normal person.

I dropped my work, flung back the tent flap, and padded down the hall to the staircase. I lived for the moment when Orion woke up. I wasn't supposed to wake him myself, but sometimes I couldn't resist; he was never ill-tempered when he awoke but seemed fuzzy and dazed as a newborn kitten. Now and then I'd jump on his cot and put my arms around him, resting my face close to his so I would be the first thing he saw of the day.

He'd always look back at me with one eye closed: "If I try to look at you with both eyes," he would say, "I see two of you."

And I would jerk my head back and forth to confuse him, to make it seem as if there really were two Astas.

"Orion," I managed to gasp now, having run out of breath near the top of the stairs, "Orion, are you up?"

There wasn't a sound from the other side of the door. I waited a few seconds, then went ahead and let myself in. At first there was nothing to see but the spartan room, with its bare walls and floor, the bureau that held the rabbit-eared TV and an assortment of over-the-counter medicine bottles, and my brother's forlornly narrow cot. Then I noticed something else—one of his feet protruding from under the cot—and I bent down to seize it in both hands.

"Orion, come out and talk to me."

It took a bit of adjustment, an unseen shifting of hips and elbows and knees, before Orion's foot retreated and his cow-licked, blinking head appeared in its place. Often when Orion fell out of bed, he couldn't be bothered to crawl back in it, opting instead to worm himself into the dark, safe space under the cot.

"Your hair!" he blurted out. "What happened to all of it?"

I touched it and smiled a modest smile. "I have the plague."

"No!"

"Yes!"

Orion wiggled his shoulders and emerged in full from under the cot. Wincing, he sat up and rested his back against the cot's frame, running his hands up and down his calves, which were bare below his rolled-up pajama bottoms. The wince became a grimace. He was forever losing sensation in his legs. "What makes you think you have the plague?"

"I have a lump."

"Big or small?"

"Small," I said. "But it'll get bigger, don't you think?"

A startling noise distracted me then. For a few seconds I forgot about my lump, looking up at the high single window in Orion's room, which had one loosened corner of tar paper *flap-flapping* outside the sill.

"I was standing on my bed to reach the window," Orion offered helpfully, following my gaze. "But I got hot and sort of dizzy. I must have leaned over too far."

"I thought you fell out of a dream."

"No, just off the bed."

"You know you're not supposed to play with the windows," I said—Mother in miniature. "You know you're not supposed to touch them!"

"I wanted to see if there's a ledge that sticks out from the window. Maybe there's one big enough to sit on." Orion had been enchanted by the idea of ledges ever since he had seen a TV man crouched atop one, hammering shingles. "But I couldn't get a good look and now it feels like I hurt something when I fell. My legs aren't doing what I want them to do."

I managed to take my eyes away from the window's exposed, frost-covered corner. "Your legs are probably just sleeping," I said, staring at them. The calves were swollen and a little discolored—almost blue. I watched as my brother pressed one, his thumbprint leaving a mark that didn't disappear for a good while. "Do you want me to sing a song to wake them up? I made up a new song."

His brow knitted in discomfort—whether at my proposal or in actual pain, I could not say—but I placed my hand on his left calf and began to sing, perhaps a little less tunefully than before:

The Spirit and the Bride say, Come, Jezebel,
Right before she fell,
Right before she fell . . .

and ended the song with a good, hard slap.

Orion made a rattling noise in his throat, which I took to be a sound of appreciation. I began kneading his calf muscles with my fist. "Is it working?" I asked. "Am I helping?"

I enjoyed attending to Orion in my mother's stead. Massaging the blood back into his muscles made me feel powerful. I liked his body, its comforting similarity to mine: the short feet, the knobby anklebones, the hip bones that jutted like handles. Then the rib cage, with its grooves and minute indentations that begged for me to dig my fingers in and get to whatever soft thing lay below. Above that, the symmetry of the collarbones, the shoulders that stood up like little bird wings, and the bumps at the backs of our heads.

More than anything, though, I loved my brother's face. I loved it not only because it resembled mine, with its full lips and abbreviated nose, but also because it was where his breath came from. His breath was warm and smelled like syrup of ipecac, reminding me of the sweet sickness of vomit.

"You're not doing that much good," Orion said. He said it rather politely, all things considered. "I'm not sure anything will help."

"Maybe a bath would make you feel better," I said and giggled—scandalized by my idea.

Only Mother had free access to the claw-foot tub in the bathroom. We were not allowed to bathe when she wasn't present, and even then, we seldom bathed more than once a week; Mother said that bathwater was dirtier than kitchen water and regular exposure to it was not good for boys and girls. But when Mother was feeling indulgent, Orion and I took baths together, and a model airplane, floating belly up, joined us in the tub. What fun it had been when Orion made shrill dolphin noises from the *Mysteries of the Sea* show and had sent the plane swimming nose first toward me!

"I miss our bath toys," I said, staring at Orion's legs; he had elevated them and, bracing himself on his palms, was scissor-kicking the air in an effort to rouse the blood. "Especially your plane."

"My F5F Hellcat! What'd it have to go and get burned up for? And my B-24 Liberator. The Liberator was the best toy of all. It was like a submarine once its wings fell off."

"Remember when Mother put talcum powder on the floor?" I wiggled my toes at the memory and impulsively reached for Orion's knobby, numb ones. "And we stepped in it—"

"And pretended we were on the sands of the Sahara?" Orion finished.

"Yes!" I cried out. "She wore her face paint and dark lipstick. 'EMOTE, children, don't forget to EMOTE,' she said . . ."

"'Especially the sheik, children . . . he's the one who really has to REGISTER EMOTION . . . '"

"He did that very well," I said in my normal voice, and I smiled at my brother. Orion, naturally, had been assigned the role of the sheik. But we hadn't played that game again. Not since my mother, in a fit of inventiveness, had given the stage direction, "Sheik, rend your shirt! Rend your shirt with passion!" and Orion, looking doubtful at first, unraveled a frayed row of stitches from the sleeve of his pullover sweater. Mother, snapping back to reality, ended the game immediately. She grumbled about this afterward as she slouched over knitting needles, though neither of us had understood what the fuss was about.

"That sand was nothing like real sand," Orion said. "Powder is powdery, and real sand is *porous*."

"It doesn't matter. You don't have to be the sheik ever again," I said. "We could act out a different movie, just the two of us. We could make a movie about finding the right medicine to cure your leg."

"It'd be as good as a science show and a mystery show rolled into one if we could do that." Orion paused, his legs frozen in midair like a cat arrested in the act of washing itself. "But how could we make a movie without Mother?"

This was a legitimate question. Orion and I did engage in movielike activities throughout the day, slurping our soup and smacking our lips with what we hoped was cinematic relish, talking to the people on TV—sometimes I leapt from Orion's cot to kiss the lips of whoever was onscreen, delicious electricity buzzing my lips. Sometimes we made movies about doing homework or hiding under the bed. But we had never consciously, systematically made a movie in which *plot* played a part, and we were used to Mother's stage directions, her sense of exactly how and when we should EMOTE. What would we do without those? Every feeling had an accompanying gesture—eyes rolled upward for atonement, hands upraised for mortal fear—there were endless correspondences, and too many emotions for us to possibly remember the gestures on our own.

Orion chewed his lip. He seemed to take counsel from the blank TV screen, a bit of flustered pink showing around his cheeks. "Could you hand me one of my bed pillows, Asta? I just might have an idea."

I handed him the one I considered the nicest: the pillow most redolent of his shampoo. I looked on as he began an elaborate manhandling of the pillowcase. He removed the pillow and, holding the empty case at arm's length, assessed it before rolling it up from the bottom and placing it over his head. It fitted his skull, more or less, with little danger of falling off.

"This detective hat will help me think," he said. "And I've already had one pretty good thought. Do you remember the TV show where people were making healing potions out of plant extracts?" He pronounced that last word, *extracts*, very carefully, and his face grew pinker still. "You remember? The one where they made a mustard plaster and put it on a man to make his chest feel better?"

Immediately I felt myself brighten. "And they made tea out of tree bark and water?"

Orion, nodding, said, "Imagine—if a little mustard plaster on the chest can work medical miracles, just think of what mustard plaster smeared over the whole body might do."

"It might seal in the juicy goodness," I said.

"You're thinking of the Chef Man. But anyway . . . we might not have any plain old mustard, but a can of something with a mustard ingredient might work the same." He waggled a sage and mysterious finger before my face. "What is it that Mother told me the other day when I was working in my math primer? 'A sum is as good as its parts.'"

"Yes," I replied, "some of the parts are almost as good."

Having received that affirmation from me, Orion pronounced himself well enough to stand. I clasped him under the armpits—he was not at all heavy—and helped him to his feet. He turned out to be more bandy-legged than I'd expected, and at one point I thought that his knees might give way entirely; but he rallied and, grabbing the bureau for leverage, inched steadily toward the wall—putting one foot in front of the other, first testing his weight on each.

At the top of the stairs he sat down, hard, and asked me to bring his pillow to him again. He wanted to place it under his bottom so he could slide all the way down the stairs without getting black and blue. I fetched it for him, then raced downstairs to await his flight; from my mooring at the foot of the stairs I stretched my arms as wide as they could go.

"Come straight down," I said. "I want to catch you."

"It's physically impossible for you to catch me like that. Put your arms in front of you like this."

I looked up at him, noting how far away he seemed as he demonstrated the positioning of the hands. I rearranged my own and shouted, "Come to me!"—the certainty of having my gesture down pat bolstered the intensity of my performance—and Orion came bumping down the stairs. As he neared me, I sidestepped, and Orion landed on all fours, his pillow softly descending behind him.

"Ow," he said, with a face full of reproof.

"You were going much too fast," I said unapologetically. "You might have killed me."

Orion let out a beleaguered sigh. His back cracked as he arched it. I arched my back as well, but no *pop*.

"I think I'll just crawl to the kitchen from here," he said. "It's easier."

Without a word I dropped to all fours and began to crawl alongside him. I thought that if I had to do that through eternity—crawl at his side until my knees and hands hurt—then there were much worse things, much worse things by far.

* * * * * * * * *

Orion and I sat cross-legged on the kitchen floor, with the countertops and all the kitchen paraphernalia—the hanging copper pans and the gaily woven potholders—miles above our heads, forgotten relics of the everyday world.

Clearing out the lower cupboard had proved to be light work, for there were only three cans left on the shelves, each one stripped of its label. We surmised that Mother was overdue for marketing; she shopped at the warehouse in town twice monthly, getting the greatest possible discounts on outdated canned goods and items sold in bulk. As for the cans' being stripped, there was no one to blame but myself for that. I'd had the idea that the colorful labels were about the right size for homemade paper dolls, and Mother agreed with me, even helping me peel some of them off and cut them into shapes. I'd thus amassed a fair number of paper dolls with the odd appellation—SAUERKRAUT or BOUILLON, though often hacked down to read ERKRAU or LLON—printed across their backsides.

"You and your dumb paper dolls," Orion said, staring at the three denuded cans. "What we need now is a way to figure out what is in these."

"How about a can opener?" I suggested.

"I don't think I'm hungry enough to eat three cans of food right now, but if we open them and don't eat them right away, they'll go bad," Orion said. "Maybe we could put everything together in one big bowl and store it in the refrigerator for later."

My brother instructed me to get the can opener out of the drawer and a large plastic mixing bowl from under the sink. I handed him the former and placed the latter on the floor. I sat across from Orion, who had arranged all three cans between his splayed ankles, and waited anxiously as the can opener dug into the first one.

"Come out, mustard," I whispered.

But we could tell right away what the can had to offer. A liquid bead of broth appeared as soon as the lid was punctured; once the can opener had made its full rotation, the severed lid bobbed indifferently on the broth.

"Chicken soup," I said.

"*Damned* chicken soup," Orion said, one-upping me.

I took the can from him and dumped its contents into the bowl until drops of broth splattered my face. I shook the can long past the point of emptiness, wanting to expel every imagined drop, until Orion tapped me on the leg. "Beef bouillon," he said, handing me a second can.

"You're supposed to wait for me before you open it!"

"Not necessarily. Sometimes the detective can go ahead without the assistant and fill her in on the details later."

Emptying the second can quickly, keeping a steely eye on Orion lest he even think of forging ahead without me, I said, "Before you open the next one . . . what do you think of saying a little prayer for something other than soup or bouillon?"

"I don't think much of it."

"But you're good at prayers. You always know what to say."

Orion gave some thought to the compliment before sighing and bowing his head over the can between his ankles. "Heavenly Father," he prayed flatly, "please give us something that isn't bouillon or soup, something with mustard, so that my legs won't be so stiff and blue and fat anymore, and so that I might have a chance of getting better. No one should have blue legs, Father, even those of us who do go standing on beds and looking through gaps in the tar paper without meaning any harm. Amen."

"Amen," I seconded.

The third can also held bouillon. For a moment I was too injured to speak. I had so hoped that Orion's idea would not fail us, that the TV wisdom would not mislead us, that God would shine down upon us and be gracious in His mustardly benediction. I hardly knew where to allocate the blame.

"It's not over yet," Orion said. "I'm not sure that the cupboard's stripped bare. It might not be *in puris naturalibus*."

"It is, too, empty," I said sullenly. I thought it was in poor form for Orion to be showing off his vocabulary at such a time as this.

In response, or rather in lieu of one, Orion turned away from me and thrust his head and upper torso into the lower cupboard, cursing ("Crikey!") as he struck his elbow on a shelf. He scanned the darkest corners for displaced cans. At last he happened upon a metal container—the sort that had a plastic peelaway lid, which, once removed, revealed a collection of teabags so old they'd gone stiff; some of them almost seemed ossified.

"Didn't the TV people say tea was a kind of medicine?" Orion said, prying a teabag loose and squinting at it. "They did, didn't they? It has all-natural herbs of the earth inside it. Here—you'd better hold this."

I clutched the can to my lap, pleased to have been given its custody.

Orion disappeared into the cupboard again. "There's something else in here," he said, muffled.

I tried to squirm closer to him, and he brushed at me with a free hand.

"Don't. You're blocking my light." He emerged holding a wide glass jar that was half filled with murky, pulpy juice; leaning in for a better look, I saw a wart-covered thing floating inside.

"It's alive," I said, revolted.

"No, it's a pickle. An old one, too, I bet." I watched Orion as he unscrewed the lid, fished out his prize, and held the thing to the light in a cursory search for visible contaminants. Finding none, he bit off the pickle's end with a satisfied, wet-sounding crunch.

"Are you sure that's really a pickle?" I asked as he swallowed the last of it.

"Pretty sure," he said, turning the jar over in his hands to read the label. "It says *pickle* right on it. It says right on the back that it's made of cucumber . . . vinegar . . . sugar . . . mustard powder . . ."

It took a second for this to register; my mind closed on that last word, *powder*, and I thought again of Orion as the sheik on the Sahara's talcum-powder sands. Then I noticed the light of small victory breaking over Orion's face.

"Oh!" I said.

What followed was a solemn procedure. Following my brother's directions I boiled hot water on the stove, soaked three of the teabags, and found a dry dishrag to absorb the pickle juice. I rubbed the teabags over his calves until his legs drooled amber, all the while admiring the perfume of the earth that rose from those steamy pouches; I dipped the rag in the pickle juice and wrung it over his face and forehead—at which point solemnity gave way to mad tittering.

"You're dripping all over the floor," I observed. "All the medicine's going to run right off you."

"I'd better be wrapped up, like a mummy."

"Or a turkey. We could wrap you up and cook you so that all of those juices are sealed in, like the Chef Man does."

"You can wrap me up and cook me for an hour. Not one minute more."

"Should I get the blanket and belts?" I asked.

Orion agreed that would be a good idea, so I ran upstairs to the bathroom to fetch a blanket and several of Mother's narrow belts. Mother had once devised a game called Rattlesnake: she'd placed us in blankets and rolled us up like crêpes, leaving only our faces exposed and securing our middles and ankles with belts. We shimmied our torsos and snapped our jaws at each other like venomous rattlers. It had made Mother laugh to see us writhe from one end of the room to the other; it was fun, even empowering, to learn that we still had mobility without the use of our arms and legs.

Orion lay waiting for me in his spreading puddle on the kitchen floor. He took the blanket I provided and allowed me to help him with tucking its edges around his body. This was a clumsy endeavor, made worse when it came time for the belts to be fastened—I had no recollection of ever having had a belt, and since it had been a while since I'd owned a pair of shoes or a coat, I was unsure how things clasped and tied—but we somehow managed to bind the blanket around him.

"What am I going to cook you in?" I asked. "The oven?"

"No, not the oven. I'll never fit between the racks," Orion said. "What about the hamper in the pantry?"

Orion writhed snakelike to the pantry while I egged him on with cries of "Toil in the Earth, ye serpent!" and "Eat dirt! It is your destiny!" Upon reaching the hamper, I emptied it of its few soiled linens and tipped it over so Orion could slither inside. He advised me to let him out at 11:00 AM, explaining in detail how to recognize it on the clock (I could not then tell time very reliably), at which hour he would have achieved the perfect state of crackling brown goodness. I righted the hamper with him inside it, left Mother's copy of the Big Movie Book propped under the lid—a little fresh air couldn't hurt him, I reasoned—and kissed him good-bye.

My step was light as I returned to the kitchen to drain the last can of bouillon. The heat was rumbling through the old baseboards at last, which for me was always proof of the day's

RESEMBLING OURSELVES

MOTHER ONCE TOLD ME, when I was too young to appreciate it, that it is only through others' perspectives that we come to understand who we are. Or, to put it her way: "Not until we're shaped by others do we end up resembling something that looks like ourselves." But I'd like to think Orion and I were born fully formed—Athena and Apollo, sprung from the head of Zeus—and we resembled not ourselves so much as each other. That was the way I wanted it. That is the way I like to think of it still.

It was perhaps because of this acute sense of kinship that Orion's hour in the hamper did not pass without interruptions from me. I could not bear to have him where I was not. I'd gone back to my Bible homework, hauling the book from the living room to the kitchen table, which was right in front of the clock; I turned from page to page in a state of distraction, paying less attention to what I read than to the minute hand's slow progress. Whenever the solitude became too much for me, I left the table and went into the pantry to see how Orion was coming along; I don't know if I expected him to rise like a yeasty loaf, but I was inevitably disappointed with what I saw each time I opened the hamper lid.

"Put that lid down," he said after the fourth intrusion. "Can't you see I'm cooking?"

No question about it: Orion did look hot. His close-cropped hair feathered sweatily around his temples, and his expression was one of unmistakable concentration.

My brother could be so willful when he was concentrating. The thinner he grew, the more frequently he engaged in what Mother called trances—the lolling-back of the head, the firm pressing of his eyelashes against his cheeks, the tightening of his hands into fists. I'd asked him once what he saw when he went into these trances, and he said, "Oh, magical things. Lots of things that are purple and blue, up in the air. And I see myself walking down a green hill."

"And who will bring white peace, that he may sleep upon his hill again?" I'd quoted hopefully. But Orion had only shaken his head, declaring that there was not a speck of white to be found anywhere in his visions.

Never having been able to see such things on my own, I envied him.

I closed the lid of the hamper and retreated on tiptoes. But how heavily I slumped in my chair once I'd returned to the Bible! I'd left it open to a plate of thirteen men competing for elbow room at a long supper table. All the men wore robes, and most seemed to have no legs; I looked from one man to the other, mentally comparing their faces to those of the actors in the Big Movie Book. What ripping silent movies they could make, these men! Perhaps the subtitles would reveal that their legs had been blown off in a battle. Perhaps their legs would have to be restored with the help of herbs applied by a clever little girl who would gladly join them for supper in the end.

"Asta?" a voice was calling. "Asta, I have to come out now." The voice had a note of urgency, I thought, glancing at the clock. The time that had elapsed was still shy of one hour. Nevertheless, I went to the hamper and opened the lid again. Orion's eyes, no longer shut, were black and slick and beseeching.

"I think I'm going to throw up," he said.

No further prompting was needed. I gave the hamper a push, tipping it right over until the lid splayed open and Orion came slowly wiggling out, a bewildered moth emerging from its chrysalis. I bent down to undo Orion's belts and he thrashed and kicked his way out of the blankets. As he got to his feet, I was right behind him and considered mentioning that he seemed to be walking well; wasn't that a good sign? But before I could offer these words of encouragement, Orion shut the bathroom door an inch before my face.

Presently I heard the sound of retching, and I opened the door in time to see my brother crouched by the toilet bowl. His vomit was nothing impressive: just the bright green bile and mucus that an empty stomach houses. "The pickle must have been bad," he muttered and hung his head as the syllables echoed against the porcelain.

"But don't you feel better, dear?"

Exactly the wording Mother used when she gave us syrup of ipecac! She swore this flushed our bodies of residual poisons whenever we got the flu, and she'd cover our heads with caresses as we gasped and heaved over the toilet bowl. We did, in truth, always sleep better afterward—growing placid and resting as soundly as if we'd been drugged.

But Orion only gave a blank sort of look, seeming not to hear me. He had some dribble on his chin, but he seemed oblivious to that too. When he did manage to find his voice again, his words were thick and a little distorted. But it was what he said, not the way he said it, that heartened me.

"You know what?" he said. "I think I do feel a little better now." And he lifted one leg at a time, looking closely to see the lean, pale flesh where the swollen blue had been.

* * * * * * * *

Vomiting had tuckered Orion out. We resorted to watching TV in his bedroom for a while, even though TV was forbidden at that hour; Mother was most particular about when we watched programs, yet sometimes she made exceptions when Orion and I weren't feeling well. After giving it some thought, we agreed that day might be one such exception.

Settling once again on the cot, my brother pulled his blanket up to his chin. I tugged at the knob of the TV set and waited for the crackle of static to subside, the dilation of the screen's foggy eye, before curling up beside him.

A basso voice intoned through the fog: "Sierra Slims makes great smokes! Just ask Debonair Don what *he* thinks! Oh, wait—you can't!" The onscreen image of a smoking, smooth-haired man in a tailored suit had a caption at the bottom: "1933–1977." The picture fizzled and faded until it was replaced by an ominous black screen and the sound of a persistent cough. "Brought to you by the American Lung Association," came a second, funereal voice.

I glanced at Orion. He often chimed in with the commercials, but now he sat silent, his brow puckered. I wondered if he had momentarily forgotten Mother wasn't there. My brother was afflicted with a bit of a lateral lisp, and sometimes Mother would try to cure him by pricking his recalcitrant tongue with a toothpick. I practiced saying my *s*'s aloud just then—"Sssssierra Ssssslimssss"—and took stock of my flawless delivery. I nodded at Orion, but he stared stonily ahead.

Although commercials were easy to memorize, Orion and I did not care much for them. I suppose this was because Mother made fun of the actors, calling them pedestrian pitchmen and saying they lacked EMOTIONAL RANGE. It seemed to be in our best interest to share her values, even if certain products— hot cereal, cake mixes (things I'd never seen, much less eaten)— gave me some emotional excitement of my own. And sometimes, though less frequently, there was the thrill of identification. As the cigarette commercial ended and a toothpaste commercial began, I wiggled one of my teeth, which had become loose only a few days before.

Fingers in mouth, I nudged Orion, and together we sang the jingle back at the screen:

You'll wonder where your bad breath went
When you brush your teeth with Hint-o-Mint!

"AND NOW BACK TO CLASSIC TV TUESDAYS," came the announcer's voice, startling me into a more attentive posture.

"Heavens, isn't this something?" I whispered to Orion. This was a phrase of Mother's that I had never understood—was not everything something?—but she always said it in such a reverent tone.

The featured show began. A gnome of a man in a checkered coat and a matching Tyrolean hat bounded on the screen and began to sing, starting the song in a twittering yodel and romping through dizzying scales from there. As he reached the last line, the camera panned across something that almost made me leap off the cot.

Children. Rows and rows of children sitting in bleacher seats. Girls in smocked dresses, their hair cut bluntly in china-doll bangs. Boys whose plump knees were made conspicuous by short pants. Children like us, and yet not like us. Children from the outside.

"HOORAY!" shouted the children in unison.

Without thinking about it, Orion and I had lowered ourselves from the cot and were inching closer and closer to the TV, our eyes devouring the antics of the gnomelike man and of the laughing, swaying, fidgeting children. At one point I placed my palms on the screen, framing the action between mouth-moistened fingers until Orion shooed my hand away.

"I can't see when you do that," he said peevishly.

"Where did all those children come from?"

"What do you mean, where did they come from? Can't you be quiet? You're ruining the singing."

The singing was now being performed by a little girl not much older than me, a girl whose thin voice and extreme unction were compensated for by a marvelous blondeness and charm and coquetry that I lacked.

"Look how she dances," I whispered. "Do you think she's dead now? Do you think this show was filmed a long time ago?"

"Probably," Orion said. But I could see that he was frowning again, that he was puzzled.

"It doesn't seem right that someone like that would get sick and die."

Orion countered, "Why shouldn't it be right? It's what *happens.*"

The children applauded by banging the fat pads of their hands together, their stubby fingers pointing upward as if in prayer. One of the boys was missing not one but two of his front teeth; it gave him a foolish look when he smiled, and I wondered with some dismay if I would look so foolish when I lost mine.

"I can't believe how many of them there are. So many children," I said as the camera pulled back.

We did not say another word as the show and its participants, blithely unaware of their fate, carried on. Neither of us paid much attention to the loose tar paper that slapped against the outside of Orion's window, or the wind that stirred beneath it, or the quiet ghostings of snow that were beginning, just beginning, to intensify everywhere outside.

BLANK SPACES

ORDINARILY, IT FELT GOOD to get through the second half of the day. Orion and I felt our spirits lift with the knowledge that Mother would soon be home. It was fun to be just the two of us up to a point, but Mother put our world into focus in a way that we welcomed.

In the late afternoon, a few hours after we'd had our soup for lunch (a full bowl's worth for me, and only a few spoonfuls for Orion), we prepared the house for Mother's return. We draped her bathrobe over her armchair alongside her white nightgown. She liked to remove her cleaning-woman's smock as soon as she got in the door and would make a number of satisfied (and, to our ears, satisfying) noises whenever she changed into those waiting bedclothes. We also placed two old soda bottles on the floor by her chair; Mother would roll these back and forth, back and forth under her bare feet—an excellent source of relief for tired arches, she said.

In Orion's bedroom we prepared things with the highest and holiest precision. Mother always watched a show or two with us before we went to bed, but she would do so only if things were arranged according to her specifications. We laid a satin comforter on the floor and put throw pillows in their respective places. Orion's pillow was closest to the TV; if it wasn't, he would announce, querulously, that the TV people's faces were all blurry.

Finally, we arranged the dining room. I did the honors of setting Mother's favorite teacup and saucer on the table, as well as a stirring spoon with a hummingbird engraved on the handle. "What do you suppose Mother will be having today?" I asked Orion.

Orion and I always guessed, with much anticipation, what Mother would bring home to eat with her after-dinner tea. She kept an opened package of something or other in her pocketbook most days, iced or sugar-sprinkled cookies, shortbread squares. We weren't allowed to have so much as a bite, since sugar reduced children's natural immunities, but we did think it a magnificent moment whenever Mother revealed what she had. We'd coax her to hold the cookies out so we could see them, and sometimes she even permitted us to sniff them. Most often they had an oily sweetness about them, like benign little secrets.

"I can't even think about food right now," Orion said, putting a hand to his stomach. "Not after that pickle. And all that soup. And you know what else? The pickle juice has dried on me, and it's forming a crust. Have you ever tried to think when you're all crusty?"

I couldn't say that I had. "The kitchen floor's crusty too," Orion went on. "You know how Mother hates a dirty floor." No sooner had he spoken than discomfort stole over me, for I *did* know. It dawned on me that Mother might have due cause for anger when she saw what our day's activities had consisted of. My laundry list of sins—everything from reading the primer to the spilling of pickle juice on the floor—seemed too great for her not to intuit. I looked to the nearest diversion—the dining room window—to keep these feelings hidden from my brother.

Orion, who had been taking a break from housework to rest in one of the dining room chairs, got up to see what I was looking at. "What are you staring at that window for? There's nothing to see." He came up beside me and watched with me as the tar paper stirred.

"I was just thinking . . . I was just thinking that it must be winter for real."

"How can you tell?"

"Because it's so cold that things must be frozen outside."

"You're right," Orion said. "That's very good. That wasn't an easy question, you know."

"Can you tell me more about the winter?" I asked, turning to him. "I like to hear about the different seasons."

"Winter follows the fall," Orion said, "and it comes before the spring. Round and round it goes, like that."

There seemed something so comforting about roundness, so harmonious and reliable. When one followed a circular route, how could one ever make a wrong turn? I began walking slowly around the table, my hand trailing along its surface. Orion—mesmerized by my movements, I'd like to think—fell in step behind me.

"And what does the winter smell like?"

"Go up to the window and smell for yourself." When I looked at him suspiciously, Orion urged, "Go ahead and put your face up to it. You can smell it right through the glass."

Feeling doubtful yet curious, I went over to the window, putting my nose as close to it as I could. The tar paper sighed and billowed on the other side of the pane, and I could not help shrinking back.

"I smelled *something*," I said. Truth be told, I wasn't sure I had—but then I wasn't sure I hadn't, either. There was a strange feeling that originated in my stomach and seeped into my heart. A presentiment, maybe. Part of me had thought the air smelled good, the way one imagined white should smell: a refreshing absence. And yet there was something about that absence—some trace of Mother's *horror vacui*, her dislike of blank spaces—that overcame me.

Or maybe it was just the bodies I imagined outside the window—human bodies piled as high as my waist. What, I wondered with a shudder, would *they* smell like? Would someone collect them and give them a final resting place before it grew dark? I was glad to be alive and inside a warm house whose lamps we turned on, come nightfall.

* * * * * * * * *

The last thing we did in preparation for Mother's return was run a damp cloth over the kitchen floor to remove all traces of pickle-juice stickiness. Orion put his head under the faucet for a brief minute and toweled his hair dry and, in doing so, eradicated the last traces of our day's activities.

All that toweling and rubbing and drying at the end of such a day left us exhausted, so when we were done Orion and I huddled together on the cot. I poked my fingers through the holes of the afghan until this pastime no longer interested me.

The blustery wind encircled the house, and we napped through it, off and on, until suddenly I sat bolt upright and nudged my brother with my foot.

"Orion," I said, "isn't it time?"

Time for Mother to come home. Then again, it was nearly impossible to gauge the time of day by the light. With the papered-over windows, we only had the vaguest sense of whether the sun had set. On fiercely sunny days, the rooms were mezzotinted a grayish-pink—but on this day they kept changing colors, growing dark one instant and silvery-bright the next.

"Shouldn't Mother be home by now?" I insisted.

"She's getting groceries," Orion said without opening even one of his eyes. "Remember the empty cupboards?"

That explanation satisfied me for a while. I lay on my back and stared at the slanting wall that loomed over the cot; I imagined that the wall was hugging me, and I did not want it to let go. But soon I felt the swooning feeling that is often the precursor of a dream. I rolled on my stomach and kicked my feet as I thought a dolphin might—in my mind, a dolphin *should* have feet—and Orion and I were in the tub, all dreamy contentment.

I'm the Sierra Slims Sea Monster, my brother said in a drowned-boy's voice, *and I've lived here for hundreds of years, eating little children alive*. In the dream I was not afraid, for even though he submerged his whole head under the water until his hair streamed like a wild tangle of kelp, I knew that in reality he hadn't had such lustrous hair in a long, long time.

Oh, Orion, you are so wise, like Solomon! Let us always live together as two velocipedes!

Little girls and jellyfish and shells, he replied, his voice glub-glubbing under the water. *There is none that I would not eat*.

I woke again to find things considerably darker. I raised my head. Orion awoke and sat up, and the afghan fell to the floor. "Mother?" he said. "Are you here?"

But the house was quiet.

Quiet at unexpected times can seem louder than noise, I realized that day. Orion and I could expertly fill the silences when we had to, but every night after sundown we'd come to expect Mother's brisk step, her muttering or half singing under her breath, the sound of running water or the hiss of her teakettle, the sound of her half dancing, half pacing across the floor as she played her record albums. Orion and I had never known a wholly quiet evening.

My brother went downstairs to check the kitchen clock. "It's almost seven thirty," he reported upon his return. "Mother should have been home two hours ago. Maybe an hour and a half, if you take out a half hour for shopping."

His tone was not exactly worried. If anything, there was a hint of excitement in it; any deviation from our normal routine was something of an adventure.

"I guess we'll just wait for her," I said.

Orion got out his flash cards with the addition and subtraction on them; I was not good at math, but I let him review the sums with me for a while. We watched the game shows that Mother usually watched with us—*Tic Tac Dough* and *The Joker's Wild*. By nine o'clock I was hungry again and heated up more soup, but Orion said he would rather wait to eat with Mother.

"Do you think maybe she came in when we were napping?" he asked as I finished rinsing out my bowl. "Maybe she came in and saw us asleep and decided not to wake us. She might have gone straight to bed."

It didn't seem implausible. "Let's go upstairs," I proposed, "and look for her."

We tried calling as we approached her bedroom door, but were mindful not to call too loudly; Mother was a sensitive sleeper who could be almost beastly in response to a rude awakening. There was also the possibility, if she had indeed gone to bed so early, that she was not feeling well; now and then she'd call in sick to work, complaining of a headache, and at such times we would stay by her bedside as long as she would tolerate, comforting her with cool washcloths for her brow and crayon drawings that depicted her face on a better day.

At the bedroom door we hesitated, neither of us wanting to open it, for Orion and I had not entered Mother's bedroom uninvited in months. The last time we had, we'd gotten into trouble. We'd decided to play with the face paints in her bureau drawer; I had long coveted the contents of her makeup case, its ovals of green eye shadow flecked with gold, the matching circles of rose-pink lip gloss and rouge still bearing the shadows of her fingerprints. Orion and I had been intrigued by a bottle of roll-on antiperspirant, with its efficient scientific shape, and had assumed it was something to be rubbed on the face. After smearing these potions over our cheeks, foreheads, and chins, we'd had second thoughts. We each tied one of Mother's silk scarves under our eyes, hoping such masks would conceal our deed—soap and water seemed more dishonest somehow, an effacement of the crime—and hid ourselves under Mother's bed. Of course she found us and dragged us out by our feet.

"Why are you hiding?" she'd asked, her words ominously sotto voce, still holding me by one ankle. Her dark eyes had acquired that glint they sometimes got when she was upset; her loose hair fell untidily over her face as she bent down to our level. "Are you a couple of little sneaks? Is that what you are?"

"Yes," we'd said in unison, which seemed the only thing to say.

"Do you know what happens to little sneaks?"

We had looked at her mutely, our eyes doubtless enlarged above the masks.

"They get eaten alive by bigger sneaks," she said, and at this witticism she'd straightened up and thrown her head back in laughter, the dark cavern of her throat offset by the brightness of her silver fillings. The laughter was so infectious that I almost smiled, but the scarf's tight fabric held my facial muscles in place.

"Do you think that's funny?" she'd said, her expression hardening again. "It's funny to be a sneak, is it?"

"Yes," we'd said.

And that is how our toys got incinerated. Mother went into our bedrooms and came out again with armfuls of Orion's G.I. Joes and paratrooper dolls and planes, my rag doll, and the toy merry-go-round that had whimsical seats shaped like swans and elephants and threw them one by one into the fireplace. She told us to stand back from the blaze, lest an errant spark come flying out at us, so we stood behind our mother, looking from the fireplace to her and back again, incredulous. It's tempting to say she'd looked *formidable*, standing there lit luridly by the flames, but in fact she looked protective: tall and erect, with her eyes austerely crinkled to ward off the light and heat.

"I suppose this is what it looked like when my mother's films burned up," Mother said, tilting her head at a speculative angle. "Everything she did, up in smoke! Her whole record. Poisonous nitrate is her whole record, children. And you are mine."

She crossed her arms in front of her chest, fondling, then squeezing, the soft flesh of her upper arms. "Feel me," she said. "I feel real enough to you, don't I? But how do we know we're really here? I mean, how do we ever *know*? We never know, do we? We just hope for the best and *pretend*."

I was afraid to touch her. What if she were a transparency of herself—a ghost? But Orion rested his hand on her elbow in a sympathetic way. She looked at him as if she were going to cry, her face working, and this shocked us more than anything that had preceded it. Yet she did not cry.

We had not dared go into her bedroom unsupervised after that. Now we hovered outside the door, rapping three or four times to see if she'd answer. There was no answer. We crept away as quietly as we'd come.

IN MOTHER'S ROOM

IT IS HARD TO REMEMBER how that night concluded. I remember it being close to midnight when my brother decided to light a few candles. Mother often lit candles in the evening. She found candlelight restful, conducive to drowsiness, and she thought that it had a soothing effect, lending gentleness even to the unkindest faces; perhaps she wanted our last image of her each evening to be so soft that we would look kindly upon her in our dreams. Sitting by the dining room window, keeping an ear out for Mother's car turning in the driveway, Orion looked tired but calm as the candlelight shadows lapped and flickered over his face.

"What do you think could be keeping her so long?" I asked him.

"She may have had more cleaning to do than usual. Or maybe there was an errand she had to take care of in town, something she had to do right away. I wish we still had a phone."

"I don't remember ever having a phone."

"In the old house we did. The one we lived in before we moved here. We had a phone, and windows you could see through, and neighbors whose houses were so close you could see them from where we lived. That was about four years ago, I think." He shook his head as if to free it of such thoughts. "Anyway," he went on, "don't worry about Mother. She's sure to be back by morning. I'm going to take my blanket and pillows and sleep near the doorway so that I can see her as soon as she comes in."

Orion blew out the candles one by one and took his bedding into the living room. I stared at him wistfully as he lay on his plumped-up pillows and bedspread; although I had no particular desire to sleep on the floor, I did not want to sleep upstairs by myself. At last I made a gesture indicating that Orion should move over. He sighed but acquiesced all the same, and I pulled back a corner of the blanket and laid my body next to his. I pushed myself against the damp small of his back, but within a few minutes I feared I would suffocate and reluctantly moved away.

Orion fell asleep almost at once. When he slept, he was as inert as the dead. His right arm was flung over his head, his hand in a loose fist. He didn't appear to breathe at all, though I could hear his heart working hard as ever, beating out from just below his shoulder blades. And every now and then he *did* breathe, in a disruptive half snort, followed by a deep, chesty cough that somehow didn't wake him.

I tried to think of calming things, restful things. Instead I found myself thinking of outside, of pigs and cows and horses running wild over the hillsides, seeking shelter from the drifting snow, and of beasts with six wings about them that never flew away. They never needed to.

* * * * * * * * *

The next morning, every one of my bones hurt from having slept in an unnatural place and position. What I rued more than anything was having slept in my woolen dress, for it had stuck to my clammy body in a most disagreeable way.

Orion had scarcely shifted position all night—he was still on his back with his chin tucked toward his shoulder, like a mourning dove. I ran a hand over his face, over his forehead—he had a very tender forehead, surprising for one with such a hard and factual mind—and down the sloping bridge of his nose.

"It's morning," I said.

"Is she home?" he said, half into the pillow.

"I don't know," I said. Then, "Maybe. Yes, I think she must have come in. I thought I heard her work shoes squeaking."

Orion and I took a little time to roll around and stretch before rousing ourselves. Anxious but still bleary-eyed with sleepiness, we got up to look for Mother, Orion tugging at his too-big pajama bottoms as he shuffled down the hallway, both of us stumbling into the walls once or twice. We passed the kitchen and looked inside—nothing.

Mother was also not in the dining room, the living room, the pantry, or the upstairs bathroom. She was not in Orion's room or in the closets or even in the tiny room I slept in (a glorified closet with a cot that matched Orion's); we checked inside my closet and under my cot, just to make sure. That left only Mother's room. The odds were against her being inside; but where else could she be, if not there? Once again we found ourselves outside her door, prickling with anxiety.

"We ought to go in," Orion said.

"I don't think we should."

"We have to," Orion said, his voice rising a little with the imperative. And with that he turned the knob.

The condition of the bedroom, the wild, ransacked look of the place, was what struck me first.

The floor was covered with upended cardboard boxes and reams of scattered paper mixed with a tangle of bikini panties and half-slips and nylon stockings (the entire contents of Mother's underwear drawer, by the looks of it). There were some empty prescription bottles and crumpled cigarette packages. On her mattress was an abandoned knitting project—skeins of unraveled pink and brown yarn exploding from headboard to footboard. The small rag rug that usually lay in her doorway was a rumpled ball in a corner next to an odd, disappointingly empty candy box. Underneath the rug, a sock was pinned to the floor— a sock with a curving toe, as if its owner still inhabited it.

Sickened, I took a reflexive step backward.

I had the feeling that Mother had occupied the room recently; I almost believed that the room bore some remainder of her scent, an improbable mingling of nicotine and tuberose. It was unlike her, though, to leave her usually spotless room in such a disordered state. The only thing that retained its usual neatness was the top of her bureau. I tried to take some reassurance from the sight of the old diamond-patterned leatherette manicure case, the tubes and pots of unidentifiable creams, and the perfume whose bottle was shaped like a blue goose-girl that one could twist in two so that the perfume might be dabbed on from an opening in her waist. These, at least, were where they should be.

As I stayed rooted to the spot, Orion peered under Mother's bed and even looked inside her walk-in closet, which we almost never opened. It was usually crammed from top to bottom with boxes on the floor and walls of clothes hanging on either side, so there was no room for us to stand in it—in other words, it held little attraction for us. Over Orion's shoulder I saw now that the closet was nearly empty. Most of the boxes had been dragged into the middle of the room. And Mother, as I had begun to expect, was not inside the closet.

"Did you do this?" I asked Orion when he turned back around. "Did *you* make this mess?"

"I was just about to ask you the same thing."

"No!" I said. "Why would I?"

"Well, if it wasn't you and it wasn't me," Orion said, rubbing his forehead absently, "I wonder if someone came in and did it, like a burglar or a prowler. Someone who came here looking for something."

"You don't think it was Mother who did it?"

"She wouldn't do this to her room, I'm sure of it. She loves this room too much."

But I was not so sure. I imagined Mother engrossed in a role, right in the thick of it, tearing things apart with a vengeance; I could almost hear the fire in the hearth rising and crackling as she fed it toy after toy. It was not all that hard to picture her ravaging a ten-foot-by-twelve-foot bedroom in a short amount of time. But when would she have done it? I remembered how tranquil she'd been the last time I saw her, speaking softly and stroking her hair in that absent caress. There had been no signs of a storm brewing then.

Orion looked on as if taking final stock of the damage and, in a resolute manner that surprised me, he picked up one of the overturned boxes and began gathering together some of the bits of paper and manila folders that lay around it. "She'd better not see this mess. How do you suppose she'd feel, coming home and seeing this? If she knew someone had broken in, she'd be worried that we weren't safe. She wouldn't want to leave us at home anymore, and then we wouldn't get any more money because she'd leave her job."

"How could someone have gotten in? Everything's boarded up, and nobody knows we're here."

"I don't know," Orion said. "All I know's they got in *somehow*."

I wanted to tell him not to touch anything in the room, for fear of a reprise of Mother's last rage. Goodness knew that a second fire, or worse, could result. Even if we hadn't been the ones to create the mess, what authority did we have to put things back? I opened my mouth to say something but closed it again. I could see that Orion was already settled and decided on the matter and that there would be no reasoning with him.

Orion said, "Maybe you can start putting her underthings back in the dresser. That's more of a girl's job anyway. After that you could start putting papers together. Bills, receipts, coupons—anything with numbers or dollar signs on it might as well go in the same box. I think that's the way Mother would do it." He paused, then added as an afterthought, "At least that's the way I would do it."

"And what are we going to do with the boxes once they're full?"

"Put them back into the closet the way they were."

Lifting heavy boxes would be a lot of work for Orion—more physical work than he was capable of. "I can carry them," I said.

Orion didn't disagree with me. I began to help him out, tackling the undergarments first and putting them back in the top

drawer of the bureau; hard work, I realized, was good at helping one to forget the immediate problem, for I found it impossible to worry about Mother's whereabouts and move objects at
the same time. Uprighting a box, I began filling it with papers,
sometimes not even checking to see what was written on them;
words caught my eye and leapt from the page but were quickly
disregarded or forgotten. There were ticket stubs to plays,
index-card recipes for zucchini and pumpkin bread, and a
piece of paper that read "Certificate of Achievement in English"
awarded to my mother in 1957; the certificate had a gold seal
and was slightly frayed at one corner. On another paper, with
the words "Progress Report: Kindergarten" typed across the
top, I saw my brother's name—*Orion Hewitt*.

"Orion, do you want to see your progress report?" I asked.

"Sorry?"

I held it out for him to see and, after looking at it cockeyed,
he frowned and shook his head. "If I were you, I wouldn't *read*
the papers. It'll take too long if you try to read everything."

"I'm *not* reading everything," I said, which was the truth.
Ticket stubs and zucchini-bread recipes did not make for com-
pelling reading.

Amid some of my other finds were unfinished sketches, to-do
lists (my mother liked lists in general), and sheets of paper that
bore only series of numbers, with geometric doodles filling
up the rest of the page. There were take-out menus and the
occasional greeting card still tucked in its envelope. One of the
envelopes was particularly thick. Mother didn't get much mail
anymore, except the utility bill or the odd flyer that was meant
for someone else; never, absolutely never, did she get thick
letters like this one. In the envelope's upper left-hand corner
was the name John Hewitt—my father's name. *This must have*

been written, I thought, *before he walked straight into the ocean.*
Glancing sideways at Orion, I took the letter out of its envelope
and tried to unfold it without making a sound. I saw that it was
a densely typed letter, which gave me better hope of making out
some of the longer words; I could not read grown-ups' cursive
writing yet.

"Dear Loretta," the typeface read. "Don't think that I'm not
aware of how lavish you are with your letters . . ." I stopped
there, for *lavish* was an unknown word, and I could see, skim-
ming ahead, that the long letter was filled with other words I
did not recognize. I turned the sheet over, then went on to the
third page and read this passage:

> And how could I not have seen? I see you in the high
> school cafeteria, bending over one of your pears—when
> did you stop doing that, eating fruit with a knife, making
> petals out of the pears? I see you near one of the trees,
> outside of school. This is so stupid—every time I see you,
> in my mind, your eyes darken with pleasure at the sight
> of me, and then I feel a little guilty for my . . . what is the
> word for it? Narcissism?

I let out a great sigh. "Narcissism" had exceeded my limited
comprehension. *No wonder our father walked straight into the
ocean,* I thought; probably no one understood what he was going
on about half the time! I would have to read the letter later, once
our task was done and after we'd found Mother. I slipped the
envelope into the front pocket of my dress and kept working.

Within minutes the first box was full. I carried it to the
closet, almost buckling under its weight, and shoved it in a far
corner. When I came back, Orion had a small notebook in his

lap that he was reading; his shoulders rounded over it and his finger followed the words along the page. "I thought we weren't supposed to be reading," I couldn't resist pointing out.

"We're not," Orion said, "but this is different."

"Different how?"

"It's a notebook of Mother's, and it might be a clue. She wrote in it just a couple of days ago. It's . . . peculiar."

"Peculiar how?"

Orion cleared his throat and moved the notebook a little closer so as to see it better. "Listen to this. This is Mother's handwriting."

January 28, 1978. I don't know how many nights I can wake up gasping for air and thinking about the children in their little beds and wondering how much longer they can make it. If they do make it, it won't be because of me. I have never felt so helpless. Where did they come from, these children? By what force of nature have they lived this long? Sometimes I don't recognize them as mine. When I was little I had a Japanese fighting fish that I kept in a fishbowl. I don't remember how I ended up with this fish, since it had these limp fins and was ugly—I prefer those little neon blue ones that are too small to really be hideous—but it must have been a gift, certainly not something I picked out myself. Not long after I got the fish, I started having these dreams about bigger fish gasping for air in shallow puddles, and I couldn't do anything to save them. I flushed my fighting fish down the toilet just so I could get some relief. It did make me feel better, but only for a little while.

Sometimes I think I'd like to go out for a long walk without telling anyone where I'm going and not stop until I get tired, or maybe not even then. I can't explain the terror of not being good enough and wanting to run away. Of not being able to be depended upon. I tried to explain it to John a few times, but in the end he was the one I couldn't depend on to stay.

Orion looked up at me; his face had paled. "It ends there," he said.

"I don't understand it. The part about the fish doesn't make any sense. And why doesn't she know where we came from? She told me I came from a seed and an egg." (I had a concrete and not unpleasant mental image of a pumpkin seed penetrating the supple yet yielding whites of a hard-boiled egg, with me as the result.)

"You're missing the point. At the end here she's talking about taking a walk and not stopping. What if that's what she did? That would explain why she didn't come back last night."

I gave this a moment's reflection. "Then it would just be the two of us."

"We couldn't get by with just the two of us."

"No," I agreed. "We need Mother."

"We should go out looking for her. She couldn't have gone far on foot."

"But how can we get out? The doors are boarded up, and so are the windows. Besides," I said, feeling my heart rate elevate, "outside's where all the poison things are. All the bodies and sicknesses."

"I know," Orion said. He looked very discouraged. He closed the notebook again and laid it on the top of the papers he'd accumulated in the box. "I guess there's not a lot we can do."

The ensuing silence was dreadful. Finally, as though to prove him wrong, to show him that I *could* do something productive, I closed the flaps of his box for him and started moving it toward the closet. I dragged the box for part of the way, then nudged it along by giving it kicks (this was easier, I found, than trying to lift it in my arms). When I got to the closet, I tried to place it exactly as Mother would have, next to the first box, flush against the back wall. I backed away a half step—less than a half step—to see if I'd done a passable job.

What happened next was rather extraordinary. The floor gave out from under me.

What does one remember about falling? I know that I felt more shame than fright at my graceless and seemingly endless descent. As my hands scrabbled for something to hold on to, there was not one ounce of the romance one expects from the heroine who falls off a craggy cliff and into the rough sea. There was only the sound of boards splintering and a series of rude thuds, the last of which was me—my body landing.

THE BEST WAY OUT
IS THROUGH

MY KNEES HAD LANDED on something sharp. I was in darkness. My feet found something to brace themselves against and as soon as my hands were free to explore I realized that I'd landed on a flight of stairs.

There was a rush of footfalls overhead, and I looked up to see Orion's face staring at me through a hole in the floorboards—a space so small that I could not help feeling a sense of wonder at having slid through it. I tried to say something, but the only sound that came out was a faint peep.

"Asta!" Orion said. "Are you hurt?"

I had no idea how to respond, being too shaken to determine whether I was genuinely hurt or not. I could taste blood in my mouth, bright and tangy, and my tongue touched the empty space where my loose tooth had been. The impact of the fall had dislodged it. I groped about, but the tooth was nowhere to be found. Had I swallowed it? I blinked back tears, as upset by that thought as I was by anything else.

"You broke right through the *floor*," Orion said, his voice conveying a degree of respect that somehow made my situation more tolerable. "Right through the floor. How did you manage that?" He ran a hand over the small gap I'd made in the floorboards. "See how thin the wood is? It doesn't feel like a regular part of the floor at all."

That seemed a given, I thought. Regular floors tended not to have stairwells hidden beneath them, didn't they?

"Maybe Mother kept all those boxes in here so we couldn't fall through," Orion said. "She was blocking off that weak patch in the floor. And you had to go and step right on it!"

"Aren't you going to help me out of here?" I asked, swallowing hard and finding my voice at last.

Orion started. "Oh," he said. "Sure. Sure I'll help you."

"I'll need a candle to see."

"I'll get the flashlight. That'll work better." But Orion seemed in no great hurry. I wasn't sure if he was sorry to desert such an intriguing sight—me, Asta, trapped like so many of the bugs I'd wooed out from under the bathroom tiles—or if he was just reluctant to leave me alone in the dark. Finally, he got up stiffly, and I listened to him dragging his feet through the bedroom until I could no longer locate him by sound. Instead, I focused on where I was, to make some sense of the mystery space into which I'd fallen.

As my eyes began to adjust, I could make out more and more of my surroundings. The air was thick, almost powdery, dense with dust and plaster. Biting my lower lip, I maneuvered my body until I was seated on one of the steps. I wiggled my toes and rotated my ankles to confirm that I still could. There was a rip in the knee of my tights and something that felt like a hot, stinging scrape on the knee itself, but beyond this my injuries seemed few. Mother would be glad, I thought, to know that I'd escaped real harm. She might even call me *a brave little soldier* or *my stalwart Pork Chop* when she saw me and heard of my ordeal. I thought then of the lump Mother had found that morning, and my fingers sought it out to make sure *it* had not been dislodged in my fall. But it was still there. I was still sick.

What was this purgatorial place I had found myself in? I wasn't afraid so much as I was curious. It felt as if I were offstage, waiting for something to happen—a cue—and I wondered if this was what Mother had meant, when telling me of her stage training, by that area that was neither on the stage nor away from it but somewhere in between. The *wings*, wasn't it called? *In the wings it's nothing but you and the sounds you hear coming off the stage—that and the knowledge that you must soon face your audience like the nakedest of emperors—my dear, I speak the truth! For all the disguises that a role might provide, it is still part of you that is bared to the world in those footlights. You can imagine that, can't you, Asta?*

How easily Mother's rounded tones could enter my mind!

Waiting on the stairs, I felt neither here nor there; the stillness of waiting was all I had. Was that why Mother hadn't come home? Had she gotten stuck somewhere, waiting, and she was planning to make a grand entrance later on?

I stood up—inelegantly, in my narrow space—and extended my left arm for balance. *When you make your entrance*, Mother had said, *you can't simply walk up onstage big as Billy-be-damned. You ride in on the waves of light! They'll carry you in if you let them!* Thinking of this, I took a tentative step down.

And down again.

It was not all that hard, I discovered, to make an entrance.

Twelve steps, all told. As I reached the last one, I almost lost my footing all over again. My arm shot out in front of me and made contact with a cool, damp surface. Protruding from it, exactly level with my hand, was a polished little nail that had a hook fitted snugly over it.

The hook was L-shaped, like an L lying on its side. How useful it was, after all, to look at everything sideways! I soon forgot about my entrance, and my sore knee, and even the dull sound of Orion slamming drawers shut in a far-off room as he looked for the flashlight. Instead, I lifted and replaced the hook from its nail, lifting and replacing, lifting and replacing; I must have done this a half dozen times.

All of a sudden there was a creak, the sickening whine of something giving way, and a crack appeared in the wall—a crack just wide enough for me to see the glittering hint of white that lay beyond it.

Snow?

I felt a glare against my back then, and I turned to face the concentrated beam that my brother was shining on me. He had climbed noiselessly through the hole and now stood at the top of the steps, seeing the same thing I saw. In this instant there was a mirroring of our expressions; I could barely see his face, but I could make out the shades of recognition—a manifestation of the same thought I was having.

"It's a door that leads to the outside," I said. "And I've gone and done it now. I've gone and opened it, Orion, and the poisons are here!"

* * * * * * * * *

It surprises me to realize how much of what came next we agreed upon, though what impresses me even more was that the outside world was available through such a *simple* means of egress.

Our initial task was to get out of the stairwell, which proved to be the easiest part of our operation; Orion's flashlight made it possible for us to find our way to the top. Together we looked at the opening I'd made and at the stairwell and wondered aloud at the boarded-off exit. Orion was convinced it had once been a back door to the house from which crooks and thieves could make an escape after they'd robbed it; I thought maybe a troll had lived under there, barred from the main house and its attractions.

The first thing I did was wipe the cobwebs and dust off my dress and face and hair. Orion helped me shake out the hem of my dress, loosing a dust ball that had found its way up my skirt. He said seriously, "I see this all as a sign."

"A sign of what?" I wanted to know.

"A sign that we are meant to go outdoors and look for Mother. It's almost magic, the way the door appeared. I think it was meant to be. I think if we dressed warmly and went out right now, we'd find her in no time."

"What about the plague?" I asked. "The bodies piled up on the streets and sidewalks. The beasts with six wings about them."

"If you're going to be a scaredy-cat," Orion said, "then I guess that means you don't want to find Mother all that much. You want us to stay here by ourselves. You want her to walk to the ends of the earth until she's exhausted and can't even remember her way back home."

I stopped swiping at the back of my dress, where particularly tenacious bits of dust had settled into the wool. "You know I don't want that."

"Then let's go out and find her. We'll look for just a little while, and if we don't see her before we get to the nearest house, we can stop there and ask the people if we can use their phone."

"*If* we can find people nearby who are still alive," I said dourly.

It was clear that we had no choice but to look for Mother, equipping ourselves for the cold however we could—but how, given our limited resources? My mind racing, I mentally reviewed Mother's outdoor attire: any of her half dozen winter coats along with a hat and scarf, a pair of gloves, and boots. She also carried a pocketbook whenever she went out, different colors on different days and different fabrics for different seasons—but I had no idea what she kept inside these or why they were essential.

Orion and I went downstairs to the hall closet to see what we could find. I pulled down Mother's second-favorite jacket (after the fox-collared one she'd worn to work): an orange and brown patchwork number with a round black velvet collar and cuffs. On Mother, the jacket stopped just at her hips, but on me it was ankle length, the sleeves long enough to cover my hands and serve the same function as mittens. Likewise, the blue down jacket Orion selected dwarfed him. We could not find any scarves and hats, so we decided we'd go bareheaded (Mother sometimes went hatless, depending on how elaborately she had arranged her hair); we settled on the coats and two pairs of boots.

Mother's boots were tall, and on us they were so big that their tops flopped helplessly over our knees and our feet slid freely over the insoles. I suggested trimming the tops down with pinking shears, but Orion thought stuffing the toes with wadded-up socks would suffice. This improved matters slightly—enough, in any case, for us to practice shuffling back and forth.

"I wish I had a pocketbook," I said after stumbling down repeated lengths of the hall. "I don't think I'm supposed to go outside without one." I was remembering all the times when Mother had bolted the front door behind her, only to scrabble at the locks again and come bursting back into the house, having forgotten her pocketbook. A second exploration of the hall closet yielded one of Mother's purses—white with pink beading and a broken rhinestone clasp—which I seized upon with much triumph, though I wished I could think of something interesting to fill it with.

"You can put the flashlight in there," Orion said as if reading my mind. "We'll need it to find our way down those stairs again."

The flashlight! Of course. Orion had left it on the side table near the front door. I placed it inside the purse to see how it fit, then spent a full minute toying with the clasp, peering into the purse's satin-lined belly, and toying with the clasp again. When Orion cleared his throat, I looked up inquiringly.

"Anything else? Is there anything we're forgetting?" Orion asked.

"What about Mother's bedroom? We didn't put the rest of the boxes away," I said, stalling.

"We'll explain that to her when we see her. She might not like it, but I think she'll understand once we tell her the whole story. Come on, Asta, don't be afraid."

"I'm not afraid," I said, drawing Mother's enormous coat around me, pulling it as close to my skin as I could. How could I be in any real danger, I told myself, with the smell and feel of my mother so close to me? "I'm *not* afraid," I said again. "I'm ready to go if you are."

It was time to go back to Mother's room, to Mother's closet. Using the flashlight to guide us, we carefully lowered ourselves through the hole and found our footing on the stairs. Lying on one of the steps was the white envelope I'd had in my dress pocket. It must have been jostled out when I fell. I picked the envelope up and showed it to Orion.

"It's an old letter to Mother from John Hewitt," I said. Then, correcting myself: "I mean from our father. I was . . . I was going to try to read it."

"Put it in your pocketbook. We'll read it later," Orion said.

In our oversized clothing, bracing our hands against the wall, my brother and I minced and hobbled down to the bottom step. We took turns tugging on the door handle; our hands overlapped at one point, and we pulled with all our might until the heavy old door opened wide and the snow flew straight into my eyes and open mouth.

It was time to begin our search for Mother.

OPEN MEANS OPEN

As Orion and I took those first few mincing steps in the snow, our mother's boots slid and squashed around our ankles, and the broken clasp of her pocketbook clickety-clacked against the beads. I found the clickety-clacking more instructive than irksome, since it was like the sound I always imagined when reading the primer—the taskmaster guiding me through the particulars of my lesson with sharp, reprimanding raps from his thorn-stick.

Outside felt like Mother's world to me. It was filled with every possible allure—things that looked good, sounded good, felt good. Not everything I saw was new to me, for the world of books and television had introduced me to more things than one might expect. It had given me images of trees, so I was surprised only by their height. I had imagined almost everything in miniature. Now it was as if a magnifying glass had been placed over the surface of the world, and seeing everything so enlarged made me realize how few things were within my grasp. The trees weren't. Not the tops of them, anyway, which touched the sun and were thus the most desirable; restricted to the lowest branches, I stopped to shake the snow off them. An acorn fell out—I didn't know what it was—and I was delighted with this gift, with its cap like a bumpy brown bowl. Soon I was stopping every few feet along the road to collect some curio or another, each of which I crammed into a coat pocket.

"Look!" I said, picking up a twig with a twisted corkscrew shape.

"Look!" I said, sighting a pigeon. I chased him down the road for a few paces, flailing my arms to get his attention—but, looking for all the world like a seagull in a nature show, he up and flew away.

The space between snow and the sky, which I couldn't dream of pocketing, was also novel to me. Unlike things at home, in our world within walls, the outside things shimmered in a vast, bright expanse. I expected to feel a tremor—a wavering signal.

But when I extended my arm, I felt nothing at all.

There were only trees and the spaces between the trees for a good long stretch. No human limbs jutting from the snowbanks, thankfully, and no men hauling bodies away. The only horror was not knowing where Mother was.

For all my brother's assured navigating, I could tell that the effort was causing him some wear and tear. The more time passed, the more noticeable was the phlegmy rattle that came from deep in his chest, and talking seemed a trial for him. After a while he stopped by the side of the road and squinted at some point in the distance. I waited for him to compose himself, stamping my feet to keep warm. Such large and clumsy tracks my feet left, in Mother's boots!

"I see part of a house," Orion said between wheezes.

"What?"

"A part of a house. A chimney," he said, extending a forefinger.

I saw what he meant then. We had a chimney at our house, too, but had never seen it from the outside—it existed as a rectangular protuberance in the corner of Orion's room, plastered and wallpapered over so as to blend in. Often Orion and I heard the thumping noises and cheeps of the chimney swifts that made their nests in there; it comforted us when they made their presence known. The chimney Orion now pointed to, visible above and beyond a pine tree down the road, was a plain brick square like those on houses in picture books.

As Orion and I advanced, the rest of the house revealed itself. It was pale green, the color of cooked cabbage speckled with brown, and not very big. Its windows were bare, and two of the front windowpanes had jagged holes in them.

On the flattened edge of a snowbank in front of the house, I saw something else—a mound of droppings, some of which crisscrossed over one another. I stopped to look at them with an involuntary little exclamation.

"Those came from inside a dog," Orion said dismissively.

"Goodness," I said. "Right out in the open?" I had hoped I would see a live dog on the road—Sally Ann's beribboned Scottie came to mind—or even a nice tabby cat. But as many times as I'd seen them depicted in books, there had never been one mention of their inability to use a toilet. I disapproved.

"There isn't any tar paper on these windows," I said after refocusing my attention on the house.

"No," Orion said. "It looks like an empty house."

"Empty why?"

"Maybe it's a dead person's house. Someone must have gone in . . . and taken the paper off the windows . . . because there's no need to protect the owners from the outside anymore." Orion put a capper on this sentence by releasing a loose cough. "It's too bad," he went on, "because if anyone still lived here, they would be our neighbors, and we could use their phone. Let's look through the window to see if there's anything left inside."

We pushed our way past some bedraggled bushes to have a look. Through one of the broken windows I saw mostly bare walls with the occasional hunk of beige-colored wallpaper clinging like strips of loose skin. The floor was covered with a large sheet of plastic and newspapers. There were three or four empty bottles, and in the far corner lay a single brick—the instrument used for breaking the windows, Orion guessed. I didn't see a telephone anywhere, and the room, though obviously lived in at one point, did not look as if it had ever been hospitable.

Orion went up to the front door and gave it a few raps. When no one answered, he knocked again. I was just about to suggest that we keep going—I wasn't liking the looks of that empty house one bit, with the plastic and the newspaper rippling quietly every time the wind blew—when Orion and I heard an engine somewhere in the distance. It was the same sound as the trucks we sometimes heard at night, from the safety of our beds.

It was hard to tell where the sound was coming from, but it seemed close by. Within a few seconds I could tell that it was getting fainter rather than nearer; I knew this because I always listened to the sound of Mother's car leaving the driveway, straining my ears for it until I could hear the hum of white noise and house noises. I knew that once the sound of Mother's engine could no longer be heard, we would not see her again for hours and hours.

We broke into a run, or something resembling one; Orion lagged behind me, and the frisk of the run was short-lived, but in a minute or two we came upon an encouraging find: tire tracks in the unplowed road. At least we had a trail before us—one that would surely lead someplace—and a path that offered our first real hope of the morning.

* * * * * * * * *

Orion and I had walked another half mile or so when the trees began to thin out. Soon we were walking without cover. We followed the tire tracks around a curve in the road, and there, stood a second house. Unlike the green house with its desolate air, this one had signs of life: a truck parked in a lot and—marvel of marvels—an OPEN sign hanging in the door. "It's a store," Orion said, as if reading my mind, and pointed to a sign next to the door: CRAZY CARL'S GENERAL STORE. WE HAVE NIGHT CRAWLERS.

Next to the front entrance a man was untying a black dog from a post. Whatever one might say about this man, it was clear even from our distance that his frame and constitution were hardly those of a sick person.

The dog, in contrast, had a narrow snout and trembling, spindly legs. It began swaying back and forth at the end of its leash as soon as it saw us, and a horrid noise came tearing out of its throat.

"Princess!" the man said. "Cool it!"

These unusual utterances commanded our full attention. As we got closer we were able to appreciate how tall the man was—and how mountain-shaped, in his bulky checked overcoat. His hat with its earflaps and his profuse beard hid the particularities of his facial features from us. The dog had begun gnawing on the leash and the man made sport of yanking it. Orion and I, having come as close as we dared, kept a tactful silence, not knowing if we were interrupting something or not.

At last, without turning his head, the man uttered more of these fantastic words. "Princess, you little dirtbag, you pretty little suck-mutt," he said, slapping the dog's sides with a friendly familiarity. Then, to our surprise, he looked straight at us and shot out, "Spoiled rotten, ain't she?"

"How is she spoiled?" Orion said, just as unexpectedly, and the sound of his voice directed at someone other than Mother or myself gave me a prickling sensation on the back of my neck.

The man looked a bit startled, as if he hadn't expected—or wanted—an answer. "Oh, I don't know. Gets too many doggie treats, I'd say." He gave us each a once-over, showing some teeth behind his beard; then he looked us up and down with the pronounced overreaction Mother's face had when she was REGISTERING EMOTION in one of her scenes.

"Think those coats fit you all right?" he asked and winked at us.

"They're Mother's," I said. "Have you seen her?"

"I don't know if I'd know your mother if I seen her, but as it happens, I only seen some kids on their way to school."

"To school? Already?"

"Sure. It's only the little kids that go in later, you know. The afternoon kindergarten."

"Oh, yes," Orion said. "I remember now."

I was astonished to see that conversation could be achieved as easily as this. I suspected my brother was bluffing, guessing the right responses rather than knowing them. I hadn't known that his acting talents could be so broadly applied.

"Least that's what I think," the man qualified. "I don't live in town. I'm over in Whitefield. I just make the delivery run. I'm the bread man. I bring the bread in my truck. I'm acquainted with the main roads down here, but I'm not acquainted with the people so much, except for Ruth and Carl at the store here, and Charlie Tobin at the store over t'other side of town. I've probably not met your ma at all."

"We're not acquainted with folks either," I said, trying to assume the same tone as the man. "Just our ma."

Orion nudged me in the ribs, but the man only laughed gutturally. "Not so many folks to know anymore. Everyone's going out to the city. It's been all but dead here since the mill shut down back in '74. Used to be a nice community. But you're probably better off not knowing no one but your ma. My own ma would be the first to tell you that a mother's love is a blessing. When I was a kid I thought that was bull caca, but it's true. She's been dead for eleven years now. Eleven years? I think that's just about right." The man looked at the sky, still scratching the fur around the dog's collar. "Well, I don't know about you, but I got a long day ahead of me, and the roads almost ain't fit for driving." He unleashed the dog in one quick flick of his thumb. She promptly rose on her hindquarters and put her front paws against the passenger side of the truck, her torso lengthening and shimmering until she resembled a slim dark trout. The man opened the door and she scampered in with a hop and a wiggle.

"Would you mind if I asked you something?" Orion said as the man crossed the front of the truck to get into the driver's side.

"Uh-huh?"

"Do you think there's a phone inside that store we could use?"

"Why, I imagine you could so long as it's a local call."

"The sign on the door says 'open,'" Orion said. "Does that mean we can walk right in, or do you think we should knock?"

"Sheesh, now, what do you think? Do you usually knock when you go to the store?"

Orion thought with visible effort. "I guess what I want to know is . . . I think 'open' means *open*. But I don't know if 'open' means open to me or for somebody who isn't me."

The man's eyes narrowed the way Mother's did when she thought we were misbehaving. "Open means open," he said. "What else could it mean?"

We watched him slide into the driver's seat of the truck, slam his door, and turn a key in the ignition. He gave us a half wave as the truck lurched backward, turned, and made a barreling exit from the lot, a grist of snow spraying us.

"I guess," Orion said after the engine was no longer audible, "it means we can walk right in."

* * * * * * * * *

The door to Crazy Carl's General Store was a springy one with a handle instead of a knob; something tinkly sounded as we went inside, and we looked up to see a little bell strung above the door, wagging its tongue at us. This amused me so much that I went back outside and came in again, just to see if I could catch the bell in midmotion. I was even preparing a third exit and entrance when Orion grabbed me by the shoulder and gestured at what lay before us.

Amazing that I could be taken with an ordinary old bell when I had greater riches in my view. The store resembled the inside of a giant cupboard. Here stood aisles redundant with shelves, each shelf holding more food than I had ever seen in my life. Signs suspended by chains hung above each aisle; I thought they might offer an instruction or an invitation, just as the sign on the door had, so I walked up and down to read each: Bread and Cereal, Soups and Canned Vegetables, Cold Beverages. These weren't instructions, I concluded, so much as they were announcements—static commercials for each product.

The last aisle, Cold Beverages, was so chilly that I went back to the canned goods, gazing upon those stacked cylinders with their maniacally cheerful labels. SpaghettiOs with a face on the label, a face with an impish tongue sticking out! Canned meat graced by a dancing, fork-tailed red devil! I almost felt ecstatic as I lifted my head to see how high the stacks of cans rose.

"Oh, Orion, let's count them!" I said.

"No," he said in an oddly indistinct voice. "You come here."

I went back to where he was standing, not far from the entrance, and saw what I had missed in my excitement over the aisles: a glass-topped counter that displayed jars filled to the brim with colorful shapes. "Penny candy," Orion explained, and he identified each jar of candy in turn: long licorice whips, peanut chews, white-dotted nonpareils, toffee sealed in tufted gold papers, glossy chocolate drops, and others. On top of the counter were such sundries as maps, cigarette lighters, and batteries—but the centerpiece of it all was an oval dish laden with round crackers. NEW! DODD'S TABLE CRACKERS—TRY ME, implored a placard propped up against the dish. I could see that Orion had obeyed the placard's call already; a good many DODD'S TABLE CRACKERS competed for space in his mouth.

Could the placard be deceptive, I wondered? Was it a trick? If the OPEN sign in the door had meant *open*, then the meaning of "try me" might be just as simple. Besides, I realized for the first time that day, I was famished. I tried one, imagining that the table cracker would be sweet, and was surprised to find it as salty as bouillon. It was nonetheless a pleasant first encounter with crispiness, and while the required amount of chewing hurt my jaw a bit, I made a smacking sound with my mouth like the ones Mother made over her tea.

"Don't eat the whole plate, you," a startlingly close voice drawled.

Orion's and my hands fell to our sides. A tall, large-boned woman squeezed through a door to the left of the counter. The woman had gray hair tied back in a plaid kerchief and was dressed in matching plaid slacks that made her sturdy legs seem even sturdier. Over the slacks was a cream-colored apron, tied in the back with a drooping bow that ended at the top of her buttocks.

"Crackers're just for sampling," she said. "Not for pigging out."

The woman's voice was low and affectless. She gave us a diffuse sort of look before ducking under the counter to produce a roll of paper towels and a spray bottle of blue cleaning fluid. "Haven't seen you kids around here before," she said, noisily unsheathing the paper towels from their plastic wrap. "Visiting from away?"

We stood there, petrified.

"No school for you today, eh?"

"What?" Orion said, his mouth still partly gummed shut with cracker crumbs.

"No school today?"

"No," Orion said. "I guess not."

The woman, who had just sprayed a fine stream of cleanser over the countertop, looked unimpressed—but Orion, after forti-

fying himself with a deep breath, went on: "We were wondering
if you'd seen our mother. Or if you have a phone we could use.
She hasn't been home. Maybe you know where she works?"

"Who's your mother?" she said with laconic disinterest, tearing off several perforations of paper towels. "You need me to
call the police for you?"

"No, I don't think so," Orion said. "Our mother's name is
Loretta Hewitt. She cleans offices."

"Offices, huh? That narrows it right down, don't it?"

I was not enamored of this woman's way of talking. Her
pinched voice sounded as if it were coming straight out of
her nose. While Orion continued to speak with her, I slipped
into the nearest aisle for another look at the foodstuffs on the
lower shelves. There I found individual cupcakes wrapped in
cellophane—cupcakes with slick brown tops and maraschino
cherries in the center. I touched one end of the wrapper, aiming
for the grace with which the bodiless hands in TV commercials
might open such a package but finally resorting to tearing the
end of it with my teeth.

"Our mother's about this tall," I could hear Orion saying, "and
has dark hair down to here—" at this point he must have waved
a hand somewhere near the small of his back—"and her eyes are
dark, too—and the last time we saw her she was wearing—what
was she wearing, Asta?"

I bit fully into the heart of the cherry-topped cupcake. "Red
rubber zip-up boots and her fox-collar coat," I said.

"What's that girl doing back there?" the woman asked, her
pitch rising. "She eating something else?"

I came forth with the ruins of the cake in my hands.

"You'll be wanting to pay for that, missy."

"I will?" I said, unruffled. "Why?"

There was a long and rather formidable silence in which I could almost hear the woman mentally counting to ten.

"Go off with you, then," the woman said, her pink complexion having gone a shade redder. "I ain't seen your mother, and the phone ain't working today anyhow, but I hope she catches up with you so she can teach you some manners."

"I know all about manners," I said with as much dignity as I could muster. "Never take the largest slice of cake off a plate . . . that's my favorite manner."

"The school bus." My brother, the mollifier, stepped in. "Which way to the nearest bus stop from here?"

"It's that way, right at the end of the road there, where the stop sign is," she said, jerking a thumb over her shoulder. She hesitated. Her tongue explored the inside of her cheek, creating a bulge, as if it were doing the thinking for her. "Listen. Do you kids . . ." she began but stopped short. Orion had already given me a push toward the door, where the little bell waited to peal at our exit.

"Why did you want to know where the bus stop is?" I asked when we were alone on the roadside again. "We can't go to school."

"Don't worry about it," Orion said. "We're not going to school."

"Then why go to the bus stop?"

"For a ride," he said simply. "It'll save us from walking, won't it?"

"ACTRESSES ARE SUPPOSED
TO BE PRETTY"

I WAS NOT PRECISELY SURE what a *bus stop* was—a place where the bus stopped, that much I could gather, but what would a bus stop look like? This question preoccupied me as we went farther up the road in the direction the woman had pointed. I was trying to take my mind off the cold and not doing a very good job of it; compared with the general store's comfortably regulated temperature, the chill outside seemed harsher than ever.

"Are we really going to take a ride on a bus?" I asked.

"Sure, if the bus driver lets us," Orion said. "If he's a nice bus driver, maybe he'll drive around to see if we can find Mother on the road somewhere. I'm not sure how much longer I can last on foot."

I wasn't sure how much longer Orion could last either. My own feet were starting to go numb and my legs were heavy and tired; these things did not bode well for my brother, whose condition was worse than mine. But somehow we kept walking, willing one foot in front of the other even when it seemed we could walk no more. The idea of curling up in a ball on top of the snow occurred to me repeatedly. I wondered if I could dig a hole in the snowbank to make a warm, insulated snow tent—a snow clubhouse—where we could sit for a while. *Hear ye, hear ye. This meeting should come to order. What will we buy with our dues?* I had almost made up my mind to try it when I saw what we were looking for up ahead: an octagonal red stop sign and human forms cavorting around the signpost.

I pointed these out to Orion, and we summoned our last bit of strength so that we could get closer and see better. As the human forms came into focus, they acquired more details—I took in puffy jackets and knitted hats with variegated stripes and pom-poms; a honey-brown ponytail here; a smart book bag there; a tin lunchbox swung in an exaggerated wave by a snow-encrusted mitten—all of these things attached to and animated by children, real children.

I could tell at a glance that the children looked nothing like the well-scrubbed ones I'd seen on the TV show the day before. I tried to remind myself that some were younger than I—kindergarteners, probably—and therefore not to be feared, but most were at least my size, or bigger, and all of them ran around in circles or charged at one another in a predatory way that demonstrated few concessions to order.

I lost what little desire I might have had to get closer to any of them. I dug my hands into my coat pocket to feel one of my new acorns, clutching it so hard that the fingers of my left hand cramped.

"They have worse germs than we do," I whispered. "Why don't we just turn back?"

I half expected Orion to say that we shouldn't—we had, after all, come this far at his insistence. But he surprised me by offering no argument, and he hunched his shoulders until they almost reached his ears.

"I think . . ." he started. His words were cut off by a sidelong look, intimidating even from afar, that one of the children shot our way. The child then delivered an attention-getting blow to the arm of the nearest boy, and that one, in turn, hit the girl next to him. Soon every pair of eyes was fixed upon us, and a high giggle burbled up and stifled itself almost as quickly.

"You!" said the one who had noticed us first. I couldn't tell if it was a boy or a girl; its voice sounded like the macaw I'd once seen on the show *Our Feathered Friends*. "Get ovah here!"

Orion and I exchanged glances, and Orion took a couple steps forward.

"Closer," insisted the macaw.

My hand on my brother's arm, we did as the child said. Up close I saw that our host had a freckled face, one that bore no further hint of gender under its quilted hood.

"Look at 'em," said another—a girl, I'd judged by the honey-brown ponytail—and the same giggle as before rose again, joined by a scattering of others eerily like it.

"They're queer," another child said. "Look at their clothes!"

"Why are you dressed like a girl?" a boy near the back of the huddle shouted to Orion.

"Is that your girlfriend with you?"

I looked from one child to another, beginning to panic. There were seven faces in all. Seven children, more than half of whom were bigger and taller than I, and at least as big as Orion. The children had squinchy eyes, made squinchier by their fat cheeks; their smiling mouths seemed lopsided, cruel, wet. In that instant I felt for all the world like I was taking part in a gangster movie, and my mind raced with thoughts of how I was supposed to act during such a hard-boiled encounter.

"That's my *sister*," Orion said.

"How come you got woman's clothes on?"

"They're Mother's," I said. "She's lost, we think. Do any . . . do any of you have a phone we could use?"

"No," said the ponytailed girl. "What do you want to do, call the police and tell them you stole your mom's clothes?"

"Thief!" the freckled one said, taking me aback by singling me out with a finger. "You took her purse, too? Does it got any money in it?"

"Mother has lots of pocketbooks," I said confusedly, trying to bring things back to a reality I could follow. "She's got a million of them, at least."

"What—is she rich?"

"Is she a movie star?"

"Is she Farrah Fawcett?"

"No," I said, wondering if the inquisitor was pulling my leg— whoever heard of a name as preposterous as Farrah Fawcett? "But my grandmother was an actress. Her name was . . ."

The explanation died in my throat as the freckled creature came up to me, nose to nose. I confirmed that she was a girl then, for she had pierced ears with tiny stud earrings in the shape of daisies. That didn't strike me as a boyish thing to wear. Her face was so close to mine that I could feel the breath expelled from her nostrils.

"If your grandmother's a famous actress," she said, "how come you're so ugly? Actresses are supposed to be pretty."

That was a very interesting, very direct question. I had never given much thought to whether I was ugly, but now that this girl had mentioned it, I realized that Mother had never once told me I was pretty. Perhaps there was a reason for that.

"I don't know," I said as humbly as I could, and the girl curled her upper lip to expose her teeth.

Jean Harlow came to mind when I looked at her. I had always thought Jean Harlow had a singularly unattractive face—doughy yet rough, with eyes that were both vacant and fierce—and something about this girl looked like Harlow to me; I'd always thought *her* ugly, but what did I know? My mother had assured me that the actress had been regarded as a great beauty—especially by men. With this in mind, I curled my own upper lip, hoping it would look glamorous.

To my complete chagrin, the girl raised one of her mittened hands and clobbered me across the side of the face. It was a poorly executed strike, dulled by the sogginess of the mitten, but shocking to me all the same.

Orion—why wasn't he doing anything? For the first time in my life he was useless to me, relegated to the back of the small crowd that was now closing around the girl and me.

"Oh, dear, are you crying?" she asked, slinging an arm around my neck. "I didn't mean to make you cry. Don't cry, little baby . . . don't cry." The mittened hand came up again, this time to dry off tears she had only imagined were there; the melting snow from her hand had streaked my face with wetness. Just as I regained my breath, the girl retracted her arm and struck me a second time.

"Dummy!" she chortled.

Some of the children were laughing, or murmuring to themselves in a gobbling sort of language. My tormentor put her arm around me again, shouldering me from the crowd with her false concern, and I decided in that moment that there was nothing I could do but surrender, or at least play along. I obligingly let a trickle of melted snow run tearlike from the corner of my eye, and she obligingly waited for it to fall halfway down my cheek before pummeling me again. The pain was much more endurable once I was braced for it.

My rescue came in the form of the yellow school bus nosing a path down the road. "Bus! Bus!" shrieked the children, and at this eruption the Jean Harlow girl unhanded me and pushed her way to the front of the small crowd. I sidled up to Orion, who was turning grayer by the minute, and took his hand. His cold fingers locked around mine.

The bus came to a full stop, and the door opened magically, folding in on itself with the quick snapping movement of a paper fan. All seven children began shoving and jostling to get on board, and I was somehow brought in step with them. Worriedly, I spun around to locate Orion while the children behind me beat my back with their fists, sending me forward.

"What do we do? Do we get on it?" I shouted.

"Listen to her," one of the children said. "Doesn't know if she's on the right bus!"

The bus didn't look like my idea of a right bus. My idea of a right bus would have had nicer passengers on it, for starters. I had no sooner thought this than one of the children gave me such a push that I was sent sprawling up the stairs, toward the bus driver, who didn't so much as look at me askance. Orion made haste to board after me, snagging me by Mother's coat sash and pulling me to my feet.

"Careful, kids. Watch your step," the bus driver said. He still wasn't looking at us. His eyes were fixed on the rearview mirror in front of him.

"Excuse me," Orion said. "Excuse me, we want to know—"

"Move it!" yelped an impatient voice behind us.

"We have to find out where—"

"Grab a seat already, Jimmy. We're running late," said the bus driver. I noticed then that he had a rose-pink mole on the back of his neck that distended like a wee, fleshy finger. It wasn't egg- or apple-sized, but goodness knew it could grow that large in a few weeks' time. How could a man so afflicted be of any use to us?

"I'm not Jimmy," I heard Orion mutter behind me.

One look down the length of the bus told us that the seats held two children apiece, although some were only half occupied; everyone began filling in the vacancies—some of the already-seated children gesticulating to friends, flagging down preferred seatmates. Neither Orion nor I was among those flagged. What few pairs of eyes made contact with mine were pebbly and bold, and it didn't take me long to learn to keep *my* eyes down.

Near the back of the bus was an unoccupied seat, and I all but collapsed into it gratefully, pulling Orion down with me. The bus driver yelled some further admonishment to the children as the last of them scurried for places. Then the door at the front unfolded shut, and the bus began to move.

Almost instantly the bus became the hottest, most airless place I could ever imagine. The cluster of children produced a heat and an aroma that I had never experienced before—all that collective breath being expelled, and with it scents that emanated from scalps and pigtails, the chalky smell of gum being torn from the backs of baseball card packages, and the silvery odor of wet winter wool.

Making matters worse was the din of voices: girls' voices, sounding shriller than mine had ever sounded in my own ears, mixed in with the coarser calls of the boys. *So this is outside*, I thought to myself. Only we *weren't* outdoors anymore, really. I had to keep reminding myself of that. We were in a sort of inside, a public inside where I not only had to tolerate other people but also get accustomed to the feel of things moving under my feet, of things moving past the windows. I dared not look out the window for fear of what I might see rushing by; instead, I looked at the children seated around us, some of whom were letting their heads bob sleepily with the motion of the bus. One girl sitting diagonally across from me caught my eye and smiled shyly. She was plump, with pale cheeks and brown hair parted severely in the middle. I looked away, afraid.

I turned to Orion and said, in my absolute lowest voice, "If it's called a bus *stop*, why does the bus keep going?"

"It stops long enough for you to get on it," Orion whispered back.

"Like a merry-go-round?"

"Sort of," he said, "only it goes in one direction. Straight ahead, not around." No sooner had he said that than the bus took a sharp turn to the right, and Orion made an on-the-spot amendment: "I mean, it can go in more than one direction sometimes, not always in a straight line . . ."

"But where is it *going*?" I interrupted.

"To school, I think."

I sucked in my breath.

"But we're not actually going into the classroom. We'll just find a grown-up who can tell us about Mother, that's all. Maybe the bus driver can tell us . . . once everyone gets off . . . " Orion's voice dwindled away, and I could tell he had little faith that we'd get assistance from the likes of the mole-necked bus driver, who continued to fuss with his radio and glance in his rearview mirror haphazardly.

"That girl who hit me . . ." I whispered.

"She's awful."

"They're all like that, aren't they?"

Orion offered no reply, which compelled me to push the issue further. "If she'd hit you," I said, "I'd have hurt her. If *anyone* had, I would have." I looked all around the bus, hoping that the freckled Jean Harlow girl had overheard this powerful sentiment, but saw no one with a hood like hers. She must have taken it off, rendering herself unrecognizable.

"I don't think you're supposed to hit people ever," Orion said. "It's not considered polite."

Politeness be hanged; I was too busy envisioning my hand making contact with the plump, dappled meat of the girl's cheek. What a satisfactory reverberation it would have made! Still, I had the good sense to drop the subject. I counted the windows on the bus; there were twenty-four of them, twelve on one side and twelve on the other.

"Is a bus kind of like a little house?" I asked, settling back in my seat. "Like a house that goes someplace?"

"You could say that," Orion said, looking out his window.

The course the bus took was narrow and winding, with little to see but the occasional broken-down barn, the branches of trees leaning and stretching toward us, the road below pitted and covered with potholes that jostled us in our seats. The other children became restless; two of them in the seat before us had begun pulling each other's hair, an act made more burlesque by their howls. Orion and I paused to look at them with interest before resuming our conversation.

"Orion," I said. "What do you think Mother will do if she gets home before us and sees we left the house?"

He gave me a uniquely Orion shrug. "I doubt she's even come home yet."

"But what if she does?"

"She'll probably faint and won't wake up for a long time."

"Maybe she'll faint and hit the floor so hard she'll fall through it like I did," I said.

Mother was a splendid fainter, so this was not an unlikely scenario. Of course, I had never known her to faint for real, but she often showed us her talent for making her body go slack, sinking to the floor in a whoosh of skirts; she said that a good hard faint was the litmus test, whatever that was, of any performer's ability. After giving the matter more thought, I had to admit that it would be less likely for her to feign a faint without the benefit of an audience; whatever would the point of that be?

"Maybe . . ." I started to say, but the sudden flutter of "Shhhh! Shhhhhh!" clipped the thought short.

"The lights are on!" chorused a few children around me. "The lights are on!"

"What does that mean?" I said aloud to anyone within earshot, paying no heed to Orion's squeeze of my arm. Sure enough, someone had overheard, for a terse, anonymous reply drifted over to me.

"It means shut up, you dummy!"

I had no idea why the appearance of a light meant shut up, but the response it elicited made me think this was serious business. I followed the upward gaze of the other children and saw that a row of small lights on the ceiling had come on.

I suppose the same thing would have happened at our house if Mother had made the grand gesture of tearing the tar paper off the outside of the windows, showing us the light. That would have silenced us, no question. But the windows of the bus still allowed in plenty of sunlight, while the artificial light was considered the thing to fear; why this illogical, topsy-turvy response?

I slunk as low as I could in my seat, and Orion slunk down with me. We were still in these slouched positions when the bus came to a stop. I popped my head up and saw that we were being deposited before a redbrick building, tall and rectangular—like a box of DODD'S TABLE CRACKERS, I thought, and I puffed up with pride at having made this connection.

"That's the school," Orion said.

"Really?"

My pleasure dissipated as the passengers stood up and began shoving and hurrying and galumphing down the aisle with a vehemence that left me feeling paralyzed. They plopped in various ungainly ways out of the bus, landing on the ground below with about as much finesse as newborn colts dropping out of a mare (I had seen this, too, on the nature show—one of its more unforgettable episodes). Orion and I didn't dare budge, waiting for the others to clear out so as to avoid being trampled, when, from the front, the bus driver said, "Everybody off?"

We remained dead quiet. I didn't want to give this man any reason to yell at us again; we needed to ingratiate ourselves with him, difficult though this idea seemed. "Maybe we ought to go

AND THEN IT'S THE END

WE DID OUR BEST NOT TO BETRAY ourselves during those moments when the bus pulled out of the school parking lot. Orion and I lifted our heads until we were at eye level with the window, unable to resist stealing a look at what we were leaving behind: a sloping embankment with mystifying architecture rising out of the snow. I lacked the vocabulary to identify it as *playground equipment*; instead I thought of these metal configurations as sculptures or, better yet, stage props, since the children playing on them were so immersed in their roles, so uninhibited.

Some of the children were slung belly first on the swings, the tips of their hair dragging in the snow. At the top of a high slide stood a lone boy, poised as an assassin, while the children below ran with sticks in their hands, trailing these in the slush that had settled around the plowed areas of the embankment—rituals of a tribe into which I'd never been initiated. I was profoundly grateful to watch them, every last one of them, recede into the distance.

"Keep sitting low," Orion said out of the corner of his mouth.

"Why?" I mouthed back. "The others are gone now."

Orion paused. "Yes, but I bet the bus driver wouldn't like it if he knew we were here."

It took a few seconds for this to sink in. "You should have moved faster," I said right in Orion's ear. "Why didn't you move to the front when everyone else did?"

"Well, why didn't you? You were the one with the aisle seat."

"I was waiting for you to tell me what to do."

"Why should I be the one to tell you everything?"

I had no answer for that. My brother and I moved from our seat to the space on the floor, shielded by the rows of gray vinyl seats in front of us. We could sit comfortably enough with our knees drawn up; I placed my forehead against the vinyl seat and felt a throbbing, a vibration that started in my forehead and ended in my rattling teeth.

At the helm of the bus, unaware of his cargo, the bus driver spoke amiably into his radiolike gadget, which seemed funny to me. It sounded as if someone were talking back to him, but the second voice was too faint for me to make out the words.

"Roads aren't bad at all," the bus driver said. "Had some trouble coming in on 95 earlier, but other than that I been surprised how easy it is."

I strained my ears, fruitlessly, to hear his party's reply.

"Yeah, it's not enough to stick it to me by making me work on my birthday. A few half dozen other things gotta go wrong too."

"He has a birthday," I whispered to Orion. "I wonder what he's getting for a present."

Orion gave me a severe, even condescending, look that suggested this was none of my business.

"I want to know," I said, attempting to justify myself, "because Sally Ann in my primer was having a birthday too. Only I never got to finish reading that story."

"Oh, that old story," Orion said. "I read it ages ago."

"Do you know how it ends?"

"Of course."

"She's not doing a damned thing for me tonight, mark my words," the bus driver said—and for a second I thought this was in response to *my* query. "Biggest gift she could ever give would be keeping her claptrap shut for one night." He delivered a rollicking laugh.

"Tell the story," I said to Orion.

"I can't."

My brother could be something of a secret harborer, or at least cultivated himself as such, but I knew he was capable of generosity with a well-spun tale when given the right encouragement. "Yes, you can. Whisper it to me."

"You didn't see that earlier?" the driver was saying in the front. "Out there on the Old Belfast Road?"

"Please, Orion—tell it to me!"

Orion maneuvered his head around the seat, glancing uneasily at the driver. "Maybe I don't remember the story as well as I thought," he said.

"You do too. You never forget."

"You ain't kidding, George," the driver was saying—he pronounced it *Jawdge*—"they been traveling from away, most likely. It's almost always *them*."

The bus driver's sudden talkativeness was beginning to annoy. I wished he would go back to talking about something interesting, like birthdays, if he had to talk at all. I was about to mouth these words to Orion when the bus slowed down; I inched up just enough to peek outside the window, and I saw that we were turning into a fenced-in lot where a few other buses stood idle, like overgrown animals left to graze on frozen land.

The driver settled into a parking spot and turned off the engine. We heard him exit the bus with a surprisingly sprightly step. Orion and I sneaked another look out the window to see where he was going. He headed toward a small brick building at the far end of the lot, pausing to fumble around in his pocket for a cigarette.

"Where do you think he's going?" I asked, observing the swinging of his arms, his shoulders relaxing with the first intake of tobacco. "Is he coming back?"

"I'm sure he will," Orion said, though I wasn't convinced of his certainty. He was staring at the brick building with a worried expression, and I could understand why. There was something not right about this solitary structure in the midst of all these forsaken buses. "Maybe he's knows we've been in here all along," I said. "Maybe he's going inside to report us."

I pressed closer to Orion, huddled there on the floor. "What if we're trapped in here?" I asked, my lips moving against his jacket's thick padding. I checked to see how this had struck him and repeated the question. "The bus door opens by itself, whenever it wants to. What if it doesn't want to? What if we're trapped?"

"We're not," my brother said. "There's an emergency exit in the back. See?"

"How can you be sure it works?"

Orion gave the impression of pretending he hadn't heard, and I studied the dark lashes lowered on his cheeks with rising irritation. After a while he rested his chin on his knees and encircled his folded-up legs in his arms. To anyone else, this might have looked like an avoidance tactic, but I recognized it as the posture he liked to assume when he was preparing to launch into a story.

In hushed, measured tones, Orion began.

* * * * * * * * *

"It was a warm, bright, beautiful summer, and Sally Ann's feet and toes were the first to wake up. 'Today is my birthday!' she sang to herself."

I looked down at my own feet and toes—they were tinglier by the minute, poor things—and tried to imagine what a warm, bright, beautiful summer might feel like. But for the life of me I could not imagine my toes waking up before the rest of my body.

"Sally Ann had looked forward to this day for weeks, and Mother had said she could have a party with some of her little friends. She mailed notes and sent them off in a bunch of envelopes. Now I will tell you what the letter said:

"'Dear Little Friends'"—Orion paused to look at me. "That's how the letter begins: 'Dear Little Friends.'"

"That's how all letters begin."

"Well . . . kind of. 'Dear Little Friends: I am having a birthday party on Saturday. I will be six years old that day. Won't you come to my house at noon? Signed, your friend Sally Ann.'"

"I'd go," I said. "I'd go to any birthday party that anyone invited me to."

"I had my own party once," Orion said.

"You did not."

"Yes I did. A long time ago, I had cake and ice cream and I got two games and a plane." Orion rolled his heavy-lidded eyes toward the roof of the bus, startling me with their inky color; the irises were flooded, occupied almost entirely by dark pupils.

"When is your birthday, then?" I challenged.

"All I remember is that the leaves were yellow and red, and it was too cold to eat outside, so it must have been in the fall," he said. "Yours is in the fall, too. You had a party right before I did."

Seeing me open my mouth in protest, Orion kept going: "You were too little to remember. You still had feet pajamas on. You didn't even know it was your birthday . . . you just stared out the window all day long, shouting, 'Cars! I see cars!' and shaking this purple cow full of coins that someone had given you. It was a *coin bank*. You kept whispering, 'Jingle, jingle,' and then you tried to sink your top teeth into the windowsill. You left tooth marks in it, and you wouldn't even sit down for cake." Orion shook his head from side to side, his expression plainly indicating that I hadn't been very bright.

"Go back to the Sally Ann story," I said, shamed by this depiction of my younger self.

"Okay, where was I? . . . Before Sally Ann's birthday, her mother said that she might have whatever she liked, excepting a pony, and Sally Ann said, 'I would like a velocipede, please, and doll with real true hair.'"

"That's the part I want to know!" I said. "What's a velocipede?"

Orion thought this over, one eyebrow cocked and the other hooded over his eye. "It's a centipede that goes very fast," he finally said.

"Oh," I said. "What's a centipede?"

"It's a bug that's the color of a penny, and it has a hundred legs and lives in the dirt."

"And in the bathroom tiles?"

"Maybe," Orion said. His eyes traveled upward again. "But it would be so much nicer to live in the dirt, don't you think?"

He offered this last with such earnestness that I couldn't help laughing. I realized then that this was the first time I'd laughed in almost twenty-four hours.

"It *would*," he insisted. "If we lived in the dirt I could dig a hole that goes from here to someplace where the plague hasn't come yet. All I'd have to do is get a map with a safe place on it and figure out how far the safe place is from here, and then I could bring a tape measure underground. When I got to the right number of inches, I'd know it was time to start digging our way out again."

"Do they make a tape measure that long?" I asked, having no idea who "they" might be. I hoped Orion wouldn't call me on this generalization.

"No, but I could add the numbers together."

I wilted a little under his confident gaze. Mathematics always intimidated me, and I was grateful when he returned to the story.

"Dolls, velocipedes . . . ah, yes, I remember what comes next. See, Sally Ann was so excited, knowing that there might be presents with paper and ribbons at the breakfast table that morning. But as she went downstairs she noticed that her throat hurt. That seemed . . . peculiar, but she got sore throats every once in a while and her mother gave her hot tea with honey, which made her feel better."

I looked up sharply.

"But as soon as Sally Ann reached the breakfast table, her mother saw her and exclaimed, 'Why, Sally Ann! Your face is plastered with red spots!'"

"Oh, no!" I nearly shrieked, forgetting where I was. "Livered spots!"

"Potato eyes!" Orion said, and the corners of his own eyes crinkled with the most inappropriate smile I had ever seen.

"Don't tell me another word," I said. "I don't think I can stand it!"

"'You will have to tell the other children that they can't come over,'" he went on in a mellifluous Mother-voice. "'There will be no birthday party for you, Sally Ann.'"

"Horrible," I murmured disconsolately. "Oh, horrible."

I covered my face with my hands. I did not like to cry—much better, I thought, to reap accolades for bravery—but I did feel as though tears were close.

"All right," Orion said after witnessing my struggle for a minute or two. "I lied."

"About what?"

"I changed some things around," he said. "The story from the primer's much duller than the one I told. Sally Ann gets every single present she asked for, and everyone has a good time at the party, and then it's The End."

"I don't think that's dull. I think it's so much better when you tell it just as it is."

"Is it?" he asked. "I like my way better."

We looked out the bus window. Up in the sky was a plane that left a cloud-tail streaming behind.

The plane moved smoothly, reminding me of Orion's cherished plane that had once swum through bathwater; in my mind, the sky became part water and the plane an excellent swimmer.

Without a word, Orion and I watched it—the whole of it—until the plane changed back to what it had been all along: only a plane that had passed us by and entered the clouds, beclouded.

* * * * * * * * *

We were so absorbed in watching the plane that we failed to notice the driver's approach, and when the bus door reopened and his footfalls sounded on the steps, neither Orion nor I was prepared.

It would have been easier, perhaps, if we'd given ourselves up then and there. To this day I cannot say why we did not—why we could not. But we were children, and frightened; for children that is reason enough.

We lowered ourselves till our chins rested on the floor and we were looking underneath the seats. Through the gap between the seat and floor we could see the driver's boots and the tip of a broom sliding to and fro in a listless stroke. His feet and the broom vanished momentarily as he swept along the aisle, but then his boots were within our line of vision again, a little closer this time—closer and closer still, until there was nothing to do but wait for him to come.

Because of what was and is to come. That's the answer.

"Follow me," Orion said. "I know what to do now. It just came to me."

"What?"

He was already starting to climb over me, making his way to the aisle. "Come on, follow me. There's no use talking to him. Let's get out of here." At that moment the driver loomed over us and his eyes locked with mine. His big, hammy hand shot out, closing on my wrist, and Orion, who had just scrambled to his feet, took off running with all his might toward the back of the bus. "Come *on*!" he huffed over his shoulder one last time, but I was frozen, my arm caught in the man's grip.

"Hold it right there!" the bus driver said to Orion, but my brother was already pulling a lever on the emergency door in the back of the bus, and the next thing I knew, the door was open and he was knee-deep in the snow. I raised myself up a little to see Orion hesitate ever so briefly, hiking up the back of Mother's jacket so he could run without tripping on it. With the jacket so held and his elbows crooked, the deep snow grabbing at his boots with each step, he might have been a comical sight, but what made it sobering was that no one chased after him. No one tried to stop him. He began a slow and laborious jog down the road—perhaps assuming I was behind him all along.

"I have to go where my brother's going," I said, looking up at the bus driver.

"You're not going anywhere till you tell me what you're doing on my bus."

"You called him Jimmy when we got on," I said. "You let us get on."

"Huh?" The driver shook his head. His broom was still half lifted, as if to strike. "What on earth's the matter with you? You shouldn't be here."

"Our mother is lost."

"Lost?"

Something about the man's voice changed then, but the damage was already done. I could not bear to look at him anymore, to see the sudden changes in him; I could not risk seeing any more unkindness, any more of that which I did not understand.

"Sweetheart . . ." the driver said.

"Leave me alone!" I said. "We have to find her, that's all. We can find her by ourselves! Just let me go with my brother!"

"You're getting yourself all worked up, sweetheart. No need for that, is there? We'll figure this out. Here, you'd better wipe, um, with this." With rough uncertainty, the driver reached into his pants pocket and pulled out a handkerchief. He attempted to apply it under my nose, and I swatted it away, infuriated.

Then the driver's intentions became clear to me. A stain of blood was on the handkerchief where it had touched my nose—a stain that opened and swelled with the luxuriance of something newly in flower.

Blood. My blood.

I raised my hand to my face, and in the exact instant that I did, a well of red plopped to the front of Mother's coat. Another followed. I felt as if I were undergoing a seasonal change, as if I were losing all my petals, helpless to stop the process.

"Tip your head back," the man was saying, but it was not his voice I was listening to.

The first sign you're dying is a bad nosebleed, Orion had said on an afternoon when we'd been safely ensconced in his room, an afternoon when our mother had been safely ensconced at work, ready to come back to us at the appointed time. *Once that first nosebleed comes, it's over.*

I did tip my head back then—not to arrest the flow of blood, in deference to the driver's wish, but to open my mouth and scream. I screamed so loudly that I went sightless and deaf to all but the sound and shape of my own cry.

BOOK TWO

THE KINDNESS OF STRANGERS

I DIDN'T HAVE MUCH REASON TO THINK of my first bus driver over the years, but when I was older and beginning to be interested in newspaper obituaries, I saw him listed among the dead. He was predeceased by his loving wife. He had been a bus driver for thirty-five years and was said to have enjoyed his work. In his lifetime he had driven more children to and from school than I could conceive of; I imagined that in all those years, Orion and I were the only children he had driven unwittingly, his only stowaways.

But I had no such capability for reflection at the time. I knew only terror as the bus driver directed me across the parking lot and inside the brick building without lifting his heavy, blunt hand from my shoulder for an instant.

He took me through a garage that reeked of mold and gasoline and into a cramped kitchenette. Pointing to a metal folding chair in the corner, he told me to sit down. I followed this order, too frightened to utter a word. I had never been in a room alone with an adult man before. I might as well have been alone with a Minotaur, or a biblical beast with ten horns and seven heads.

The bus driver kept an uneasy distance from me as I took my seat. It was almost as if he were as afraid of me as I was of him. It would have been hard for him not to have noticed how I was shuddering from head to toe as the blood continued to trickle from my nose, albeit at a slower rate than before; at one point he handed me a fresh wad of napkins with clumsy solicitude. "Easy does it," he mumbled. "That bad old nosebleed'll be gone before you know it."

And despite my belief that he was saying whatever he needed so the tears would stop, it turned out he was right. The bleeding subsided. My tears, and some of my terror, subsided along with it. I felt curiously drained, and somewhere in the back of my mind I could hear Mother's voice saying—no, purring—*I felt wonderfully emptied out, afterward.*

The bus driver tried to smile at me, the corners of his mouth not quite lifting all the way up. "There, now, that's better," he said. "What can I get for you? Whyn't I make you a cup of hot chocolate to warm you up?"

"All right," I said. Why not? It seemed, all at once, as though time had stopped. I could sit there forever in my mother's over-sized coat, hunching my shoulders for warmth and clutching at her pocketbook, and no one would miss me. With no one to note my absence, what did I matter? Sniffling a little, I watched the bus driver prepare a cup of hot chocolate, which was something I couldn't recall ever having had before; he tore open a paper packet and poured a powdery substance into a cracked mug that said MERRY CHRISTMAS on it. I tried not to stare too much at the fleshy mole on the back of his neck as he added water to the mug and heated it in an oven he called a microwave. ("The nuker," he explained, and he laughed a dry little laugh, as if this were a joke I should understand.) He served the hot chocolate alongside a paper plate holding three small, hard cookies that he said might be stale but seemed perfectly edible to me.

"I need to make a phone call," the bus driver said. "You okay for now? You seem to be doing good. I'll be just in the next room for a minute. Holler if you need anything."

"Okay," I said woodenly. I knew that I didn't have enough left in me to holler under any circumstance, and I had no particular reason to believe he'd be back. In my mind's eye all I could see was Orion dropping down into the snow, the snow pulling at his boots, trying to devour him. Alone with my snack, my hands still trembling around the mug, I was surprised by the hot chocolate's sweetness, and I'd drunk most of it before the man came back into the kitchen.

I only half heard the bus driver as he told me his name—Mr. Levesque—and apologized for how he'd reacted to finding us. "I seen you kids, and it startled me is all," he said, pulling a chair out as if he intended to sit down in front of me; then he changed his mind. "Gave me a shock. I'm not a mean person by nature, anyone can tell you that. How old are you? About five?"

"Seven," I said, looking somewhat ostentatiously into my empty cup and setting it back down on the table. Mr. Levesque took the cue and went to get me a second cupful. I wouldn't have dared to hint for seconds back home, but home seemed far away.

His back to me, stirring the powder into the water, Mr. Levesque asked, "So where do you and your brother live?" He asked it in a very conversational way, as if he were inquiring about my favorite color, and I told him that we lived in Mother's house. "Do you know the address? The street number?" he asked, and I told him that I couldn't remember it, but that there had been a boarded-up house and a general store farther down the road from us.

At his urging, I tried to answer the question of why we got on the bus. I had already explained bits of it between hiccupping sobs while we walked to the garage. But all I could think of was Mother, and now of Orion, who was goodness knew where. Someone needed to find him before he strained his poor lungs any more. I tried to express this to the bus driver, but my voice kept catching and thickening at parts of the story, making it harder and harder to talk.

"Now don't get yourself in a state," Mr. Levesque said at last. "We'll sort this out. I got a guy, a patrol cop, sent out to look for your brother. And do you know Officer Shelton? He's coming to talk to you. He's a neighbor of mine, a policeman. If you were big enough to read you'd probably have seen his name in the newspaper."

"We don't get the newspaper," I said. "But I know how to read a little bit, if it isn't in cursive."

"Do you, now," the man said, more as a comment than a question. "You like reading? We got a couple magazines somebody left here. You want to look at them while we wait? You want to look at them and maybe have some more of them godawful cookies?"

I said yes to both and ended up with a copy of *Time* magazine (the cover looked a bit warped, as if someone had read it in the bathtub) and three more of the hard little cookies. I nibbled and sipped and turned the pages, trying to sound out the longer words in my head and trying to guess meanings from the photos: *President Carter pardons most Vietnam draft dodgers. In Helsinki, Soviet skaters Sergei Shakria and Marine Tcherkasova are the first skaters to perform a quadruple twist lift.* I stared at the long names in this last sentence until my eyes almost crossed from the effort and looked at the picture of a couple in sequined, theatrical costumes that, in the case of the woman, showed a lot of leg. I tried not to pay attention to Mr. Levesque, who was trying not to look at me, having hoisted himself up to sit on the countertop, his legs drumming against a cupboard and his eyes continually darting to the clock on the wall.

I had finished the last cookie and was almost done with the magazine when a tall, stout man in a dark blue uniform and a short, slight woman in regular clothes came in, stopping in the doorway just long enough to scrape the snow off their boots. Mr. Levesque met them at the door and shared a few words with the man, speaking in a whisper that rose and fell almost apologetically. "I thought it was a prank," Mr. Levesque said at one point—that ugly word, *prank*, jumping out. The officer nodded understandingly and then pretended to notice me for the first time. He did an exaggerated double take. His keen blue eyes bulged out for emphasis.

"Who's *this* little girl?" he said in a voice that came deep from his belly. I was embarrassed on his behalf, embarrassed for his bad acting. "I'm guessing you must be Esther?"

"Asta," I said and spelled it for him. I had known how to spell my name since I was eleven months old, and I was glad to have a chance to show this off. "Well then, Asta, I'm Officer Shelton," he said, taking a yellow pad out of his pocket and writing something down. "This lady here—" he said, pointing to the woman behind him, a quiet woman with short brown hair that feathered up from under her knitted cap, "is Miss Shelton, my sister. She happened to be visiting when Mr. Levesque here called. I don't suppose you know if your last name is spelled H-e-w-i-t-t?"

"Yes, that's right."

"We understand you were out riding the buses," he said.

"Only one bus," I said. "But I wasn't by myself. My brother was with me."

"So we heard. We were lucky enough to pick *him* up down the road. This time of year you can't go running off and not leave footprints, right?"

"Where is he?"

"He's out in the car with my partner, resting up. Getting warm. Probably picking out some tunes on the radio."

"That's good," I said, then wondered if it was. Would Orion have been better off if the police hadn't picked him up so quickly? Would he have found some cellar or basement to sleep in overnight or have built an igloo-like shelter out of frozen snow? No, I didn't like to think of him experiencing an igloo without me—the thought made me jealous.

"Your brother's not talking right now, Asta, so if you don't mind, I'll just ask you a couple of questions. It's your mother's name I am wondering about. Is your Mother's name Hewitt too? Yes? And do you know her first name?"

"Loretta," I said.

"Pretty," the officer said, writing it down. "And you don't know her address?"

I shook my head.

"Telephone number?"

"We don't have a phone."

"Do you go to school? Somebody at school might have an address for you."

"I don't go to school. I take my lessons at home on account of the plague."

"What plague do you mean, honey?" This from the woman called Miss Shelton. In contrast with her brother, her voice was thin, almost nasal.

"The one I have now," I said.

Officer Shelton and his sister exchanged glances. "Miss Shelton is a trained nurse," the officer said to me. "She can take a look at you in a minute and find out why you're having that nosebleed we heard about. But first I'd like to ask you a few more questions, if you think you're up to it."

"Okay," I said. "But we'd better hurry. We have to keep looking for Mother."

"I've got people on the lookout right now, dear." The officer pronounced it *dee-ah*. "Mr. Levesque was good enough to tell me the little bit that he knows. Now, is it just your mother and brother who live with you? No daddy? No other brothers or sisters?"

I told him that my father was dead and that there was no one else in the family. Both my parents had been only children, I told him, and I hadn't known any of my grandparents, not even Lucia Lively, the great silent-movie actress who had met an untimely end. But I would have liked to have known her, I told him.

The police officer, scribbling in a fury, asked me more questions.

He asked if I knew when I was born. He asked if I remembered how long we had been living at our house. I said that I didn't know and couldn't remember back very far.

I told him about falling asleep and realizing that Mother wasn't there and waiting until the next morning to look for her in earnest. I told him about the hidden stairwell and putting on

Mother's clothes and leaving the house. He saw that I was holding Mother's pocketbook in my lap—clinging to it, really—and asked if I were carrying anything inside it; I opened the beaded bag to show him the flashlight and the assortment of acorns and the letter from my father. "I didn't get to read very much of this yet," I said of the letter. "Orion and I were going to read it later."

The officer skimmed a paragraph or two and said, "That's all right, dear. I'll just take the letter for safe keeping."

Out of the corner of his mouth, more to Mr. Levesque than to me, he said, "The address on the envelope is Scituate, Massachusetts, but the letter was mailed years ago. Still, may as well have someone put a call in and see if there's a record of electricity service issued to anyone named Hewitt there."

"How often do you get these nosebleeds, Asta?" he asked, turning back to me as though there had never been an interruption.

"Never," I said. "Today was the first one. I guess it's the first sign that I'm dying."

"Oh, I don't know about that," the officer said, suppressing a laugh. "Would you, Ginny? Do you know anything about that?" He appealed to Miss Shelton, who had quietly stepped forward during this interrogation and was now standing right next to me. What was she sneaking up on me for? I wondered.

"A nosebleed usually doesn't mean anything serious," she said. "Lots of children get nosebleeds for lots of different reasons. I'd like to take a quick look at you, Asta, just to get your blood pressure and listen to your heart and take your temperature. None of those things will hurt," she added, probably seeing the worry flicker across my eyes.

Was she going to look for more lumps? I thought that maybe I should help her out a little and point out the lump near my pelvic bone, but then I thought I'd best say nothing about it for fear of insulting her intelligence. I had seen enough medical shows on TV to know that a trained nurse could find such things on her own.

The bus driver and the officer went out into the garage, and in a few minutes I could hear their low voices and smell tobacco wafting into the room. Miss Shelton asked me to take off Mother's jacket, and she stood back and looked me up and down. "You're a little thing, aren't you?" she said, more to herself than to me. "Do you get enough to eat at home?" She casually wrapped a cuff around my forearm and tightened it until I was afraid that the arm might burst like an orange when it's squeezed. "Do you feel hungry sometimes?"

"I think so," I said. "We like to be hungry, though. It's good discipline for us."

She cocked her head, tightened some more, listened. "Mmm," she said. She slid a cold stethoscope under the loose neck of my dress and listened to my heart. Officer Shelton came back in, alone, after Miss Shelton had smoothed my dress down. She turned her head and said in a low voice, "There's a mild arrhythmia. I'd like to see her get an EKG and some blood work."

Blood work sounded like the most rigorous kind of work imaginable. I wasn't at all sure I was up for it. "Where would we do that?" I asked. "At a hospital?"

"Sure, a hospital," Officer Shelton said in a sportive way. "Have you ever been in a hospital before, Asta? It would be a good idea to have a doctor look after you while we look for your mom."

I thought of the hospital waiting rooms I'd seen on some of the medical shows. The odd hum of the rooms, with people both languid and tense—expectant, anxious, bored. The excited comings and goings of doctors and nurses. "All right," I said. "That might not be so bad."

Officer Shelton asked if I wanted to go to the hospital in the squad car with him and his partner and Orion or ride with Miss Shelton in the emergency van they'd come in. Without hesitating, I said that I wanted to ride with Orion—even though riding in an emergency van sounded like more fun.

Miss Shelton helped me back into Mother's coat and took me by the hand to lead me outside. This made me uncomfortable—I didn't need to be held by the hand just to walk a few feet—but I felt it wouldn't be nice to reject her. As we were leaving, I saw Officer Shelton having a last word with Mr. Levesque, who had emerged from the garage, tucking a book of matches into his front shirt pocket. I was able to make out the following: *Hewitt house . . . right off the old Shaw Road . . . some property up there . . . says a woman lives by herself in one of them . . .* before Miss Shelton opened the squad car door for me.

Another police officer was sitting behind the steering wheel of the car. By the looks of him, I thought with a germ of hope, this police officer might be Mexican—there was a unit about a Mexican boy named Manuel in the section of my primer called "Children from Faraway Lands," and on one especially entrancing page Manuel could be seen blindfolded and beating the stuffing out of a piñata.

"This is Officer Tagliaferre," Officer Shelton said.

"Hello," I said to him, and then I saw the dark, small shape of my brother in the backseat, clumsily wrapped in a blanket. "I want to ride in the back, please. With *him*," I said to the officer, pointing at the brother shape.

Officer Shelton opened the door to the backseat, and I slid in next to Orion. He had the blanket pulled around his head so that only his eyes, a tuft of his black hair, and part of his tender forehead showed. "Are you all right?" I asked him.

Orion made a sound that was neither a yes nor a no.

"He ain't talking," the officer who looked like Manuel said, in a way that was probably meant to be more helpful than judgmental. "He ain't feeling too good right now."

"Of course he's not," I said. I put my arm around him, or around the blanket-covered Orion-shape, and I felt his shoulders rise and fall as he expelled a little sigh. Even under the blanket, I could feel the hard little stones and articulations of his spine.

From the front passenger seat, Officer Shelton asked me if I wanted the radio turned up, and since Orion wasn't saying anything, and the officer seemed to want music, I let him play with the tuner until he found a song he liked. When Mother listened to music, she usually played show tunes, jazz, or blues—Billie Holiday and Sarah Vaughan were her favorites—and I liked those songs too, with their inspired rhymes that paired words like *glamorous* with *amorous*—but the officer chose a pop music station, one which crackled and hissed for a moment before homing in on its signal.

There is something particularly magical about listening to music from a car radio while looking out a window at a vast, open sky. It was starting to get dark—and the dark, as I remember it, was the most beautiful, pregnant darkness I had ever seen. I held on firmly to Orion. On the radio, a man with a keening voice was singing about a yellow brick road. I couldn't understand most of the words he sang, but I understood the word *good-bye* and knew that this good-bye was terribly mournful, tragic even. As I sat there in the squad car with two men I didn't know, my mother gone and my brother seeming far away, I felt my heart and throat fill with a sadness, a sadness so tangible it almost felt good.

* * * * * * * * *

At the hospital, Orion and I were taken to separate rooms and things began to happen in quick succession. It was almost as though I experienced those hours out of body, my self hovering at some high point near the ceiling while the corporeal me sat on a table, attended to by medical staff. The doctor asked me to strip down to my underpants, which upset me, and had me dress in a paper robe. He asked me to breathe in and out deeply while he put a cold instrument on my back. Then a nurse applied what she called a *blood pressure cuff*, even tighter than Miss Shelton's cuff, and took a little rubber-tipped hammer and whacked each of my knees with it. When nothing happened, she whacked again, and without warning I burst into tears. I had the vaguest awareness of Miss Shelton in the corner of the room, her voice floating over to me.

It's just to test your reflexes, honey. It doesn't hurt you.

And I, crying harder: *But it hurts my feelings.*

I heard words back and forth: *pretty dehydrated . . . concerned about electrolytes . . . she's in better shape than the brother.*

From my position on the ceiling, the room tilted, slanted, spun in a slow circle. The little girl with the shorn hair and the round face and the angular body had a puckered, unattractive, splotchy face when she cried. Then the world opened up and became not a place of quiet, virtuous illness but of violation and public pain. It stayed that way for what felt like a long time.

* * * * * * * * *

I don't know if they gave me something to make me sleep, but I know that I dreamt. In the dream I was standing in a long, unlit corridor near an unfamiliar door. Orion was with me. I could tell from his appearance that we'd somehow grown older; I felt an aching in my bones at having shot up so quickly, at having become a gangling person in grown-up clothes that pulled against my skin. Orion knocked on the door. We seemed to have no real expectation of anyone opening it. But the door opened a crack, and a greeting that was both singsongy and affirming came out. The woman behind the door showed herself. Her dark hair was twisted up in pin curls, and a floor-length chenille robe hugged the sinews of her body.

It's a funny hour to come a-calling. Don't you think it's a little late? my mother asked, looking first at me and then at Orion. *Are you hoping I'll ask you in, or are you just going to stand there with your bare faces hanging out?*

It was Mother—our mother—behind the door; she had aged, but we recognized her. God, did we recognize her! And she, of course, recognized us.

I woke up and found myself in a small white room. Light oozed in through a window, and I instinctively moved to press my forearm against my eyes, to blot the brightness out. But my forearm didn't cooperate. There was something attached to me, I realized—long tubes sticking like tentacles out of my bandage-covered hand. I tried to shrug the tentacles loose, but they held fast. With a sinking feeling I realized that the doctor had no intention of letting me free anytime soon.

"Hello," a somehow familiar voice said. *Mother?* I thought for one split second. I looked in the direction from which the voice came and saw Miss Shelton in a chair by the side of my bed. She was reading a paperback book with the title *Sheila Levine Is Dead and Living in New York*, but when my eyes met hers, she set the book down spread-eagled in her lap. "How are you feeling?" she asked.

"Tired," I said. "I've never felt so tired before." And it was true. I had slept so heavily that my head hurt; I had put all my energy into a deep, ferocious sleep. "Why are you here?" I asked, not out of rudeness but out of genuine curiosity. I had expected to wake up in a room alone.

"Somebody ought to be here, oughtn't they?" Miss Shelton retorted.

"I don't know."

"Well, I do."

She looked as if she hadn't gotten much sleep herself. I studied her face, which was more exposed now that she'd removed the knit cap; she might have been the same age as my mother, not quite as girlish as I originally thought. She had a puffiness under her eyes and not an ounce of makeup on, even though a little concealer might have done her a world of good. "I was dreaming about my mother," I said before I was aware I was going to. "It . . . it seemed like it was real."

The corner of Miss Shelton's mouth moved in an enigmatic way. "Maybe you heard us talking about her and your mind decided to put her in your dream."

"You found her?" I said, and I tried to sit up a little. I don't know how I knew. Maybe something in Miss Shelton's face gave it away. If I had not been so tired, I would have felt ecstatic. Instead I felt a dulled sense of relief. Miss Shelton, her trouser-clad legs slightly parted (even then, I had the vague thought that this was not the most ladylike way to sit), cupped her hands together and leaned as far toward me as she could.

"Do you know what the word *coincidence* means?" Miss Shelton asked.

"Yes," I said. "It's like a surprise."

"Kind of," she said. "That's a pretty good definition, actually. We found your mother by a coincidence. She'd been discharged from—let out of—the hospital less than an hour before you were brought in. I'm surprised you didn't meet each other coming and going. She was in a car accident—not too bad of an accident, just hit her head and got a broken rib, so they kept her overnight for observation, mostly to see if . . . Why are you looking at me like that?"

The dulled relief had expanded into a richer, more pleasurable feeling. Of course that's what had happened! Why hadn't I guessed? Mother hadn't meant to leave us alone; she had been heading home to us, just as she did every night, when an accident happened. I was almost giggling because I felt that Mother had been somehow vindicated, but I sensed that Miss Shelton would not understand this even if I tried to explain. "I just feel glad," I said.

"I'm sure you are. You must be happy to know your mother's all right."

"Yes," I said, even though there was more to it than that. "When is she coming to see me?"

"I don't know. The police will want to talk to her for a while, I'm sure. After that, I can't say what'll happen. I did hear she's been asking to see you and your brother."

"Where did Orion go? Why didn't they put him in here with me?" I looked around the ten-by-twelve hospital room with its little sink and bathroom, the window with venetian blinds that looked like rows of slitted eyes fixing on me with distrust or disdain. "There's enough space here for us both."

"He's in his own room. He's needing a little more care than you," Miss Shelton said. "You're going to be discharged tomorrow or the day after, whereas Orion might be here for a few more days, getting his strength back."

"What does *discharged* mean again?"

"It means sent home." Miss Shelton's shoulders twitched as if her own words had bitten her. "Or sent out of the hospital, if not home."

At that moment a nurse came in with a chart. She was almost as wide as she was short, with flyaway hair and a hectic complexion—the kind of woman who always speaks louder than necessary, especially around children. "Somebody's awake!" she bellowed cheerily.

"I was just telling Asta when she might be discharged," Miss Shelton said.

"Things are moving along," the nurse said. "There's a few more test results the doctors are waiting on. Your doctor will tell you this himself, but just to put your mind at ease, I can tell you that all your tests so far have been just fine. You're in good health overall. They were a little worried about your heart, but the tests show that everything looks good."

"Amazing how resilient the human body is," Miss Shelton said to the nurse in a low murmur.

"It *is*, isn't it?" she bellowed back.

"What about my lump?" I asked.

"Pardon?" The nurse, who had been taking a plastic wrapper off a thermometer, looked startled.

"My lump," I said, gesturing toward the lower half of my body with the hand that wasn't hooked up to tubes. "I've got a lump here."

"I don't know what you mean, honey. A lump? What lump?"

"The plague I have. That Orion and I have. The thing that's making us sick."

The nurse and Miss Shelton exchanged glances. "I don't know what you mean," the nurse said again.

"You've got nothing out of the ordinary," Miss Shelton said.

It was as if a pall came over the room. My eyes narrowed until I could hardly make out the outlines of Miss Shelton or the cheerful, rotund nurse. They were liars, the both of them. I shut my eyes hard—so hard they spasmed—so I wouldn't have to see either one of them anymore.

AN ANGEL BLOWN IN
FROM HEAVEN

THE FOLLOWING MORNING Mother was brought in to see me.

I say "brought in" because Mother did not come alone. She was escorted by a silent, barrel-shaped man in shirtsleeves who had even shorter hair than mine (although mine, thank goodness, was growing a bit more every day). My day nurse, Leslie, was at Mother's other elbow. I could tell she had no intention of leaving us alone; she, the strange man, and I were the audience for Mother's entrance.

And what an entrance my mother made, breezing through the door like an angel blown in from heaven! Despite the grimy-looking bandage on her temple and the fact that her hair was tied back with the kind of plain rubber band one sees in butchers' bundles, she was still resplendent in her red rubber zip-up boots and the fox-collar coat—radiant, even, as her eyes took in the sight of me.

"How's my Pork Chop?" she said, her voice carrying across the room. "Give me a hug, but oh, not too hard, my rib is broken." I barely had a chance to put my arms around her before she pulled away from my light grasp to address Leslie. "You're her nurse? I have to tell you, she looks *much* better than I expected. Not half so *pinched* as she looked before."

Leslie cleared her throat. In a low voice—but not low enough to go unheard by anyone in the room—she asked, "Is this your mother, Asta?"

"Oh, yes," I said against my mother's hair, for Mother was hugging me again—a fuller, more proper hug this time. Her coif, simply arranged though it was, was stiff with hair spray and tasted bitter against my tongue. I was reminded of the time I had scratched an itch in my ear and then put the finger into my mouth, inadvertently sampling some earwax. The taste was almost the same.

"What's that supposed to mean, *Is this your mother*?" my mother asked, disengaging herself once more and straightening to her full height—which was not very tall for a grown-up, admittedly. I straightened up a little in my bed too, as though her stage direction—PROUD POSTURE—had been issued. She pointed toward me, then laid her fingertips against her breastbone, her wrist arched. It was a gesture meant to convey earnestness, I thought—one of many I'd seen in the Big Movie Book. "Who else would I be? Look at us and tell me we don't have the same eyes, the same coloring." Mother faced me now, still using the same gesture, which struck me as superfluous— she didn't need to appeal to *me* in that way. "Asta, tell them I'm your mother."

"I did already."

"Mrs. Hewitt, you've gotta understand that we needed that

confirmation from your daughter," the barrel-shaped man said. Leaning against the doorjamb, he exuded weariness, as though he'd witnessed scores of scenes like this since his day had begun.

"Now that you've got your confirmation, please show enough courtesy to give me a moment alone with my child," my mother said.

Nobody, but nobody, could refuse my mother when she assumed such an imperious tone. The nurse and the man conferred briefly and agreed to wait outside my room for a few minutes. "If you need anything," Leslie said to me in parting—sounding a little sour, I thought—"I'll just be out here by the door."

Alone with me—or as close to alone as our interlopers would allow her to get—my mother sat in the chair at my bedside and gave me a searching, almost hungry look. I imagine that I gave the same look back. For some reason, my eyes were drawn to her mouth. I saw that her lipstick had dried up, leaving her with a red-flecked residue on her lips, but apart from this, her face was lovely, and her gaze was like a warm bath.

"Are you all right?" I asked her. "I heard you were in an accident."

My mother laughed ruefully. "The other day, when I was driving to the warehouse to buy groceries, going up the Old Belfast Road, I hit a patch of black ice and the car rolled over. They say that your life flashes before your eyes when something like that happens. Mine didn't, and it's a shame—it would have been interesting to see all those things I've forgotten from the past. But never mind little old me, I want to talk about *you*, Pork Chop—about your health."

"I'm all right."

"Are you? That's funny, they've been telling me you're mal-nourished. Out of all the health problems you've had, I should think that this would be the least of them! You've always been small-boned for your age, just like me when I was a child, but I fattened up later. By twelve, thirteen years old, I'd eaten one too many whoopie pies and had to go on a diet. You will too." She drew in a deep, unsteady breath. "Have they been telling you things about me? They're saying *terrible* things about me as a mother. Do you think I'm a bad mother, Asta?"

"No," I said. I shook my head and said it again, smiling a little at the very idea. "No!" All I could do was shake my head in that idiotic way and look at her—I couldn't look at her enough. It was as if a movie star had stepped off the screen, except bet-ter, for the movie star wasn't just someone you'd admired from afar but known in your heart all your life—known in a way you couldn't express.

"I don't profess to be perfect. I know that I'm not. But I can promise you that if I'd been kept in the hospital for one night longer, I'd have let someone know about you and Orion being alone in the house. I thought you'd be fine for one night and part of a day." She looked at a point just above my shoulder, her eyes turning pretty with a sheen that was not quite teary. "Never in a million years would I have expected to come home to an empty house! I thought someone must have come in and kidnapped the both of you . . . I thought maybe the kidnapper would come back to get me, and I was so afraid. By the way . . . did I ever tell you my mother, Lucia Lively, was cast in a vampire movie with a plot like that once—*The Vampyr Wife*? 'Vampyr' with a *y*. She got mostly edited out, of course, but to hear her tell it, she got to do a really delicious scream in one scene, and it happened right after a *thing* jumped out of a closet. Can you picture it?"

"Yes," I said, picturing Lucia Lively as I imagined her, with saucer-sized eyes flashing wildly in the dark, her plump hands fluttering near her face. "What happened next?"

"Never mind that. What *I* experienced was worse—worse than someone jumping out of a closet! I saw a hole in my closet floor and knew you must have gotten out. And for a moment—I shouldn't say this, but just for a moment—I felt something like relief. Not relief because you and Orion had let yourselves out rather than being kidnapped, although that was certainly part of it, but relief because you were *gone*. Do you understand what I mean?"

"Yes," I said again, but it must have sounded unconvincing.

"How can I explain it? It's like . . . it's like once something you love is gone it is kind of a relief—you never have to worry about losing it again. It's already lost."

"But I'm not lost," I said.

My mother laid her slender hand over my bandaged one, just managing to avoid the IV tube.

"It's like with your father," she said. "When he was finally gone, it was a relief. But then there's another part of me that still doesn't function without him. I was looking for his letters, up in my room, the morning of the accident. I felt like I *had* to find them, and I was getting myself in—kind of a state, looking. I'm afraid you must have thought me a terrible slob, leaving the room that way."

"Not at all," I said.

"Anyway," she said, "you can be sure I was on my way to the store down on Bond Street to make a phone call reporting my children missing, when these two police officers banged on the door and just about gave me a heart attack. Now they're trying to make it sound as though I would have never reported you missing—that I was *negligent*—when all I ever wanted was to keep you and Orion safe."

This made me uneasy, for the use of the past tense sounded all wrong. *All I ever wanted.* "Mother?"

"Yes, Asta?"

"The doctors haven't said anything to me about my lump. They haven't said anything to me about the plague at all."

My mother sat so still that I wondered if she'd heard me, but after a minute I understood that she was only thinking hard, parsing her words. "Doctors lie," she finally said. "They obfuscate."

"What does that mean?"

"It means they don't want to see the things that you and I and Orion see. The sickness all around us. There are people who deny God, too, just because they can't see Him, and that's *truly* negligent. What kills me," she went on, "is that the doctors speak as though I made your health *worse* when I only wanted to make it better. I only did what I thought was best for my children. And now I see you in the hospital getting fat and rosy already, the way children do, and I think that maybe the things I did *were* wrong."

"I don't think so," I said. "I think they were just right."

Mother moved from the chair to the edge of my bed. "You're a good girl, Pork Chop," she said. "I'm not sure I've told you that enough." Then she kicked off her shoes and curled up alongside me. She folded her hands under her cheek, like a little girl who has finished saying her prayers and is ready to be tucked in. Her eyes were bright as two shiny black buttons. I mimicked her posture, tucking my free hand under my right cheek, and found myself wanting to laugh, for I felt as if we were sharing a secret.

"Mother?" I whispered. "Is it true about the farmers letting the pigs and cows and horses go free to eat what's left of the dry, dead grass? And the animals having six wings about them and being full of eyes within?"

"How did you remember all that? Do you like thinking about the pigs and cows and horses going free? And the beasts with wings?"

"Sometimes," I said.

"Then you should hold on to those thoughts. Hold on to what gives you comfort." There was a ruminative silence on her end. "Do you know what would bring me comfort, Asta?"

"What?"

My mother caressed the back of my stubbly head. "Bringing you home today, that's what. But I don't think it's going to be that easy. Orion isn't even ready to leave the hospital."

"Have you seen him?"

"I did, but he was sleeping. I'm not sure if he knew I was there. Actually, I was worried that he knew but was pretending not to know, if that makes any sense. He looked as good as Freddie Bartholomew in *Little Lord Fauntleroy*, if the Little Lord had been wearing a hospital johnny," Mother said. "You needn't be afraid for him. For us. We'll be together again as soon as this mess is sorted out. No matter what stunts these poisonous case workers try to pull, we're going to be okay."

My mother closed her eyes. I waited for her to say more, but after a long lull, I wondered if she had fallen asleep. Her fingers were interlaced with mine. Matching the rhythm of my breathing to hers, I closed my eyes too. The next thing I remember is the nurse and the man helping her out of my bed, and the nurse,

her mouth a white, humorless line, straightening out the depres-
sion Mother had left in my sheets. I ached for her already.

* * * * * * * * *

From my hospital bed I watched the contestants spin the big
wheel on *The Price Is Right*—a show I'd never seen before—
and waited for the nurse to take me out for my second heart
test since being admitted to the hospital. The big wheel looked
heavy, monolithic, like the picture of a Ferris wheel I'd seen
in the primer—I could imagine each number on the big wheel
having a creaking little seat attached to it and passengers lined
up to pay a fare. I was still trying to watch the wheel when the
nurse helped me onto a gurney and rolled me out of the room.
My IV stand—the Skinny Kid, some of the other nurses called
it—dragged along at my side.

As was always the case when I went from one part of the hospital to another, I felt as though I were going on a grand and ter-
rifying excursion. The walls and floors gleamed a hostile white,
relieved only by the brown plaques on the wall in memory of Dr.
So-and-So or in gratitude to Mr. Such-and-Such for his gener-
ous donation. The nurse was pushing me down the hall when
she stopped suddenly and said, "Wait, I left your chart behind.
Stay here."

Even though I could walk on my own just fine, it would never
have occurred to me to get up off the gurney unattended. Docile
and flat on my back, I looked at the pitted ceiling, the unforgiv-
ing fluorescents overhead, which were dotted with blue-black
flecks that were probably trapped flies. I heard a sigh and lifted
myself on my elbows to see who had made it; at the far end of
the hall was another unattended gurney—another poor soul

who'd been told to "Wait just a minute," I guessed. I could see feet sticking out from under the white sheet; the toes pointed away from each other, forming a V like those of a ballerina about to make a plié. I was glad that I wasn't looking at a dead person's feet. The hospital was doubtless full of dead people. Just two nights prior, I had heard a child—a girl, it sounded like—in a nearby room, and her wail had reached such decibel levels that I couldn't sleep. But in the morning no sounds came from her room. I could only assume that she'd died and been taken away—a thought that hadn't upset me as much as it should have. I was just glad I wouldn't have to hear her screaming anymore.

I stared at the feet and waited for Nurse Leslie. After a while I saw one of the feet shift—hardly more than a twitch, as though a light breeze had tickled it. I made a game of continuing to watch for any further activity, but there was none. At last Nurse Leslie returned and we started down the hall again. "Away we go," she said, trying to sound jaunty but still puffing from having sprinted to my room and back.

As my gurney rumbled past the feet I'd been watching, I turned my head and caught sight of a small, dark head against a blue-paper-covered pillow; I saw a snub nose and ink-colored eyes. Before recognition could kick in, the head shifted to study the fluorescent lights overhead. But a moment later I realized that my brother and I were on the same floor of the hospital.

"Orion," I started to say over my shoulder, but it came out as a croak, and seconds too late.

"What's the matter?" asked Nurse Leslie, continuing to plow the gurney through the corridor.

"What do you mean?" I said innocently.

"You made a sound back there."

"Oh," I said. "It wasn't anything."

make the same mistake; I'd recognize him right away and say something meaningful. *Fancy meeting you here,* I might say, which was something Mother used to quip when Orion or I walked into the bathroom while she was using it. Or, if we swerved to avoid each other in the doorway: *Want to dance?* (This last greeting might not have made much sense, though, if we were both on our gurneys, flat on our backs.) I tried to sneak a look into each room I passed, hoping to catch a glimpse of my brother in one of them, but I never did. In one room I did see an old lady lying on top of her bed, nude from the waist down. "Isn't she cold?" I couldn't help asking my Nurse Leslie, who glanced in herself and then hustled me off to the laboratory for more blood work.

From what little the nurses had told me and from what I'd overheard, I'd learned that Orion was alert and conscious but still not saying a word. His doctors believed he was perfectly capable of speaking—he had passed every neurological test he had been given—but until he opened his mouth and uttered a syllable or two, it would be hard to tell the extent of his problems.

I wondered if our trek in the snow had frozen his throat, but the nurses thought this wasn't at all likely; speech came from the *brain*, they said, and his seemed to be functioning perfectly. He spent most of his time in bed, reading and playing puzzles—complicated puzzles, they told me, not ones for children. There was another sign, too, that his mind was sound. Orion had another patient in his hospital room, I was told—a little boy who was prone to coughing fits. On one occasion he had coughed so much that he couldn't breathe and began to turn purple, prompting Orion to buzz for the nurse. A person whose brain was frozen wouldn't have known enough to do that, Nurse Leslie told me, and I clung to this reassurance.

I had a hunch that Orion was just saving his voice for when he could talk to me or Mother, not wanting to waste mental energies on someone who wouldn't appreciate him. Heaven knew that the nurses and their barrage of well-intentioned questions and comments—"How are we feeling today?" "Nice morning, isn't it?"—were enough to turn any sensible person mute. I imagined him sitting up in bed, taking everything in, missing nothing, stockpiling details to share with Mother and me later. The day when we'd compare all the stories we'd tucked away would be a fine day indeed—a day worth waiting for, I was sure.

* * * * * * * * *

Immediately following my discharge from the hospital, I stayed in the home of Miss Shelton and her roommate, Jane. How this arrangement came about is not entirely clear to me. Perhaps Miss Shelton volunteered to take me in, or perhaps she had received outside pressure to do so. She and Jane lived on the outskirts of Bond Brook in a one-story, two-bedroom house shared with a slobbery dog named Ginger who divided her sleeping time between the two ladies' beds. I slept in the living room on a foldaway couch that sagged in the middle and had a crinkly plastic sheet over the mattress.

For the first day or two I was leery; it was Ginger who drew me out of my shyness. She was a standard poodle whose unclipped, grown-out coat gave her the look of a sheepdog, and she followed me in subservience around the small house, her black eyes hidden in an underbrush of fur. What I liked most of all was her ability to take direction. When I said, "Sit," Ginger sat without moving a muscle. When I said, "Stay," she stayed! "REGISTER EMOTION," I said, and she whined with convincing mournfulness. She wasn't so bad, I decided, even if she did smell a bit funny (she had a penchant for killing woodchucks, then rubbing her body joyfully all over their carcasses before rubbing herself on me).

Miss Shelton continued to work for the duration of my stay while Jane, who was a children's librarian, took time off to watch me. I wasn't used to adult supervision during the day, and though it seemed a bit unnecessary, I didn't altogether mind. Jane was plump and pretty, with a tendency to wear loose tunic-style dresses, her long, mouse-brown hair tucked into a bandana. She tried to teach me how to knit, and I didn't have the heart to tell her that Mother had already tried and failed to teach me; my mind always wandered once I'd knitted a row or two, and because of this I had never been able to create anything more impressive than an amoeba-shaped potholder. She taught me how to play Chinese checkers and Life and Connect Four, though we had to play at the table; if we played on the floor, Ginger, with her goatlike tendency to eat anything, would chomp on the game pieces. Jane gave me library copies of *Tikki Tikki Tembo* and *Bread and Jam for Frances*, and I found them both tremendous. Still, I liked none of these things as much as my Bible, my primer, and my Big Movie Book. As much as I tried to describe these and to impress upon her how much I missed them, she made no visible effort to hunt them down for me.

One might have expected me to feel displaced living in a regular home without my mother and brother. In hindsight, I think I must have been too shocked for sadness or even confusion. There were oddities, of course—moments that almost broke through my stupor. There was the evening, for example, when Miss Shelton and Jane were watching the local news, and I saw a photo of myself and another of Orion on the TV screen.

"A nine-year-old boy who, along with his sister and mother, comprises the group now known as the Bond Brook isolates, is in stable condition at Sibley Memorial Hospital," the heavily made-up anchor lady began, but I was staring too hard at the pictures to hear the rest of what she said. I could see that the photo of me was old, for I had long hair, but Orion's snapshot was even older; in it he looked no more than my age, maybe younger. I wondered how the TV people had gotten these photos and why Orion's wasn't more recent, like mine. Miss Shelton got up and changed the channel before I could see or hear anything else.

"What is an isolate?" I asked, thinking that it sounded like something cold, something icy.

"It's getting late," Miss Shelton replied. "Why don't I go get you the new pajamas we picked out?"

Once Miss Shelton had left the room, I turned to Ginger, who had wedged her bulk next to me on the couch. "Did you know that I'm famous now? It's true—I'm on *TV*," I whispered, giving her time to let this news sink in. "But what's an isolate, Ginger?"

Strange phone calls happened at all hours. "She cannot be interviewed. Have some consideration. She's a *child*," I heard Miss Shelton say once, then hang up. Since I was the only child in the house, I knew she was talking about me, but I wondered who'd want to talk to me. To be honest, I was a little afraid of the telephone with its abrupt ring and the tinny voices that came out it; I shrank away whenever it rang.

I cowered, too, whenever someone knocked on the door; even though the visitor most often ended up being a friend of Jane's or Miss Shelton's, I never shook the feeling that people were dropping by in hopes of getting a look at me, the *isolate*. Once, during dinner (a dreadful soybean casserole that I had trouble choking down—Miss Shelton and Jane were the first vegetarians I had ever known), someone knocked on the door, and Miss Shelton, after peering through the curtain at whoever was on the stoop, told me to leave the table and hide in a back room, as far away from the door as possible, until she came to get me. The only people who came to visit me were Officer Shelton and a lady he brought along who carried a briefcase and asked about my home life.

Being of a curious mind, I had questions for them—questions about Mother and Orion. Namely, when was I going to see them? And when was Mother going to bring us home? No one gave me any satisfactory answers, though the lady with the briefcase did tell me that Mother had gone away for a while to rest. I thought this over, picturing my mother in an elevated hospital bed, her hair fanned out against fluffy pillows, her hands arranged prettily against the covers, and realized I liked to imagine her this way. One couldn't come to much harm if one stayed in bed all day, and worries can't come when one is asleep.

On the fifth day at Miss Shelton's house, a cardboard box arrived and with it some news that shed more light on my situation.

The contents of the box were minimal, mostly consisting of things taken from our house. There were two of my dresses, one for winter and one for summer; my two old cardigan sweaters; several pairs of tights and underwear; two pairs of pajamas; a toothbrush; and the ivory hairbrush that had been given to me a long time ago, which I wouldn't be needing now that my hair was so short. There was also the Bible, the primer, the Big Movie Book (bless Jane—she *had* been listening to me), and a shoe box filled with the can-label paper dolls I'd made.

Mother's beaded purse with the flashlight and acorns were tucked in the bottom of the box; the letter from John Hewitt wasn't inside the purse anymore—not such a loss considering I'd had trouble reading it on my own, but I took a moment to grieve for it anyway. There were other papers, though, including a birth certificate and a Social Security card, both with my name on them. And there was a little map of a town with a funny name: St. Germaine. The box was presented by Officer Shelton to Miss Shelton—not to me—but as she opened it, I peeped over the tabletop and recognized my things. I was allowed to look at them, running my fingers over the upraised gold lettering on the cover of the Big Movie Book, while in the next room Miss Shelton consulted in whispers with her brother.

After Officer Shelton left, she told me to sit down at the kitchen table. She said she had something she needed to tell me. "Is it bad?" I asked. I imagined it to be something about Orion, or Mother, or both.

"It's not bad. It's good, I think. We've found a relative of yours—someone close by." Miss Shelton went on talking, but I sensed something nervous in her prattle, and this made me nervous too; I only caught snippets of what she was saying, but I remember hearing that the relative lived in St. Germaine, which was forty-five minutes away from Bond Brook. Aunt Bernadine was the relative's name.

"I haven't got an Aunt Bernadine," I said. The truth was, I hardly knew what the word *aunt* meant, but I thought I remembered a chapter in the primer in which Sam and Nan had visited their Aunt Dot.

"Eh, but it seems that you do. Your father had a sister, Bernadine Hewitt. She's Bernadine Lacombe now. The police talked to her, and she's looking forward to having you in her home for a while. She has a nice large house—much bigger than here." Miss Shelton went on talking, telling me about the big backyard and the spare bedroom and Aunt Bernadine being a nurse at a middle school, until I interrupted her: "Is Orion going to be there with me?"

She shook her head. "I don't think so. It looks like he'll go to a different home for a while."

"I can't go where he is?"

Miss Shelton shook her head again, looking genuinely regretful.

"But that's not fair," I said.

"Maybe not, but you need to take that up with your aunt, not with me."

My eyes traveled back to the cardboard box. The shoe box filled with paper dolls jutted from the top of it, one blue-and-silver paper lady poking out. I remembered that Mother had helped me cut out that one. She had given the lady a pair of platform shoes and a swingy bell-shaped skirt because, she had said, you never know when a girl might have an occasion to go dancing. Miss Shelton was saying something else, something about Aunt Bernadine's house or the town of St. Germaine, but I shut her out. I picked up the blue-and-silver paper lady and held her in my palm. I tickled her feet to watch her dance, to watch her giggle and point one slipper-clad foot at me. *I'd recognize your face anywhere*, I said—not out loud, but silently, to myself—*anywhere in the world*.

* * * * * * * * *

Bernadine Lacombe drove up from St. Germaine the next evening. She was a heavyset, ruddy-faced woman with a cap of blonde hair cut in a shag that had perfectly curled-under ends, giving her the look of a mushroom. She had a jovial, hearty sort of manner from the start and a smile that showed square, remarkably even white teeth. It wasn't hard to imagine her giving spankings with her strong, fat hands and forgetting what she'd been angry about a moment later.

She brought me a doll—a rag doll with a calico sunbonnet, an apron, and plaited yarn hair—and this gesture made me want to cry because the doll was beautiful and Aunt Bernadine was being nice to me, and at the same time I feared that she didn't really mean it, that she wasn't giving me the doll because she thought I would love it but because she felt it was something she was supposed to do. I hoped I was wrong.

"You don't look a thing like my brother," were her first words to me, spoken as she held me at arm's length. Her fingers dug into my elbows as she appraised me.

"You don't look a thing like my brother, either," I said, and at that she let out a big honking laugh that made me shrink. Jane was with me that evening, skulking around curiously (and for the most part unobtrusively) in the background, stepping forward every now and then to put her two cents in or exchange banalities with the older woman ("How was the trip up from St. Germaine? We've had a warm spell here, for February.")

She directed Aunt Bernadine and me to the living room, saying that we would be more comfortable there. I sat on the same couch I slept on and Aunt Bernadine managed to shoehorn herself into the foam chair a few feet in front of me. (Jane had told me, not without pride, that this chair had been in a small plastic package when she'd bought it, and when she opened it the chair had expanded like bread dough rising—a most ingenious invention.)

"Well, we're family, all the same," Aunt Bernadine said, abruptly picking up the greeting I thought she'd dropped. "You probably wonder why I never visited you before. Truth is, I didn't even know John had kids. I lost touch with my brother— with Johnny—when he was still a kid himself. He was a few years older than me, and he did his own thing. I'm not gonna lie to you, he was a little bit crazy from the start. My parents wrote Johnny off, said he was a lost cause, but later, when we heard he'd died, I could tell Mum was sad about it. Not surprised, but sad. She didn't live long after that, and my dad passed three years later."

I sat patiently through this account, waiting for some greater, more illuminating point. There was none. "It makes sense, him marrying a woman like your mother," she went on.

"What does that mean?"

She twirled a finger near her ear. "She'd almost *have* to be a little different to take him on. Not that Johnny wasn't a smarty. He was very smart in school, read up a storm, but no sane girl would have him. Lucky for you, you're young enough to stand a chance. With a little bringing up, there's no reason why you can't have a normal life from now on. I've got two sons of my own, and they're as normal as can be. Nice, normal boys. I always thought it'd be nice to have a girl. They wanted me to take that brother of yours in too, but with two boys in the house already, I can't take on another one just yet."

Jane, who had paused in the doorway, cleared her throat. "Maybe you can tell Asta a little bit about where she'll be living," she said. "I'm sure she has a lot of questions."

I didn't have any questions. How could I have questions when I didn't know what to ask? But Aunt Bernadine, it turned out, needed no direction. Her patter was endless. She was a widow, she said, and her nice, normal sons, Kevin and Wendell, were fourteen and twelve years old, respectively, but they looked enough alike that people sometimes mistook them for twins. She lived in a large house and paid the mortgage through a combination of funds left by her late husband, her school nurse job, and rent from two college students who lived in private rooms on the third floor: "The girl, Pam, is the more personable of the two. You'll probably see her coming and going. The boy I don't have too much to do with," Aunt Bernadine said. "Pays his rent on time, that's all I care about." She told me she'd been thinking about getting an even larger home, turning it into a boardinghouse proper, but probably not till her boys were out of high school.

As for the town of St. Germaine, wasn't I lucky to have a chance to live there? I would like St. Germaine, she said, because it wasn't a dying town. It was being kept alive by a thriving community of Québécois immigrants and their English-speaking children, good working-class folks all. Why, they had just built a new McDonald's and a Dairy Queen and a Shop-Rite on Eastern Avenue, and they were planning to put in a JC Penney next! There were three elementary schools in town, but I was to go to the one called Germaine Cousin—"And if you want my opinion," she said, "that's the best of the lot. The Roy School has hippie teachers, and the other one's in the bad part of town where all the welfare kids go."

Aunt Bernadine was planning to enroll me in school. Was I really going to be staying with her that long?

"I don't think I should go to school," I said.

"You wouldn't be the first kid to say that," she said. "But nice try."

"Mother wouldn't want me to go. She says there are lots of germs there."

"What in the world are you talking about? Anything bad that goes around, they give shots nowadays so you don't catch nothing. Worst thing you're going to catch in school is head lice or a cold."

Aunt Bernadine beamed at me, smug in her conviction. I tried to stare her down, but she bested me easily, and my gaze dropped back down to the doll in my lap.

"Besides, I'll be making decisions for you for a while. Not your mother. She's in no shape to make decisions for anyone, from what I hear. Now," she said, leaning toward me so close that I felt the touch of her hot, wet breath, "anything else you want to know?"

THE LACOMBE HOUSE

IN THE LACOMBE HOUSE I had my own bedroom. I would later find out that this room had been occupied just months earlier by Aunt Bernadine's elderly mother-in-law (*mémère*, as she was known to her grandsons), who'd been sent to a nursing home in a near-vegetative state following her third stroke. The room smelled of sachet and mothballs, and its decor called to mind its previous, much older inhabitant: the ecru-colored wallpaper had a gold-leaf pattern stamped on it, and an old white dresser had drawers that groaned in agony each time they were opened and shut. Next to the bed stood a matching night table with a lamp on it, its shade like an inverted tulip. On the bed was an old quilt with once-white borders that had turned gray from age and several embroidered pillows and shams, more attractive than they were functional. Across from the bed was a window that offered a view of the driveway and the sloping yard, with a row of barren crab apple trees to mark off the property line.

I saw all this on my first day. When Miss Shelton brought me to the house, no one was home except Aunt Bernadine, who was expecting me. Kevin and Wendell were at friends' houses and wouldn't be home until dinner. Miss Shelton had an aversion either to prolonged good-byes or to staying at the Lacombe house a minute longer than necessary and didn't even linger to have the cup of coffee Aunt Bernadine offered her, but she did help me take my coat off, and she gave me a hug before she left. "Be good," was all she said to me in parting.

That was nervy of her, I thought. Only Mother was allowed to give me such directives. Still, I recognized that Miss Shelton and Jane had been kind to me. "I'll be good," I promised her.

Once alone, I was free to explore as much as I liked. Aunt Bernadine told me so, in her hearty way. She said I could go up to my room to unpack my things. She didn't comment on the fact that my "things" fit in one small gym bag, which had been loaned to me by Miss Shelton. Nor did she offer me a tour of the house, except to point out a few irregularities.

"See the front door here? To lock it behind you when you're going out, you got to twist and pull this thingie at the same time," she said, jerking the brass-plated knob to show me what she meant. "And the toilet in the upstairs bedroom? You've got to jiggle the handle to make it flush right. Not a great big jiggle, just a little one."

Everything else in the house, I assumed, would be self-explanatory, easy to figure out. But the house itself would take some getting used to. Whereas our house had low, cracked ceilings and slanting plaster walls that leaned down to meet me, the Lacombes' paneled walls were straight as pins, meeting each high tin ceiling at perfect right angles.

In the room that was to be mine, I put my rag doll (which I had grown more fond of over the past few days) on top of my new bed. I put the primer, the Big Movie Book, and my box of paper dolls on top of the dresser, and my ivory hair brush went next to them. My pajamas and underthings went into my dresser, and I hung the two dresses in the closet and laid a brand-new pair of Buster Brown shoes (a gift from Miss Shelton and Jane) side by side on the closet floor.

With my belongings thus unpacked, finding myself made uneasy by the way they seemed to stare at me in expectation, I stepped out into the hallway to see what the other rooms were like. The black telephone jangled shrilly when I walked past, as if I had set it off; my insides seized up in horror for a few seconds. Soon I heard Aunt Bernadine's voice downstairs, punctuated by laughter. Whom was she talking to? I reached out for the telephone, not quite daring to touch it but fingering the tightly coiled cord. I wondered if Mother had a phone where she was. Would it be possible to call *her*, to speak to her and make *her* laugh?

Farther down the hall was a spacious, modern-looking room—the boys' quarters, I guessed. There were bunk beds against one wall, clothes heaped all over the floor, and action figures meticulously lined up on shelves. On the walls were sports pennants, posters from *Star Wars*, and a magazine clipping of a red-haired model in form-fitting short-shorts. I saw a bookcase in one corner and went over to it, hoping for books but instead finding stacks of *Mad* magazines, *Captain America* comics, and, on one shelf, something that truly shocked me—a real skull, yellowed with age. I'd seen pictures of human skulls on various science shows, and I doubted this was a person's—I guessed it to be the skull of an animal, though I couldn't tell what kind. Its eyes were far apart, the eye sockets small, and instead of a flat little nose cavity it had a long snout that gave the head a triangular shape. A dog? Somebody's dear old pet? My stomach lurched, and I backed out of the room.

In the hallway was a narrow stairwell leading up to the third story. Glancing over my shoulder to see if anyone was watching (I don't know why this mattered, since Aunt Bernadine had given me clearance to look through the whole house), I skimmed my fingers along the railing as I took the stairs. There was not much to see, as it turned out—just one long hallway with a hardwood floor and a door at either end of the hall. In front of the door nearest me was a square of purple shag carpet—a welcome mat of sorts. Behind the door I could hear the faintest treble of a radio playing and a girlish voice singing along; I guessed this must be the room rented by Pam, one of the two boarders Aunt Bernadine had mentioned.

I migrated down the hall to the other room, which had no mat in front of it. If I had not already known that a second tenant lived upstairs, I would have assumed that this room was empty. There was a funny, stale smell like that of a dead mouse emanating from it. Orion's room almost had that smell sometimes, when his bedding went unwashed for long periods. The door was cool to the touch, and I wondered about the boarder who lived there—perhaps he was a quiet sort who was lax on hygiene and read books behind his cold, closed door. Perhaps he was like *us*. Perhaps he liked movies.

I tiptoed back to the second floor, stuck my head in Aunt Bernadine's room, saw nothing of interest, and then scoped out the upstairs bathroom. It was much larger than the bathroom at our house, which had been large enough only for two people to stand in it at the same time—big enough only for me to sit on the floor, tub-side, while Mother took her bath. The most interesting feature in the Lacombes' bathroom was not the sunken tub, the lavatory with gold faucets, or even the toilet with the blue fake-fur seat cover—it was the immense linen closet that had three doors and took up the length of one wall.

The inside of the closet was transected horizontally by long shelves. I lay on a shelf and stared at the one above it, pretending they were bunk beds. If Orion had been in the house with me, he would have fit nicely on the top bunk, I thought. I imagined him lying above me: The sound of pulling an old blanket up to my chin was the sound of him kicking his feet out from under a blanket. The steady sound of my breath was the asthmatic wheeze of his. The sound of my heart was the logy *lub-dub* of his heart, ringing out with startling power in the depths of this closet, our house within a house.

* * * * * * * * *

I met the nice, normal Lacombe brothers right before dinner. Aunt Bernadine positioned them in the front hallway and bawled, "Asta! Come meet the boys!" from the bottom of the stairs, as though I were their date and they'd come jointly to court me. I had, of course, already inspected the framed school photographs of them in the downstairs den, so I had some idea of what to expect. Both boys were blond like their mother, tall for their ages, with matching freckled faces. The older one, Kevin, was a little taller and rangier, with yellow bangs flopping over his forehead; Wendell was stocky and sported a crew cut. Neither boy made eye contact when he was introduced to me.

"Kevin's Mr. Basketball Star," Aunt Bernadine said, putting her hand on his shoulder. "Wendell's good at basketball too, but soccer's more his game. And they're not just good at sports—they can draw, too, and they're musical. Wendell just started guitar lessons. You can learn a lot from them."

"My mother can draw," I said. "And Orion and I are both musical. We make up our own songs." Kevin looked at his younger brother and, in a gesture of supreme indifference, rolled his eyes back in his head—it was the best eye roll I had ever seen. Up close, Kevin had a less-than-perfect complexion, with a rash of pimples on his cheeks and some pockmarks where pimples had come and gone. I had a feeling I wasn't meant to notice any of this, so I politely looked away.

"Go upstairs and wash your hands, both of you," Aunt Bernadine said to the boys. "And change out of those clothes. Soup's on in five minutes."

There was a rush to the stairs, involving some shoving and what sounded like a couple of muffled swear words. With a prompt from Aunt Bernadine I went to the dining room table by myself and waited for them. I said a silent prayer—a dinner prayer—in my head; I had learned to do this at Miss Shelton's, for she and Jane did not pray aloud at mealtimes the way Mother and Orion and I did, and that, to me, seemed an oversight. *Our Father*, I prayed inwardly, *who art in Heaven, Howard be thy name. You are great, you are good, and we thank you for our food.* If Orion had been there, he would not only have said the words aloud but also submitted a much more distinguished prayer. I hoped God wouldn't mind my meager offerings.

For a few minutes the table was silent as we bent over plates of damp spaghetti with tomato sauce and iceberg lettuce wedges. Then Wendell grabbed a bottle of salad dressing and, addressing his brother, said, "Hey, Pencil-Neck . . . what do you think would happen if you poured this whole bottle over your face? I dare you to find out."

"He's not going to find out," interjected Aunt Bernadine. "Oil and vinegar dressing? Do you know what that would do to his acne?"

"That's the point. I'll give him two dollars if he does it."

"You don't have two dollars to give."

"I do too. I got money for helping clean old Mrs. Fortin's attic." Wendell put the dressing down on the table—*thwack*—and shoveled spaghetti into his mouth until I feared he might choke.

"Well, save your money for comic books, then. Or whatever it is that you buy."

"I wouldn't have done it anyway, idiot," Kevin said. "Not for two bucks. Maybe for five." I thought Kevin looked a bit hurt. He had the same look on his face that Orion sometimes got when Mother corrected his *s*'s.

Aunt Bernadine snorted. "Why don't you try saying something nice to each other for a change? Your cousin's going to think you're a couple of animals. Asta," she said, shifting her attention with an alacrity that scared me, "you need to eat faster than that. The boys are almost ready for seconds."

"She's a real slow eater," Wendell said contemptuously. "She eats one piece of spaghetti at a time!"

Having my eating habits pointed out made me want to hide. I was used to eating any way I wanted to. And I was used to taking a long time to eat, savoring each bite, knowing there wouldn't be seconds—knowing it might be twenty-four hours before I could have another meal. Bravely, I threaded another strand of spaghetti around the tines of my fork and brought it to my mouth, hoping that the shakiness of my hand would go unnoticed.

A tall young woman appeared in the kitchen. I was grateful for the distraction, and the two boys, looking her over from top to bottom, seemed grateful, too, though for an entirely different reason. The woman wore flare-legged jeans and clogs and a slouchy old fisherman's sweater that was too big for her— long enough to be a minidress—yet somehow she still looked lean and elegant. She tossed her shoulder-length hair in our general direction as she opened the refrigerator's freezer compartment.

"Hey, Pammy," said Aunt Bernadine. "Plenty of food here if you want to pull up a chair."

"That's okay, I'm going out for dinner. I just wanted some ice," said Pam, glancing at the spread on the table. Her gaze fell briefly on me and then she looked away.

"This is little Asta, you've heard about her. And Asta, this is Pamela Millstein, she rents one of the rooms upstairs. Pam's in, what, your second year of college? Studying art?"

"Art history."

"Art history, can you beat that! You got a date tonight, Pam?"

"Yup," the girl said, flexing an ice cube tray and prying loose some cubes.

"With Dave?"

"No, with Judd. I'm not seeing Dave anymore."

"Judd the Stud," Wendell said, and he and his brother laughed as though he'd said something uproarious.

"Was I talking to you? I don't think so," said Aunt Bernadine. Then, to Pam, "Don't mind those clowns. They're as full of poop as two Christmas turkeys. And listen . . . Pammy? If you're coming in late tonight, see that you don't stomp up the stairs and wake everyone up. Are you sure you don't want some of this spaghetti? You know I always make enough for an army."

"No thank you, Mrs. Lacombe," Pam said. I had the impression that she didn't dislike Aunt Bernadine, despite all the woman's bluster. She smiled as she sipped her water.

Wendell's eyes followed her as she left the room. When she was well out of earshot, he piped out, "You know what? Kevin's friend Bob's brother went to high school with her, and he said that if she had as many ding-dongs sticking out of her as she'd had stuck in her, she'd be a porcupine."

"I told you not to repeat that!" Kevin said.

"Best you don't," Aunt Bernadine said, giving each boy the evil eye in turn. "That is disgusting. I don't like that kind of talk. Although I will say this much, I feel sorry for Pam's parents. Can you imagine paying for her to get that art-history degree just so she can make time with a different long-haired hippie boy every week? They'd be better off spending money on something she can use in the real world. She could be a veterinary tech, maybe, if she likes hairy critters so much." Aunt Bernadine got up and started stacking plates. "Done?" she asked, removing my plate before I could answer. I wasn't finished, but I was relieved to have the food taken away.

"Don't we get any dessert?" asked Kevin.

"Gee, I don't know. Do you think you deserve any?" Aunt Bernadine opened the freezer and took out a box of ice cream, slamming it down on the table with what I guessed was mock annoyance, though with her it was hard to tell. She scooped up great cold gobs of vanilla ice cream into bowls and distributed some spoons on the table before us. "Eat all of this," she said to me, putting a bowl where my plate had been. "You've got to keep your weight up if you don't want to go back to the hospital."

"Did they give you an IV in the hospital?" Kevin asked, looking right at me for the first time. "I had one of those once. They stuck a needle in my hand."

I started to answer, but Aunt Bernadine said, "Now, boys. Asta doesn't need to be talking about that."

"I don't mind," I said, which was true. I liked talking about the hospital. Miss Shelton and Jane had always steered the conversation in a different direction whenever I mentioned it, and this frustrated me; there were things I wanted to talk about, things I had seen and wondered about during my stay. But Aunt Bernadine was already changing the subject; standing at the sink, preparing the dinner dishes for washing, she told me in a booming voice about the local women's club she belonged to, which planned community projects every Monday and Thursday night. "I have to be there tonight because we've got our quarterly finance report, and I'm the treasurer. I handle the *moola*."

"That's nice," I said. I didn't know what else to say.

"Maybe you can help me wrap a birthday gift for my secret pal tomorrow, huh, Asta? I'll let you pick out the bow. I got 'em in all colors. Boys, don't forget to do these dishes. Asta, bedtime for you is seven thirty, but I won't be home before eight. The boys'll let you know when it's time for bed. And boys, remember what I told you."

Over my ice cream I caught sight of Wendell's face. He shot a look at his older brother, the corners of his mouth twisting down into a scowl, and then his face went back to its normal, rather slack expression.

"You hear me?" Aunt Bernadine said.

"Yeah," the boys said, more or less in unison.

"Good," she said.

She patted me on the head on her way out, perfunctorily, as though I were a dog—a dog who might make her hand smell foul if she petted it too hard or too long. I thought of the animal skull in the boys' bedroom, its flat cranium and long snout, and a shudder rippled through me before I could stop it.

* * * * * * * *

Later that evening, Kevin showed me how to use the TV. "You sit here," he said, gesturing toward the sunken couch in a way that suggested I wasn't to move from it. Not that immobility was a terrible prospect—the TV set was much bigger than the one at our house, and its pictures were in color; I imagined it could hold my attention for a long while. I sat down as I was told, my eyes trying to adjust to the lurid reds, yellows, and oranges as opposed to the reduced, shadowy images they were used to. Kevin flipped the dial a few times, looking for a suitable channel, until he stopped at *The Joker's Wild*. "There, that ought to be okay," he mumbled.

"Mother and Orion and I watch this show," I told him.

"Great," Kevin said. "Whatever you do, don't mess with the fine-tuning." He bolted back upstairs before I could say anything else, and soon I heard the boys' loud voices as they conversed in their bedroom and in the upstairs hall. Music thumped and pulsed from a stereo system, and there were several thuds, as if the boys were moving heavy furniture. Over the music and the general ruckus I could hear someone—Wendell, probably—trying to pick out some notes on a twangy instrument and not doing a very good job of it. I tried to concentrate on the TV program, wishing Kevin had shown me how to turn up the volume. In the midst of all this, Pam clomped downstairs again, this time in a denim skirt and a tight stretchy blouse under a pea coat, with a purse slung over her shoulder. I saw her out of the corner of my eye as she headed for the door.

"Bye," I said.

"What?" She looked at me, taken aback. "Bye-bye, Esther."

I didn't correct her.

The TV host looked different in color—a little older, I thought, and a little too ruddy-complexioned. But the commercials were shown to their best advantage, and their products seemed so much more desirable—and accessible—in color. I saw an advertisement for a pale orange Cool Whip–based dessert (just add cling peaches!) and an ad shilling McDonald's Quarter Pounders with Cheese, with plenty of red ketchup dribbling out the side of the bun. Everything looked positively decadent. During a commercial for Rice-A-Roni ("the San Francisco treat"), I left the couch long enough to have a look in the Lacombes' refrigerator. After a steady diet of lentil and soybean concoctions at Miss Shelton's, I thought it important to know what kind of food Aunt Bernadine kept on hand.

In the refrigerator I saw milk, some sort of red fruit juice in a big jug, packages of hot dogs, sliced bologna, American cheese singles, individual cans of chocolate pudding with flip-top lids, and various items stored in different-sized Tupperware containers. Most were unfamiliar to me. It didn't look like real food—more like the food that TV people eat—and the sight of it made me feel excited and slightly queasy at the same time

Back on the couch, I looked around the room for other telling details. The coffee table had a few unevenly stacked newspapers on it and beneath them a couple of books. One of them said *St. Germaine-Watertown Telephone Directory* on the spine. I pulled this out and began rifling through its onionskin pages. There were no pictures in it at all, no visual clues, but I soon detected the pattern of the names in tiny type; I turned to *H* and looked up the name *Hewitt*, to see if my surname was represented. There was a Hewitt, Dwayne, several Hewinses, and even a contrary individual who spelled the name H-e-w-e-t-t. There was no Hewitt, Loretta, and no Hewitt, Orion, either. Another idea came to me. I looked for the word *hospital* a few pages beyond the Hewitt listings, but there was nothing there.

I heard someone coming down the stairs and immediately shoved the telephone directory behind one of the pillows on the couch.

It was Kevin, returning to inform me that it was almost seven thirty. "Mom said to make sure you put your pajamas on and start getting ready for bed about now."

"Okay," I said.

"She also said to make sure you pee." He lowered his voice. "She doesn't want you to wet the bed."

"I don't wet the bed," I said. I could feel my face flushing at this implied—and unfounded—accusation.

"That's what *you* say. You need to wash your face and brush your teeth, too. And you'd better brush them good, because Mom won't want to pay for your cavities. She doesn't want to pay for anything of yours unless she *has* to. Especially since you're not the kind of girl she was expecting."

I looked into blue eyes that were mostly covered by floppy blond bangs. I couldn't find any evidence that he was joking. "All right," I said.

I tried not to pay attention as Kevin followed me up the stairs and stood outside the door while I used the toilet, but it was impossible to ignore. I could almost hear him breathing out there, waiting to make sure I did what I was supposed to do. I was convinced he could hear me wadding up the toilet tissue and wiping myself, and I was mortified. The toilet's flush was thundering, incriminating. I brushed my teeth for an extra long time and spat three times so he could hear that, too.

In my bedroom the bedcovers were pulled back and some of the shams and throw pillows were neatly lined up on the floor next to the bed. One of the boys must have done it, I thought, or, more likely, Aunt Bernadine before she left.

Was I really not the kind of girl she had been expecting?

What had she been expecting?

I crawled into bed and pulled the blanket over myself. Kevin shut the bedroom door, although I would have preferred to keep it open, and I was left alone in the dark. The pillow under my head was not as soft as my pillow at home, and the bedspread had a strange, vinegary smell. I was aware of the boys on the other side of the door; Wendell had stopped playing his guitar, but the bass from the stereo still thumped through the walls like a sinister heartbeat. As my eyes adjusted to the darkness in the room, things began to take on shapes I didn't recognize. I got up and turned the tulip-shaped lamp on to purge the room of these shapes and shadows and insinuations. I had just gotten back under the covers when my doorknob turned; I opened one eye and saw Kevin standing in the doorway.

"Your light's on," he said tersely.

"It's the dark," I explained. "I can't sleep in it."

"Tough," he said and switched off the lamp. I could see him mostly in shadow, backlit by the hall light.

"Kevin?" I asked as he started to turn away.

"What?"

Without even realizing what I was going to ask, the words tumbled out of me. "What is that skeleton in your room?"

"The skull, you mean?" I could feel Kevin smiling in the dark before I caught the wet-looking glint of his teeth. I was startled by the readiness of this smile. "It's a pig skull."

"Oh."

"Were you in my room? You seen my pig skull?"

"Yes."

"You want to see where I got it from?"

"Okay," I said. "I guess so."

"We'll have to go outside," he said. "So go downstairs and put your boots on. I'll meet you down there."

"I thought you said I had to be in bed."

"It'll only take a minute. Just don't tell Mom I let you do this."

I didn't know what to expect as I waited downstairs with my boots on. I only knew that the tide seemed to have turned and that I'd been given an opportunity to be in Kevin's good graces. He came downstairs with his brother a moment later. Wordlessly, Kevin and Wendell and I made a procession to the backyard. I hadn't thought to put on my coat, and it was freezing out, but I knew enough not to complain. I followed the boys to the far corner of the yard, just past a thick tree stump where the land began to incline a little. Kevin broke off a branch from one of the nearby crab apple trees and used it as a pointer. "Right about here," he said, tracing a line in the snow with a branch, "is where they used to bury the pigs. People who lived in this house before us had a pig farm. The one you seen in my room's the fourth skull I dug up. Mom threw away my first ones, but she doesn't know about the new one yet. If you tell her anything about it, you'll be sorry. In the spring, when the ground thaws, I'm going to get more pigs."

"Me, too," said Wendell. "I haven't even gotten my first one yet."

I wondered what Orion would think of this, with his interest in scientific things. He would probably know something about the bones that even the brothers didn't. He might even be able to identify parts of the pig skull by their proper anatomical names, and if he didn't know the names, he'd make up new ones that had an authentic sound.

"Why are you crying?" Wendell asked.

"I'm not," I lied.

"Aw, go back to bed," Kevin said in a disgusted tone. "And remember what I told you: Don't say anything about what you seen."

I went back to my room and lay on my side in the dark, pretending to sleep. I was still awake when Aunt Bernadine came home, and I heard her come upstairs, clucking at the boys. She pushed my door open, and I kept my eyes closed, willing myself not to move a muscle.

"Did she go right to sleep?" I heard her whisper.

"Pretty much," one of the boys replied.

I continued to keep my eyes closed while Aunt Bernadine washed up in the bathroom, and I did not stir when I heard her bedsprings protest under her weight as she lay down. I heard the boys close their bedroom door. Only after they had been quiet a long time did I open my eyes. The sky outside my window was heavy with moonlight. I got up and opened the bedroom door without making a sound. Out in the hall I could hear the deep breathing of the boys and Aunt Bernadette snoring; the air was filled with the deep breath of sleep.

I went into the bathroom, opened up the linen closet, and crawled onto a shelf, covering myself with a half-unfolded tablecloth with a tasseled hem. I tried to pull the door closed behind me, but it did not shut all the way, and a sliver of light came through. I watched this sliver, saw it flicker and wax and wane like a candle flame until Orion slipped through it and settled on the bunk above me, shifting around on top of the old linens until he'd found a comfortable position. He sighed a sigh of great unburdening.

This will be our hiding place, Orion whispered to me, *okay?*

Okay, I whispered back to him. And then I, too, was asleep.

TRIBULATION

FOR THE NEXT FIVE DAYS, Aunt Bernadine hired a babysitter to stay with me from early morning till midafternoon. My sitter was a seemingly mute elderly woman who had a passion for crocheting and butterscotch candies; she teetered back and forth in Aunt Bernadine's old rocking chair and tolerated my company during a solid lineup of soap operas, which she watched with such candy-sucking ardor that I could hear the butterscotch clinking against her teeth. At two o'clock, Kevin and Wendell came home from school and took over till Aunt Bernadine's workday was done.

On the best days, the boys carried out their babysitting assignment with slipshod obedience; neither Kevin nor Wendell paid much attention to me; sometimes they even seemed to forget I was there. But other times they remembered me all too well and competed with each other to see who could execute the best taunts and tortures.

One afternoon, Wendell, the stouter and physically stronger of the two, pinned me against the floor in a wrestler's pose—quite apropos of nothing—and worked a thick rope of spit and phlegm out of his mouth, letting it hang and undulate inches over my face. Whenever the rope thinned out and elongated to the point of breaking free, Wendell slurped it back up, swallowed, and started all over. This routine had Kevin doubled over and me nearly in tears; it would get replayed many times on subsequent afternoons.

Sometimes Wendell was at a friend's house, and during those times Kevin could be almost civil to me. Once, breezing through the kitchen and taking a banana out of the bowl, Kevin said, "Want one?" I was so touched that I took the banana and ate it without saying a word. But an hour later, Wendell came home, and he and Kevin chased me around the house with fresh new terrors they'd concocted. So went my first week at the Lacombe house.

During my second week, after I had endured follow-up doctor's visits and a round of immunizations, Aunt Bernadine registered me as a student at Germaine Cousin Elementary School. I was less than overjoyed. As much as I'd envied Orion's brief foray into formal education, my mother's depiction of school as a hotbed of germs was uppermost in my mind, and the need for shots and immunizations seemed to support this line of thinking. I also thought of the children I'd seen at the bus stop, especially the girl who had struck me in the face, and worried that the children at Germaine Cousin would be no better behaved.

"Why can't I just keep staying home?" I asked Aunt Bernadine. "I've been staying home all these years."

"And a lot you have to show for it," said Aunt Bernadine.

"What is three hundred and seventy-two minus two hundred and eighteen?"

"I don't know."

"What's the capital of Maine?"

"I don't know."

"What do plants need in order to grow?"

"Pots?"

"I rest my case," Aunt Bernadine said with great self-satisfaction. "You aren't educated. You'll be lucky if they don't stick you in kindergarten with the babies."

I didn't think that was fair, for I knew a lot of things that other children probably didn't know—things that even Aunt Bernadine might not have in her knowledge base. Besides, I had already paid a visit to the school to be tested on my skills and the testing had gone swimmingly. The woman administering the test had shown me pictures of simple objects and asked me to identify them. At first I thought she must be joking, for the pictures required no thought at all: there was a dog, and a ball, and a pair of scissors, and a school bus (I was lucky to have a reference point for that one), a piano, a clothes hanger, and a candelabra. "Good for you," the lady said when I submitted this last answer. "You could have just said 'candle' or even 'light.'"

It was determined that I was not to be stuck in kindergarten with the babies. They put me in second grade, with the understanding that I would get a tutor for math. I was assigned a teacher—a Miss Thibeau—and a classroom: Room 2B. I read this when Aunt Bernadine showed me a copy of the school registration form, where she'd written down my name and signed her own with a grown-up flourish. "Lots of kids in your class, it looks like. It's a big school," Aunt Bernadine said, sending a wave of apprehension through me. "Maybe you'll even find a friend."

"I don't think anyone will want to be my friend."

"What kind of attitude is that? You got to think positive."

"Why?" I asked.

"Because the world likes positive people, that's why."

"What would make me positive?"

"You could smile more, for one."

"You mean like an actress?" I asked.

"Sure, like an actress," Aunt Bernadine said.

In the upstairs bathroom mirror I practiced my actress smile. THINK POSITIVE, I told myself, trying out a new stage direction—but it didn't work. The smile wasn't convincing. The tooth I'd lost during my fall through Mother's floorboards had begun to grow back in; bigger and yellower than the baby tooth had been, it was canted at an unattractive angle. If I stared in the mirror long enough, the flesh of my face seemed to disappear, and I saw two hollow eyes and a dark slab where my mouth was. *Would anyone like me?* I wondered if anyone could.

* * * * * * * * *

One good thing about Germaine Cousin—if I'd been forced to point out one good thing—was that I would not have to take a bus to get to it; Aunt Bernadine's house was easily within walking distance. This gave me some consolation as I set out for my first school day, dressed in my old brown jumper and my new brown shoes and gripping a brown-bag lunch packed by Aunt Bernadine. Following orders from his mother, Wendell walked me up the street to the school. He glowered as we left the house, and I was sure he wouldn't say a word to me the entire way. But as soon as we were out of the driveway, he pointed to a house three houses up from the Lacombes' and said, "Did you know a little old crazy lady lives there?"

"No."

"Well, she does. Her name's Ramona, and she moos like a cow whenever she sees somebody coming up her walk. I used to deliver her newspaper."

This was the longest set of sentences Wendell had ever said to me. "Really?" I asked, delighted by this disclosure.

"Yeah. I know almost everyone in this neighborhood. That yellow house up there on the right? Everyone used to say it was haunted. Then a guy who called himself Matthias moved in and started up a Satan church. He had this special satanic medallion that he wore—it was like the size of a plate. Whenever we walked past the Satan church on a Sunday morning, we'd hear this weird chanting coming from inside, and the dog would be howling like someone was beating it half to death."

"Is the Satan church still there?"

"No-sa. Matthias got run out of town."

"What about this house here?" I asked, pointing.

"Oh, that's where the hillbillies live. There's eleven kids in that family, and all of 'em are stupid. That's why the house looks so run-down. Because they're hillbillies."

Wendell kept up this talk until we reached the crossing-guard lady at the top of the street. I was just beginning to feel closer to him when he handed me off to the crossing guard as though he couldn't wait to be rid of me; his own school, Cleeves Junior High, was up the street about a quarter mile.

"Did you have a good breakfast this morning?" the crossing-guard lady asked without even asking my name or introducing herself. She was a pigeon-breasted woman with short graying hair and a somewhat daft look behind her wire-rimmed glasses.

"What?"

"Did you have a good breakfast? Orange juice?"

It came out sounding like *ornjoose,* all one word. I couldn't imagine why she would want to know. I had had toast with jelly for breakfast and a glass of milk—bread and milk and jelly were luxuries that I was still getting used to, now that my palate had been expanded to include things that didn't come in cans—but what possible use could this information be to her? "I didn't have any orange juice," I said cautiously.

The crossing-guard lady tsk-tsked as though this reply disappointed her. We walked together between the freshly painted white lines of the crosswalk until we were at the opposite side of the street and I was making my way, suddenly and quite consciously alone, down the path that led into the school yard.

The school yard was almost a duplicate of the one Orion and I had seen when we'd hidden in Mr. Levesque's bus. At least the playground apparatus was the same. As I got closer I heard the *scree* of rusty swings pitching back and forth and could see children crawling and writhing on a jungle gym; one monkeylike boy dangled upside down from a pair of parallel bars, and an old merry-go-round undulated precariously as children steered it in a circle. Girls turned plastic-coated jump ropes. Boys, already filthy, further sullied themselves by wrestling in the March mud, where the snow had begun to melt.

I took a breath. I looked at everything.

As much as there was to see and hear, what really got my attention was the one quiet, stationary thing in the corner of the playground.

An oak tree bristled in a corner by a chain-link fence, yards away from all the activity. Through the fence one could see the street. At the base of the tree, I could just make out a dark-jacketed figure in profile turned toward the street. It seemed to be watching the two lanes of traffic go by.

I walked toward the tree as if pulled by a magnetic force. Then I slowed down, tiptoeing as though I were tracking a squirrel or a bird or a creature who might take flight as soon as he spotted me. Suddenly I knew for sure whom I was walking toward, and I began to run; I ran so fast that it was I who almost flew.

There, with his back against the tree trunk, was my brother.

"Orion!" I said, trying to bring myself to a stop and sliding in the dirt like a baseball player, but without the athletic panache. Sprawled on the ground before him, mud *shlurping* into my Buster Browns and caking onto my tights, I didn't even think of getting up.

Orion looked down at me. He had a book propped open on his lap in the desultory manner of someone who had been distracted and lost his place. I expected him to look as amazed, as elated, as I felt—but his black eyes danced over me, skimmed me, and then looked again at the traffic beyond the fence.

I refused to feel slighted. I was far too jubilant. "You're *here*," I burbled. "I didn't know you'd be going to school with me! Is this your first day too?"

His eyes settled on me. He shook his head. *That no-talking brother of yours*, Aunt Bernadine had said. I wasn't about to let a little thing like no-talking get in my way. "You started earlier?" I guessed, sitting up so that we could see each other eye to eye. "You've been going here for a while?"

Orion held up his hand, palm facing me. "Five days?" I guessed, counting his fingers.

Orion nodded. He looked at me more directly now, and the blank look in his eyes was fading, replaced by something else—not just alertness, I thought, but a hint of relief. Relief that I understood him. It made him look very much like the Orion I knew, even though the hollow, malnourished look was almost gone, and the eyes themselves peered out from behind new eyeglasses—I had never seen him in glasses before. He shined with something that I attributed to cleanliness.

"Do you like it here?" I asked.

He shrugged. "What are you reading?" I asked, and he picked the book up off his lap and held it up so that I could see the cover: *The Complete Works of William Shakespeare.* "That's a pretty big book. Does it have *As You Like It* in it?" I asked, and he nodded.

Having divined that he would only give yes or no answers, if that, my mind raced for what else to ask him, what else to tell him. I wanted to choose my words carefully, conveying only what was most important. "Have you heard from Mother? Do you know where she is?" When he responded with neither a nod nor a shake of the head, I tried another tack—a question that in some ways seemed even more important: "I have conversations with you at night sometimes, especially when I'm hiding in Aunt Bernadine's linen closet. Have you felt me talking to you?"

His eye contact steady now, Orion nodded. I couldn't help it—I jumped up out of the mud and threw my arms around his neck. He didn't resist, nor did he hug me back at once. His arms went around me gingerly and only tightened when he seemed to realize I wasn't going anywhere. The book slid off his lap and plumped down on the ground, but he did not reach over to pick it up right away.

"Am I going to see you every day now?" I asked. "I won't mind going to school so much if I see you every day. Please tell me I'll be seeing you a lot."

He shook his head. I would find out later that I would see Orion only in the mornings, before the first bell. That was the only time all six grades were out on the playground at once; the younger pupils had lunch and recess separately from the fourth and fifth graders, who were considered too old to consort with the likes of us.

A bell sounded. Orion got up, collected his Shakespeare, and gestured for me to follow him. Children abandoned their play and thundered toward the school entrances. Orion walked me over to the school's north side, where the younger children were lining up. He then pointed to the south end of the building, pointed back to himself, and waved. *That's my entrance over there. Where the bigger kids go.* I could almost hear him say it, just as I felt, if not saw, the smile that had not quite surfaced on his face.

As for me, when Orion left to line up with the other students, it was *I* who was grinning from ear to ear. School might be bearable if it meant I could spend a little time with Orion every day. What had I done to deserve such a gift? My cheek muscles actually smarted from the effort of smiling. I smiled broadly—a real smile, not an actress smile, so dazzling in its execution, so contagious in its effect that the teacher holding the door open smiled herself and said, "Someone looks chipper this morning."

"I'm *wonderful*," I said. And in that moment, I meant it with all my heart.

* * * * * * * * *

Room 2B held approximately twenty-five children—my fellow pupils for the remainder of the school year. A girl with long black braids that hung down her back sat in front of me, and when I listened to the roll call, I learned that her name was Ing Tran—a marvelous name! To my right sat Jacob Bunham, a boy who had coarse, papery skin and a tendency to rock back in his seat. The girls in the class were the ones I noticed most, for they all had prettier hair and clothes than I did (except for one girl, Maria Sidelinger, who looked as if she hadn't combed her hair in a while or given her clothes a recent scrubbing and from whom a sour-milk smell emanated). My hopes rose even as I tried to squelch them. Children who looked that clean might have a passing acquaintance with manners, mightn't they? They had to be at least *somewhat* respectful.

My teacher, Miss Thibeau, was younger than I expected; she was, I would later find out, one of the few teachers at Germaine Cousin who wasn't a nun. She had thick, auburn-colored hair and wore lip gloss that made her lips look wet and peachy. She smiled and laughed a lot, and when she laughed, her full breasts shook up and down under her fuzzy sweater. Although she didn't look a thing like Mother, something about her careful makeup and pretty clothes made me miss Mother with a brutal, stabbing pain. It was suddenly very important for Miss Thibeau to like me.

But as the school day progressed and we were led from subject to subject and lesson to lesson, I saw that Miss Thibeau didn't smile *all* the time—several times during the day I caught her looking in my direction and scrunching up her pretty face. I couldn't imagine why. True, I had muddy tights and was picking my nose, but why should this cause such a nasty face?

After a brief, perplexing math drill (addition and subtraction), Miss Thibeau announced that we were going to watch a filmstrip. A boy, taller and stringier than the kids in our class and called "Ethan the helper," came into the classroom to set things up. He yanked down all the window shades and pulled down the rolled-up movie screen until it obscured the chalkboard. "Don't forget to turn off the lights, Ethan," Miss Thibeau said to the tall boy, and he got up again to flick off the switches. A couple of kids giggled as the lights went out, and one witty child yelled "Boo!" but I sat in the darkness with my hands folded neatly, wondering what sort of film we were going to see. I was hoping for something with Shirley Temple in it; I'd seen pictures of her in the later chapters of the Big Movie Book but had never seen her in action. Or maybe it would be a silent movie—Mary Pickford in *Little Annie Rooney* or *Rebecca of Sunnybrook Farm*, her long sausage curls hanging out from underneath a bonnet. I hadn't known that movies were a regular part of school, and it came as a nice surprise.

The film, however, turned out to be about ocean waves. It was pretty to watch, but it didn't have any actors in it—just a man with a deep voice describing what was happening in each picture. Each time the man finished talking about an image, there was a loud and rather rude-sounding *beep!* and Ethan the helper took that as a cue to advance to the next frame. I was a little disappointed in the film at first, with its absence of drama and its dearth of actresses in pretty dresses, but there was still something thrilling about sitting in the dark with a group of people, our eyes all riveted to the same spot, the room so quiet it seemed as if we were holding our breath, waiting for the next frame to show us something really spectacular. I could see, to some small degree, why Mother loved movies.

After the film we had a music lesson, and Miss Thibeau tried to teach us to sing a song about Peter's flowing spring. A skinny girl sitting behind me sang in a squeaky, breathy, off-key voice complete with vibrato and trills; if she kept that up, I thought, she was going to injure herself. The boy to my right sang like a buzz saw. I moved my mouth along with the words but made sure not to let any sound come out. Miss Thibeau came up to me at one point and put her ear next to my mouth to hear what kind of voice I had and was met with warm, soundless, jelly-scented breath. She shook her head in disapproval.

Released from the classroom for lunchtime, I came through the cafeteria doors in the single file behind Maria, the messy-haired girl, who was peacefully sucking her thumb. The lunch monitor intercepted me as I followed Maria, informing me that people with cold lunches had to sit at one of the two long tables at the front of the room, while people with hot lunches could sit wherever they wanted. There were a lot fewer of the lowly cold-lunch crew than of the hot-lunch students, and I turned out to be the only one with an exotic lunch: my aunt's leftover bean chili in my thermos and cornbread wrapped in waxed paper. All the other kids had plain peanut-butter sandwiches and carrot sticks or a bruised apple or store-bought cookies. I made a mental note to remember to ask Aunt Bernadine if she had any pears; next time, I could bring a pear and a little knife to make petals out of the pear. "What are you *eating*?" a girl asked me in an accusatory tone, and I pretended not to have heard. So far I had gone all day without speaking a word to any of my classmates, and I intended to keep it that way. The only time I had spoken was to Miss Thibeau, telling her *here* when she read the roll call. Even that seemed a needless lapse into speech—could she not see the small girl in the corner, waving her hand?

Recess followed lunch. As the other kids paired up or formed groups, I sat alone under the tree that I had already begun to think of as Orion's and mine, watching the traffic go by on the other side just as my brother had. I made a little game with myself of counting the cars that passed in the lane closest to me. While I was in the midst of this game, two girls came up and asked me if I wanted to hold one end of a jump rope for them, and I said, "No thank you" in my most mannerly tone— thus breaking my vow of silence.

Back in class after recess, with most of the students breathless, their hearts still out on the playground, Miss Thibeau said we were going to continue a social studies unit on the Bushmen of Africa, and she played a record with Bushman poetry on it. The school record player was more up to date than Mother's, and a rich, mellow sound came from it. One of the poems went as follows:

Hunger is bad.
Hunger is like a lion.
Hunger is bad.
It makes us eat locusts.

I sat there waiting for the poem to continue, only to find that it had ended. Perhaps the Bushman poet couldn't find a word to go with *locusts*, I thought. *Hocus pocus*? No, that wouldn't do. Mother wouldn't have considered it a very poetic poem at all. This thought made me smile for the second time that day.

The last lesson of the day was religion, and Miss Thibeau read a passage from the Book of Revelation, which I knew to be the final book of the Bible. I wondered what we would do in religion class once she finished reading that book; would she go back to the beginning and start all over with Genesis, or would she keep us on our toes by going out of order? I folded my arms on top of my desk and rested my chin on them, listening to Miss Thibeau's voice:

> A great and wondrous sign appeared in heaven: a woman
> clothed with the sun, with the moon under her feet and
> a crown of twelve stars on her head. She was pregnant
> and cried out in pain as she was about to give birth.
> Then another sign appeared in heaven: an enormous red
> dragon with seven heads and ten horns and seven crowns
> on his heads. His tail swept a third of the stars out of the
> sky and flung them to the earth. The dragon stood in
> front of the woman who was about to give birth, so that
> he might devour her child the moment it was born.

Miss Thibeau looked at us. "What do these lines make you think of?"

"It's like a horror movie," a little boy near the front of the class said. "Like *The Exorcist*."

"It is scary, isn't it? What do you think of the dragon? He isn't exactly a little love, is he?"

"No," chorused several of the children.

"Do you think the woman is going to get away from the dragon? Let's read on and find out, shall we?" Miss Thibeau looked around, winced at me briefly (I had planted my finger up one nostril again), and resumed reading:

> She gave birth to a son, a male who will rule all the
> nations with an iron scepter. And her child was snatched
> up to God, and to his throne. The woman fled into the

desert to a place prepared for her by God, where she might be taken care of for 1, 260 days.

Miss Thibeau looked up again. "Who do you think the woman's baby is? The one the Bible calls 'a male' who will rule all the nations?"

The hand of the curly-haired girl next to me shot up. "Moses?" she said.

"No, not Moses, but good try. Who is another well-known male baby in the Bible?"

"Jesus," two children said at the same time.

"That's right. Jesus. And if the baby is Jesus, then that would make the woman Jesus's mother, wouldn't it? Why would she go to the desert for such a long time?"

I withdrew my finger from my nostril, considering the question. I liked the image of God preparing a place for Mary in some remote area, a place fortified with all the amenities she could want—snacks and liquids and warm blankets and books and TV—while she waited out the dragon.

"She needed to get away for a little while when things were bad, and she could come out again when things were about to get better," I heard myself say.

Miss Thibeau nodded vigorously, not minding that I had forgotten to raise my hand. "That's very good," she said, looking at me as if for the first time. "Things get worse before they get better. The 1,260 days, when it occurs, will be known as a time of tribulation—the time of trouble before Jesus's return to earth in great glory."

A couple of the children nodded, but most looked glassy-eyed. I was proud of myself for having spoken up and supplied a correct answer. I leaned back in my chair with a sense of accomplishment. Between this and my morning with Orion, it was shaping up to be a decent first day of school.

* * * * * * * * *

At the end of the day I walked by myself from school to the Lacombe house. I hung up my coat and my new-old Spiderman book bag—a castoff of Wendell's—by the door. Aunt Bernadine wasn't home yet, but I expected the boys were, for the middle school got dismissed a half hour before the elementary school. I found Kevin at the kitchen table, bent over a notebook, with several dozen uncapped Magic Markers spread on the table around him. A weedy boy with braces sat beside him, so close that the two boys' heads almost touched.

"Hi," I said.

Kevin looked at me, then at his friend, and said, "Hey, Doug. Have you met my cousin?"

"You mean Medusa?" the friend said, and his odd staccato laugh sounded like gunshots, one after the other: *pop-pop-pop*. Kevin tried to swallow his laughter but didn't wholly succeed. His shaking shoulders betrayed him.

I waited for them to finish, rubbing the back of my head, where the short hair was growing in patchily. I looked at them questioningly. Kevin's friend, having recovered his breath, looked right back at me. (Or at least one of his eyes did—the other eye was slightly crossed, the pupil pointing inward—poor fellow, his face was just stuck that way. A fine one to be calling me Medusa!)

"What are you standing there for?" Kevin finally asked me, swallowing. "You want something?"

"I was wondering what you're drawing."

"We're making comics about an intergalactic mission to save the world," the friend said. "Anything else you want to know?"

I hesitated, thinking this over. "No," I said. I had thought of telling Kevin or Wendell about Orion, but my instinct told me to keep this information to myself. They would probably just find some way to make fun of us.

"Maybe you should go play or something," Kevin said. "We're kind of busy here."

"Where do you want me to go?"

Kevin pushed his floppy blond bangs out of his eyes and looked up at me with such cold, unadulterated annoyance that I felt as though I'd been slapped. "Go play in your *room*."

I went upstairs and sat on my bed, kicking off the Buster Brown shoes. More than feeling insulted at having been spoken to coldly, I was hurt that he hadn't asked me how my first day at school had gone. I had had no real reason for thinking he would ask—in the two weeks that I'd been staying at the Lacombe house, he had asked me very little—but I'd thought that our common school-going experience might give us some pretext for conversation.

Just as I had every day since my box of things had arrived, I took the Big Movie Book off my dresser and opened it on my lap. The book was always such good company. The black-and-white photos of the legends of the silver screen gazed back at me in large-eyed benevolence. Even the vamps (like Theda Bara and Nita Naldi) seemed to regard me generously.

That one was famous for taking baths in champagne, I heard my mother say as I turned to the photo of the pouting actress whose lips were blackened just in the center to give her a bee-stung look, her layers of false eyelashes looking like the dismembered legs of a spider. *And that one was eaten by her dachshund after she died. They were pampered, those girls!* And the boys, too, apparently—I turned another page and saw Rudolph Valentino as the sheik, with a striped headdress on, sneering, the whites of his eyes visible. He didn't look much like Orion at all. In another photo he was dressed as a toreador and had a nobler, restrained, thin-lipped look. He was very versatile, I thought.

Suddenly, I could feel that someone was watching me. Looking up, I saw Wendell leaning against my door frame. His solid, blocky figure took up most of the space. "Hey," he said.

"Hello."

"So you had your first day of school today, huh?" he asked.

"Yes," I said, with more eagerness than was probably becoming. Perhaps things would go better with Wendell than they had with Kevin; he, at least, was showing some interest in how my day had gone, and our morning talk had gone so well. "Miss Thibeau is my teacher."

"Miss Thibeau, huh? She must be new. Does she know that you still pee your pants?"

If Kevin's comments had felt like a slap, Wendell's almost knocked me off the bed.

"What?"

"A teacher ought to know something like that about her student. Maybe me and Kevin should call her up and tell her."

"Please don't. I told Kevin already. It isn't true."

"And does she know your mother's in a—a crazy house?"

"She is *not*," I said primly, before giving myself a chance to think through the wisdom of this. "I think you're as full of poop as—two Christmas turkeys!"

Everything happened very quickly after that point. Wendell lunged into my room, swiping a pillow off my bed. He pinned me against the mattress and mashed the pillow into my face before I knew what was happening. The Big Movie Book plummeted to the floor with a despondent-sounding thud. I could feel Wendell pressing down with the pillow against my nose and mouth. I became aware that I could not take a breath and that it was getting hotter and hotter under the pillow, and I began to scream, or try to; I heard feet running up the stairs. Either Kevin or his friend whooped close to my ear, yet still somehow sounded very far away.

"He's smothering her!" Kevin's friend said.

"Aw, you better stop, Wen," Kevin said a few seconds later. He sounded almost loath to offer this advice. "She's gagging under there."

And as quickly as the assault had started, it ended. Wendell got off me. The three boys watched with mild interest as I rolled onto my side, gasping for air. One of them said something I couldn't make out, and the other two guffawed.

"You okay?" Kevin asked. "Asta?"

I didn't respond. Wendell heaved the pillow back onto the bed, where it landed next to me, and the three of them left the room together.

"I bet she tells Mom," I heard Kevin say as they went down the hall. "You're gonna be in trouble."

"That faker. I only had that pillow on her for like two seconds."

When the boys were downstairs again and I had caught my breath and dabbed at my watering eyes—they were watering from the pressure, I told myself through gritted teeth, not from tears—I remembered the Big Movie Book. I got down off the bed to see if it had been injured. The impact of the fall had warped its spine, and a page containing one of my favorite pictures of

Myrna Loy dressed as a Chinawoman had gotten crumpled, but it was otherwise unmarred. I sat on the floor with the book for a long time, smoothing out the ruined picture, speaking to Myrna in what I hoped was a soothing whisper: *You're all right,* I assured her. *You're all right.*

* * * * * * * * *

Aunt Bernadine came home from work later that evening with a handful of mail and a bunch of pamphlets that she dropped on the kitchen counter. "So how do you like second grade?" she asked me, posing the big question that both her sons had failed to ask. I no longer felt like answering it.

"It was okay," I said.

"Learn anything?"

I thought very hard. "I learned about Bushmen."

"Who?"

I told her and explained how hunger had made them eat locusts. "Yuck," she said, making a face. "Be glad you're not them, then. You got any homework?"

"No."

I expected her to ask if I had seen Orion, and I was wondering if I should answer her honestly about that or tell a bald-faced lie. But she didn't ask. She just nodded in a businesslike way and said, "Why don't you help me grate cheese for tonight's supper?"

I had never grated cheese before, but Aunt Bernadine showed me how, emphasizing that I must be careful not to grate my knuckles along with the cheese, for nobody likes the taste of grated skin. While we worked side by side—she was chopping tomatoes next to me, and I tried not to feel queasy at the sight of the slimy red fruit—I asked her, just to make conversation, if she'd seen any sick kids at school that day. She told me that she'd been kept busy; one kid had fallen down and broken her tooth on an old tree stump, and a boy had thrown up on the floor during health class. "American chop suey," she said, balefully.

As the block of cheese wore down to a small nub, I kept looking at one of the pamphlets at the top of the mail pile. There was a picture of the Virgin Mary on it; I recognized her by her blue hood and glowing skin. Above Mary's head the words *The Magnificat* were written in an elegant pink script; I asked Aunt Bernadine if I could have the pamphlet.

"What? Oh sure, I guess so," she said. "Take 'em all. It's just some tracts someone stuck in the door at school. Maybe you can give 'em to those nuns at Germaine Cousin. Who knows? You give those tracts to your teacher and you just might earn some brownie points."

"Thank you," I said. But I had no intention of giving the tracts to Miss Thibeau or anyone else at Germaine Cousin.

That night, after everyone else went to sleep, I got out of bed and took my flashlight and my Magnificat pamphlet into the closet. I had postponed reading it until that very moment, knowing it would sound better in the closet, with Orion (as I imagined him) listening in the bunk above. Whispering my way through each line, I felt electrified by the flow of the words, the way each sentiment built off the one before:

My soul doth magnify the Lord,
and my spirit hath rejoiced in God my Savior.
For he hath regarded the low estate of his handmaiden:
for, behold, from henceforth all generations shall call me
    blessed.

For he that is mighty hath done to me great things; and
    holy is his name.

The electric feeling traveled through my body, galvanizing
me completely by the time I got to the words *for, behold, from
henceforth all generations shall call me blessed.* I recognized this
as a grand, prophetic statement, even if I didn't know what it
meant; I tried to read as a great actress might read it, throat-
ily, while still keeping my voice low enough that it would not
be heard outside the closet door. The Virgin Mary had been
a nobody, not particularly *blessed* for the first part of her life,
and the same could be said of me, couldn't it? I was about to
start reading it again from the beginning when I heard someone
coming up the stairs. I switched off my flashlight and flattened
myself against the blankets until I heard the footsteps moving
on to the second stairwell.

It was the upstairs tenant. Not Pam, but the other one: the
quiet one whose room seemed so closed off, the one who paid
his rent on time. Once in a while I heard him at night—when
I was supposed to be asleep—and whenever I did, I couldn't
help thinking that he always had the tread of someone taking
pains to go unheard. He skulked around the Lacombe house the
same way I did. Did he, too, live in fear of being humiliated by
Bernadine and the boys? *Poor upstairs tenant,* I thought with
something like affection, flicking my flashlight back on and
breathing easier. Sometimes I imagined us meeting by accident
in the hallway and nodding at each other stiffly but with recognition, the two hunched little spiders of the house.

A FRIENDLESS CHILD

By my third week of school I had learned a number of things both in class and at home. To the surprise of everyone but myself, I turned out to be a quick study; like the proverbial sponge dipped in warm sudsy water, I absorbed. I drank things up like someone with great thirst.

In class I learned what a haiku was, how to count by tens, and how to make dinosaurs out of newspaper strips and flour-and-water paste.

At home I discovered Kevin had a crush on Pam; one afternoon, after Pam had taken a shower on the second floor, Kevin and Wendell went in with a plastic baggie and collected all the little hairs that curled around the drain. ("I'm going to put these under my pillow," I overheard Kevin boast.) I also learned that crank calls made to people randomly picked from the phone book could while away dull hours. "I just want to let you know that your mother dresses you funny and you smell like a *ham*," I overheard Wendell say into the phone one night when his mother was out, pinching his nose to disguise his voice. Then, seeing me standing in the kitchen doorway, he flexed, making like he was going to take a swipe at me, and he and Kevin laughed when I predictably flinched and cowered.

"Wait, don't go away. You want to do one?" Wendell said, holding out the receiver.

"Oh, man, that'd be classic," Kevin said.

Do one? One what? "I guess so," I said.

The boys coached me through the script I was to follow, and Kevin dialed a number. An old lady with a tiny voice answered the phone just as Wendell thrust it next to my ear. "Hello, Mrs. Perry?" I said in my deepest, most melodiously Mother-like voice. "This is the electric company, and we're calling all the houses in your neighborhood. I need you to turn off all the lights in your house."

"All the lights in the house?" the old lady croaked.

"Yes," I said. "And when you've turned them all off, please come back to the phone."

"What? I can't hear you."

"When you've turned them all off, please come back to the phone!"

I waited several minutes until the lady came back, puffing.

"Have you turned them all off?" I asked.

"Yes, they're all off."

"Dark, ain't it?" I said and hung up the phone, fast. The boys were howling with laughter on the sidelines. I giggled too, pleased to be included in this little drama, even though part of me was already feeling sorry for the tired, bewildered old lady and regretting having to use the word *ain't*.

Avoiding conflict was another skill I'd acquired, both in the classroom and out of it. Miss Thibeau still sometimes gave me funny looks in class, but the looks softened when I offered correct answers during religion or language-arts classes. The other children, sensing I was different, left me in peace for the most part. They knew I liked to spend recess by myself and mornings with Orion at our preferred spot under the tree, weaving leaves into the chain-link fence. (This leaf-weaving activity took up a great deal of time, but our efforts were paying off; we now had a wall of leaves over one whole section, so that when cars drove by on the other side of the fence, they disappeared, as if passing through a tunnel, only to reappear where the wall had stopped.)

Now that March was ending, winter was turning into spring, just as Orion had said it would. *Round and round it goes, like that.* Despite my regimented school schedule, many of my hours bled indistinctly into one another; days remained almost formless, meaningless, without the routines Orion and I had established at Mother's house. And I missed Mother very much—more and more as the days went on. I missed her movie talk, her gossip about which of Mack Sennett's Bathing Beauties had thunder thighs or dimpled knees. I missed her laying an arm across my shoulders and pulling me to her in a quick sideways hug or giving me an affectionate smack on the bottom as she sometimes did when her mood was good. I missed her laugh, the way she tucked the tip of her tongue behind her front teeth when she smiled at something funny.

"Tell me a story," I asked Aunt Bernadine one night as we stood side by side at the counter, rolling dough for a *tourtière* pie—a local specialty made with spiced ground pork in a crust.

"What do you mean, a story?"

I thought for a while, rummaging around in my head for something appropriate. "A story about my dad when he was little."

"I don't do those kinds of stories," Aunt Bernadine said.

Not to have stories about one's own brother? That seemed impossible.

On another evening before dinner, as Aunt Bernadine scrubbed potatoes in a pan in the kitchen sink and I shelled beans into a bowl, I asked her, for the first time, if Orion would ever be joining me at the Lacombe house. I had dreadfully mixed feelings about this. I wanted him with me more than anything in the world—but how horrible would it be if the Lacombe boys were mean to him the way they were mean to me?

"Why should I know what's going to happen to him?" Aunt Bernadine responded. "He's got a caseworker handling all that stuff. I don't know nothing about it. Where would I put another boy, anyway?" Without looking up from her work, Aunt Bernadine pointed in the direction of the kitchen counter and said, "That reminds me. There's a letter come for you. I left it on top of the cookbooks with the rest of the mail."

"Who is it from?"

Aunt Bernadine's expression gave nothing away. "You tell me."

Orion, I thought. Who else would it be? I dried my hands before rooting out the envelope that had been placed on top of *The Joy of Cooking*, right underneath a utility bill and a flyer from a retail furniture outlet proclaiming, "EVERYTHING MUST GO." My name was written on the envelope in a familiar, light hand; I recognized the distinctive *s* in Asta, with the lower part of the letter descending below the baseline and looping around like a ribbon. This wasn't my brother's handwriting—not even close, for my brother wrote in all block letters. These loops belonged to my mother.

"That's from Loretta, right?" Aunt Bernadine sniffed. "I'm surprised they let that woman write letters where she's at. I'm surprised they even let her have a *pencil*."

"Why? What's wrong with pencils?"

"They're sharp," Aunt Bernadine said. She pronounced it the Maine way: *shahhhp*. "Never mind. What do I know, anyway? I suppose you'll want someone to read that letter to you, seeing as you can't read."

She wasn't exactly volunteering to do the job for me, I knew, but even if she had been, something about her tone made me want to keep the letter as far from her as possible. "I can read it," I said, putting it in the pocket of my jumper. "I'll do it later."

"Suit yourself." Aunt Bernadine's mouth twisted up as though someone had wrenched it out of place. "Why don't you go read it now, and give those beans a rest." She rubbed the potatoes in the sink with such ruthlessness that I felt sorry for them.

I went up to my room, deposited myself stomach-first on my bed, and held the envelope for a while. I held it between my hands—then, flipping on my back, I held it between my ankles and my upraised feet, just for variety. The envelope was cool and smooth against my skin. As I pried open the flap, I thought about my mother's tongue moistening the seal with little licks, like a mother cat washing its young. Inside the envelope were several small sheets of paper, covered on both sides with cursive writing in an ink so blue and dense it was hard to tell the paper had once been white. How could Mother have forgotten that I couldn't read cursive? Did she even remember anything about me anymore? Had I been a different sort of girl, I would have cried for all my frustrations, but no—I was still a brave sort most of the time.

I placed the letter on my chest. I watched it rise and fall with each inhalation and exhalation and decided that it almost didn't matter if I could decipher the letter or not. It had still been written for *me*. I ran my fingertips over the garlanded cursive, feeling where my mother had pressed down in her effort to say something only I was meant to know. After a while, my fingertips grew warm—warm enough to itch, then hot enough to burn—until I felt as though I had some sense, however faint, of what she wanted to tell me.

* * * * * * * * *

Aunt Bernadine had been wrong in saying I couldn't read. The last few weeks had brought an increased comprehension of words and the way they worked together on a page, and thousands of new stories availed themselves to me.

In no time at all, the book Miss Thibeau used in reading class—a text entitled *Dogs on the Go*, which had seemed so exciting when it was first issued to me—was no longer challenging enough. Every Friday afternoon Miss Thibeau took our class to the school library and encouraged us to check out a book we hadn't read before. It was overwhelming at first, being faced with so many choices. Most of the books in the library were slender, with large, blubbery print and primary-colored pictures on each page; I couldn't imagine how even the most simpleminded child could find them difficult. I enjoyed looking at picture books, but I hungered for something more substantive—something I could spend an entire week reading until library day came around again.

One Friday, after browsing the shelves for almost the entire library period, I selected one of the few really thick books: *Little*

Women. While it was still not as thick as Orion's volume of Shakespeare, I needed two hands to hold it, and that seemed as much of a selling point as any. I opened it and read the first sentence: "'Christmas won't be Christmas without any presents,' grumbled Jo, lying on the rug." This line made me want to read more. Right away, I wanted to know who Jo was and why she was grumbling (to say nothing of why she was sprawled out on the rug like a boy despite the contrary, feminine evidence of her ballooning skirt, as seen in the drawing that accompanied the first page). "I'm going to write a book report on this," I told the library lady, Miss Mello, as she stamped the card in the back of the book and smiled disbelievingly.

I had some difficulty reading *Little Women*; there were whole passages that didn't make much sense to me, paragraphs in which the meaning fogged over, but I refused to be defeated. I devoted six days of my life to sitting by poor Beth's bedside as she went into the Valley of the Shadow, and I saw the three surviving sisters married off. The following Thursday, when Miss Thibeau handed out book-report forms, still warm and staticky from the mimeograph machine, I was ready.

I gave special thought to what I would write. I decided to skip the room allotted on the page for a drawing, filling the whole sheet with words:

Book: Little Women by Louisa May Alcott
Book Report by Asta Hewitt

Little Women is a big book that was written a long time ago. The four March sisters Meg, Jo, Beth, and Amy wear long frocks with aprons in most of the pictures. Jo is a tomboy and has a dress that gets burned up. And also a dirty glove that she has to carry in her hand all

scrunchered up, at the Ball. One part that was my favorite was when Amy the youngest sister has all these limes
she brings to school. I don't know anyone who likes
limes that much. I don't think I ever eaten one before.
The Father is away in most of the book and that is where
the title Little Women comes from. Because the girls and
Marmee grow up and become Ladies while they wait for
Father to come home. There is a boy in the book named
Laurie. He has a girls name and Jo has the boys name!
Maybe thats why they are best friends! I thought they
would get married, but Laurie marries Amy and Jo mar-
ries an old Proffesser. He can't even speak good English.
And I forgot to tell you, one of the sisters even dies.

In conclusion, I think Little Women is a good book.
The author Louisa May Alcott makes it so funny and sad
you can almost see the four sisters standing before you
like Actresses in a Movie.

The report was not complete. I wanted to go on from there,
expanding the idea of the actresses in a movie, but Miss Thibeau
told us to pass our papers forward. She'd been going from student to student, admiring everyone's drawings, but she hadn't
had a chance—or perhaps hadn't cared—to look at my work.
Still, I had the feeling that mine might be a strong report; with
the exception of the aborted ending, it said what I wanted it
to say. And I was proud of myself for using "in conclusion," a
grown-up phrase I had picked up somewhere along the way.

At recess, still feeling proud of myself, I crouched under
Orion's and my tree. The bare ground was showing more and
more signs of green. There were now leaves on the trees to weave
into our fence, not just the desiccated ones from last autumn

that had lain under snow all winter. I plucked some of the leaves off our tree and wound them around the wire of the fence in the spot where Orion and I had left off that morning. As I wove, I tried making up my own unrhyming Bushman-style poem:

These are the holes
That open to the world
Like hundreds of eyes.
Like potato eyes, only uglier.
It is good to . . .

I paused at this point, searching for a word that gave a rough musicality to the free verse and at the same time becoming aware of someone making decidedly unmusical sounds in her throat. Standing behind me was a bigger girl with Maria Sidelinger from my class—Maria, the girl who sucked her thumb—and I saw that Maria was crying. She hid her face behind her pink, unmittened hands. The white hood of her spring jacket formed a peak on top of her head that somehow made her look vulnerable, like an ice cream cone in the sun.

"No one will play with my sister," the bigger girl said. "Will you play with her?"

I deliberated on this, noting that Maria Sidelinger had not asked me herself and would not look at me while I weighed the pros and cons of playing with her. I didn't have any particular objection to the fact that she smelled bad and sucked her thumb and cried easily, but I didn't see how I could incorporate her into my play. I didn't see how I could recite my words from the Bible and cast spells and make up poems and build my leaf wall with someone other than Orion.

"I'm sorry," I said after a long pause, looking at the older Sidelinger girl and then at sobbing Maria, who didn't flinch at my response; it was almost as if she had been expecting it. "I just can't play with her. I have some important things to do right now."

The elder sister looked like she wanted to give me a piece of her mind but didn't know how to go about it; her mouth opened, then closed shut again, and she led her sister away with her hand on her elbow, giving me one last condemning look over her shoulder. "Sorry," I said again. I hoped Maria would find someone who was willing to play with her, but I doubted it—I was the only other child without playmates at recess, the *only* other one who wasn't paired or tripled or quadrupled up. I was a *friendless* child, I realized with a start. I had never viewed myself in that light before. I missed the companionship of like-minded people—Mother and Orion when he was communicative—but had no use for their lesser substitutes. That made me friendless by choice, which was not a bad way to be—preferable to the alternative, to being a child left wanting.

Shaking my head, I watched the cars passing on the other side of the fence. On the corner across the street, I saw the crossing-guard lady standing alone. In her dark navy uniform, her shoulders were as round and hunched as an owl's. She seemed to be looking in my direction, but her eyes went through me, the light glinting off her glasses. She was waiting for someone, I thought, but who? There would be no children to help across the street for hours.

THE UPSTAIRS TENANT

LATER THAT AFTERNOON I came home to a nearly empty house. Aunt Bernadine was off at one of her women's club meetings, and Wendell was at a friend's, leaving only Kevin upstairs doing homework at his desk. I checked in on him, trying to be covert about it, and he surprised me by inviting me in and showing me the poster he was working on. "It's for the science fair," he said, holding it up. "It shows skin cells and how they heal after a person gets a cut. What do you think?"

The panels depicting the four stages of healing were done in vivid Magic Markers, and the skin cells were enlarged, looking more like wet bubbles about to pop than anything one would find in the human body. "I think it's very nice," I said.

"I think it's great," Kevin said. "I might even win a prize."

"I hope it does," I said.

"What are you going to do today? It's a nice day to play outside."

I had license to do whatever I wanted, but since Kevin was being pleasant to me, I felt I ought to take his advice. I decided to spend time in my favorite section of the backyard, close to where the property line ended, near a row of rocks and an old tree stump. A few days ago, I had removed one of the light, flat rocks and placed it on top of the stump, making an altar from which I could give recitations or deliver grand pronouncements when the mood struck me.

On this day my plan was to recite the Magnificat in its entirety. I had memorized it for this express purpose, believing that such beautiful lines could only be done justice if spoken outdoors, the way I imagined Mary had said them originally. (It was hard to picture her praising the Lord from inside a linen closet, even if she'd had the finest linen closet in all of Galilee, which she probably hadn't.) I got about a third of the way through, forgot what came next, and decided to begin again from the beginning. I made my voice even humbler and more grateful-sounding (a slight quaver did the trick): "My soul doth magnify the Lord . . ."

"Are you Catholic?"

Right away I knew that although the speaker was male, it wasn't Kevin or Wendell; the voice was softer than either of theirs and cracked on the word *Catholic*. I turned and saw a thin, stoop-shouldered young man standing close by. His hands were clasped behind his back, and his dark brown hair swept up from the widow's peak on his high forehead. "Are you Catholic?" he asked again.

"What is Catholic?"

"It's a religion," the man answered. "Like, where you believe in saints and go to church and all that stuff." His voice had a hoarseness to it, a not-unpleasant quality that might have come from a cold or might have been permanent.

I gave this explanation serious thought. "I like saints," I finally replied. "I don't go to church, though. I've never been to church."

"I don't go either," the young man said. "Not since I was a kid."

Somehow this admission, this confidence, made me feel as though I could trust this stranger, even though my heart was racing at having been surprised by him in Aunt Bernadine's yard. "I heard you praying," he said as if reading my thoughts. I expected an apology to follow—*I didn't mean to startle you*— but none was forthcoming. Sneaking another look at him, I saw that his pronounced eyebrows were even darker than his hair, and beneath his eyebrows his narrow, slanted eyes were an indeterminate color. He wore regular clothes, an untucked shirt and army pants, but no jacket even though the air was still cool enough to warrant an outer garment.

"Aren't you cold?" I asked him.

"No," he said. "Not really." He was not just looking at me, he was *studying* me, I was sure, studying me keenly, with a look that was partly bemused and partly something else. *Acquisitive.* The air around him had both a heavy, sweet smell and that odd, stale smell I'd noticed outside his room. He inspected my altar, looking at it from every conceivable angle. He reminded me of Orion as he did this—it was just like Orion to look over my handiwork with a critical eye. "What's this you've got going on here? Are you trying to make a table?"

"An altar," I clarified.

"Is this like your sanctuary?"

I nodded, liking the sound of the word without fully knowing what it meant.

"Cool," he said. "You should nail a couple of boards on top of the stump here. It'd give you a better surface. Did you lift that rock yourself?"

I told him I had. He seemed impressed, then said, "You should be careful though. You could get hurt lifting those things. Last fall I used to like to come out here and turn some of those big ones over to see if there was anything underneath I could photograph. It was insects I was looking for. Insects in their natural environment." He smiled—though it looked more like a grimace—and pointed to the heavy-looking granite rock in front of him. "Under that rock there I found a bug that had a face and teeth. It was kind of snarling at me. I tried to cut it in two, just to see if that would kill it, and the pieces regenerated."

"What does *regenerated* mean?"

I'd expected the man to look apologetic, to think he'd lapsed by using such a big word in front of a child, but he remained unfazed. "It's a scientific thing."

"Is it like metamorphosis? We're studying insects in school, and we learned how caterpillars turn into moths. Metamorphosis means *change*."

"So it does," the man said, his grimace turning into a wide smile. His front teeth were crooked, and one of his incisors was dull—chipped. The imperfection, combined with his narrow eyes, made his face look wolfish. "You're a smart girl, aren't you, Asta?"

"Yes."

"And a pretty one, too."

"I'm not!" I said, outraged at what I saw as a gross exaggeration. "I'm not pretty. Nobody thinks I am. But how did you know my name?"

The man laughed, a low husky sound. "I didn't even tell you mine. I'm Leon," he said and stuck out his hand. I didn't know what to do, but he took mine and shook it—his fingers were lean and tapered—and then didn't let go. "Your name's easy enough to remember. You have a—a famous dog's name. Your brother's name is unusual, too, but not as unique as yours. Have you ever seen *The Thin Man*? One of my favorite scenes is where Nick tells this guy that his dog will tear him to pieces, which is a bunch of bull . . . have you ever *seen* that dog? He couldn't tear anyone to pieces if he tried." He laughed again, more quietly now, and I was torn between wanting to pull away and liking the sensation of the stranger's long, cool hand in mine. Then he let go, and his hand dropped back to his side.

"I haven't seen *The Thin Man*," I said.

"That's okay," Leon said. "Did you know I live on the third floor? I rent from your aunt."

"Oh!" I said. "You're the upstairs tenant!"

"You should come up and say hi to me sometime."

"I did once, sort of. I went to see what was on the third floor. But I didn't think you were home."

"Come sometime when I *am* home. I have something up there I think you'd like to see. Better not tell your aunt, though— I don't know how she'd feel about us talking. I don't think she likes me much."

"She doesn't like me much either," I said, and Leon laughed again, a laugh almost as inviting as his handshake.

"I'll look for you sometime, Asta. Have fun out here. And be careful lifting those rocks."

I didn't take my eyes off him as he crossed the lawn, removing something from his pocket that must have been a house key. It was the upstairs tenant, all right—the person I'd wondered about. Here was someone who knew about things I knew— saints and movies—someone who could be a source of good conversation, if only he hadn't been in such a hurry to leave. I had a strong urge to follow him, to take our discussion further, but I knew that I couldn't. I was just a little girl, and he was a man. I guessed him to be eighteen or nineteen years old.

* * * * * * * * *

"Do you know the name of the man who lives upstairs?"

I asked this of Aunt Bernadine that evening over dinner. The question was more of a test than anything else; I had heard him introduce himself as Leon, but somehow I wanted verification from her. "Of course I know his name," she said disdainfully, revealing the wad of mashed turnips that she'd just shoveled into her mouth. "He writes me a check with his name on it at the end of every month."

"What's his name? I forgot." I tried not to sound too curious, studying my expressionless, upside-down face on the back of my spoon.

"Leon."

"He's *Leonard* Sicart. Leonard the sicko," Kevin said, with a sneer in his voice. "He likes to be called Leon, like Leon Spinks, except he isn't black."

"You don't need to be calling him anything, got that?" Aunt Bernadine said, pointing at both me and Kevin with her fork. "That boy is not right in the head. Touched. One time I caught him in the yard with his camera taking pictures of some dirt under the crab apple trees. Looked like it'd been freshly dug up. When I asked him what on earth he thought he was doing, he said that the picture was for a *photography* class and that he wanted it to look like a grave site. He said he'd been taking a series of pictures featuring *dead things*. Then he got this look on his face—I can't even describe it. It's like he'd gone simple. I said his name a bunch of times and he acted like he couldn't hear." She forked up the remainder of the turnips on her plate. "Soon as the summer comes around, I'll get Mr. Touched-in-the-Head out and another student in his room."

"Speaking of touched in the head . . ." Wendell said, looking at me meaningfully, then leaving the sentence dangling.

"What?" Aunt Bernadine asked, casting a distrustful glance my way.

"Asta thinks she's the Virgin Mary. I heard her a few days ago in the backyard praising the Lord."

"Now that's just silly," Aunt Bernadine said this more to me than to Wendell. She reached across me for the butter dish. "We aren't in biblical times anymore, honeybunch. You aren't the Virgin Mary. You're an ordinary girl."

That was clearly the end of the conversation about Leon and the end of the conversation about me. Inside, I blazed with fury, an emotion so alien I almost didn't recognize it—I only knew that there was something in me that wanted to come tearing out and rip into Aunt Bernadine. How dare she say I was ordinary! She didn't even know me! *She didn't know what great things were in store for me.* I finished the rest of my dinner in silence. No one noticed any difference. It was rare for me to say anything at mealtimes.

* * * * * * * * *

The following morning on the playground, I told Orion about my encounter with Leon. I had already told him a little bit about

Pam, just to give him a fuller picture of life at the Lacombe house, and I was glad now to be able to describe the other tenant. I liked sharing nice things with Orion, in the rare event that I had nice things to share; conversely, I never spoke of Kevin and Wendell and the way they sometimes treated me, for I thought that might make him unhappy. "Leon reminds me of you," I told my brother. "A *lot*. He even has dark hair and dark eyes. Except he's older. He likes looking at bugs and taking photographs of them. If you had a camera, isn't that something you'd like to do? He invited me to visit him in his room." (I didn't tell him Leon had said I was pretty. For some reason, this was information I felt I should keep to myself.)

Orion looked only moderately impressed, but at least I had his attention. "I still don't understand how he knew our names," I continued. "Do you think I should ask him about it? It's not right that he knows so much about us when we don't know anything about him."

Orion tapped the book he had in his lap. He had moved on from Shakespeare and was now carrying *Great Expectations* everywhere he went; a bookmark shaped like a caterpillar with the word *bookworm* cross-stitched on it bulged from the middle of its pages.

"Are you saying Leon read about us?" I asked. "Like in the newspapers?"

Orion slouched, taking on a glazed, almost slack-jawed expression, and I knew that he was pantomiming the way a person looks when watching TV. "Or saw us on the news?" I guessed. "Maybe that's it. But I feel like it's more than that—like he *knows* us. Do you think I should ask him about it?"

Orion nodded thoughtfully.

"I think so too," I said.

Having received precisely the answer I wanted, I vowed to myself that I would question the upstairs tenant at the next opportunity.

However, the following week was filled with many distractions. In school, we were expanding a social studies unit on the American presidency by making miniature replicas of the White House, and I was writing my first-ever short story, which was about a fairy and a lamb. It filled up two sides of my wide-ruled yellow paper, and I took such care with my words that I found myself erasing and rewriting every one, leaving so many smudges that the entire composition looked like it was superimposed on a gray storm cloud. It wasn't until the next Friday night that I decided to take Leon up on his invitation.

It was by pure chance that I heard him come in, for I'd fallen asleep at my normal bedtime and woken up only because of an upsetting dream. In the dream I was walking back to Mother's house, carrying a box of my things, but when I got to our road, our house wasn't there—only a great, scorched crater where the house had once stood. I woke up agitated, a clammy sweat on my chest and neck and stomach, and fanned my nightgown away from my body, letting the cool air in. I would have given anything for some scented, absorbent cornstarch powder. Mother sometimes dusted me with it to make me more comfortable when I got sleep-sweats.

I heard the front door open and the familiar light click as it was shut. There was no question in my mind who had just come in. No one but Leon and I shut doors quietly in the Lacombe house.

Getting out of bed and inching open my bedroom door, I could see that the boys' light across the hall was off. Aunt Bernadine snored extravagantly from her master bedroom at the end of the hall. With motive and opportunity in alignment, I decided to waste no time; I advanced down the hall, going up the second staircase so that I could be there, waiting outside his room, when Leon arrived.

I felt a rush of adrenaline as I heard Leon climb the stairs and watched him turn on the hall light so that he could see to use his key. I was almost close enough for him to trip over, but he still hadn't noticed me. Not wanting to startle him, I decided to make my presence known. "Good evening," I said just as he turned around. He jumped anyway, his shoulders squaring and tension knotting his features, and for a second I thought I'd made him angry.

"Hey," he said. "Asta. What're you doing here?"

"I wanted to talk to you," I said. Then, as a reminder: "You said I should come by sometime."

He let out a deep breath, almost a sigh, his face reorganizing itself into the same mild expression I'd seen a few days before. "True," he said. In the semidarkness his eyes looked narrower than ever—I could hardly see the irises—which gave him a peaceful, sleepy look. "D'you want to come in?" he asked, opening the door a fraction wider. The sweet smell that clung to him wafted out from his room. Suddenly, the door at the opposite end of the hall opened, and Pam, her head wrapped in a fluffy powder-blue towel, glared. As she looked from Leon to me, her expression changed, but something in her attitude did not quite relent.

"Oh," she said in her breathy little voice. "I heard someone talking. I didn't know who it was."

"I'm sorry if we bothered you. Asta came up here to talk to me for a minute."

"I was already up. I just—I just didn't know who was there."

Pam looked at me, her strategically arched eyebrows giving her a look of greater astonishment than she might have actually felt, and shut the door.

"She thought I was bringing a girl home," Leon whispered as he pushed the door all the way open and felt around for the light switch. "She was hoping to see something interesting."

I wanted to tell him, *I am a girl*, but I knew I wasn't a girl in the way that Pam was a girl, and shyness came over me.

Leon's room was more commodious than I'd imagined: I had pictured something the size of my own bedroom, but he had a built-in kitchenette and a closet-sized bathroom. The living room was filled with clutter. A low table was covered with overflowing ashtrays and tissues that looked like they had been used to blot paint from a brush. Underneath and around the table were a broken eight-track tape with the ribbon pulled out, a chess board with half the pieces missing, and a three-quarters-empty bag that read "Cheetos" across the front of it. Newspapers and magazines were against the walls in stacks taller than I was. In the far corner of the room was an unmade mattress and box spring with no bed frame. A picture of a wild-haired, rather crazed-looking man glared at me from the adjacent wall. I asked Leon who the man was, and he laughed his hoarse laugh.

"It's Charles Manson. Only one of the most high-profile criminals to emerge this century."

"I never heard of him."

"Being a little kid and all, you probably don't follow that kind of news much." Leon took off his coat and let it fall where he stood. Its zipper clinked against the hardwood floor. "I don't have company much. Can you tell? Sit. Make yourself at home." He pointed to some lime-green cushions on the floor near the low table. He had no chairs. He hunkered down on the cushion across the table from where I had seated myself and waited for me to speak.

"You're right, I don't follow news much," I began, "but I know about movies. My mother and brother and I used to act them out at home. My mother says . . . " Disarmed, I stopped myself, seeing the open way Leon was smiling at me; the amiable crookedness of his teeth made him look very interesting.

"What is it that your mother says, Asta?"

"She says we have two choices." I took a moment, trying my hardest to remember exactly what Mother had said on that last day, the day before everything changed. "We can . . . we can conduct ourselves as if we are watching a movie, or we can conduct ourselves as if we are acting in a movie and leave the rest of the world to . . . hang."

I was embarrassed to repeat the words. I knew this was the sort of sentiment that Aunt Bernadine or Miss Thibeau or Kevin or Wendell would scoff at, yet Leon accepted it as if I had stated something commonplace. "What does that mean to you?" he asked.

"I don't know," I confessed.

"I don't know if I know, either, but I like your way of looking at things. I've always said that a person can learn a lot from movies, and especially from images—from the things you see. Like photographs, for instance—they can tell a story."

"Like in the Big Movie Book."

"Huh?"

I explained the book to him. The descriptions of the silent actresses in still photographs seemed to alternately intrigue and amuse him. He snickered a little—but not in a mean way—as I described some of my favorites: ethereal Marie Doro with the flowers in her hair; doomed Olive Thomas looking so wide-eyed and innocent (and not a bit like a dope fiend) under her straw bonnet; vampish Lya de Putti, who was more beautiful than Theda Bara but less famous in the end. "You really know all about those old-time stars. That's kind of sweet," Leon said. "Hey, do you want a Coke?"

"Okay," I said. Leon got up, and while he was getting a glass from a cupboard, I drew my knees up to my chest and gave another surreptitious look around the room. On a bulletin board that hung next to his bed, Leon had tacked up a number of photos that were difficult for me to make out from where I was sitting. One seemed to be of a shirtless young boy lying on his side, turned away from the camera. Returning with the Coke, Leon caught me looking at the photo and said, "That's a picture of my little brother when he was getting a spinal tap. I took it when I was fifteen and he was nine. I guess it'd seem gross to most people, but it was one of the first pictures I ever took with any serious intent. I'm taking photography in school right now, trying to get my portfolio together. Just got back from a late class, in fact."

"That's good," I said politely, even though I had no idea what a portfolio was (or a spinal tap, for that matter).

Leon handed a full glass to me and walked over toward his bed. I took a sip and coughed, surprised by the bubbles.

"Coke is carbonated," Leon said. "Maybe I should have warned you." He knelt down, felt in-between the mattress and the box spring, and pulled out an oversized, leather-bound book. "Here's a few more of my pictures. A lot of these are just for me —I'm not even going to turn them in for class," he said, resuming his spot on the cushion across from me and laying the book between us. He opened it to the beginning and began telling me about some of the photographs in his soft, husky voice. "This one doesn't look like much of anything. It's just a rope, see, and the rope's being pecked by a sparrow. But it's the rope Frank Witham used to hang himself. The Witham murders were a big news story a few years back; I guess you're too young to remember. It's the bird that gives the picture a little something extra. Do you see how it tells a story?"

I did. There was no comparison, really, between the effectiveness of my attempt to describe the silent actresses' beauty and that of the photo I was seeing now. Even without knowing who Frank Witham was—and even without that giveaway word, *murders*—I could sense something dark and forbidding.

"This one here is a picture of what's left of the trailer where old Mr. and Mrs. Hensbee used to live. It burnt down while they were watching TV. They never even made it out of their La-Z-Boys. You can see how damaged the trailer is on the outside; the inside, as you can imagine, was much worse. My photography professor says that my pictures don't have any subtext, but I disagree—I think they're nothing *but* subtext. I know that doesn't mean anything to a kid like you," he said, sounding almost frustrated about this. "*Subtext* is a pretty big word."

"*Metamorphosis* is bigger," I said, "but I know that one." I sipped my Coke, watching Leon turn the laminated pages. There were numerous photos of bulbous insects and country graveyards whose tombstones had been bleached by the sun. I wondered if *subtext* meant "something that isn't pretty." One dark lock of hair had fallen in front of Leon's face, refusing to stay put; I watched, interested, as he tried to smooth the hair back on his high forehead while turning more pages with his other hand.

"Who is that?" I asked, stopping him at a picture of a little girl standing barefoot, with what looked like a lake or a river behind her. She was wearing a long, nearly translucent white nightgown with a lace collar, and the picture seemed to have been taken at nighttime. "*She's* pretty."

"That's Deanna," he said. "She's my dad's friend's daughter. She was one of my best subjects. You like her spooky eyes?"

It reminded me so much of something Mother would say—*sweet Jesus, look at their eyes.* I looked at them. Although the photo was black and white, I could tell that the girl's eyes were a very pale blue or a very steely gray. "It's like her eyes are peeling you right down to your core," Leon said. "Like you're an apple core, right?"

On the next page was another picture of Deanna lit by moonlight. At first I thought my eyes were playing tricks on me, for it looked as though she wasn't wearing any clothes. She was curled up like a ball, her buttocks and her pointy little shoulders visible. Her face was turned toward the camera and her eyes flashed silver, as defensive as an out-thrust knife. "Nice, isn't it?" Leon asked.

"Is she naked?"

"Nah," he said, laughing. "She has a bathing suit on. Her family owns a lake house." He reached over and turned the page a little more quickly than I would have liked. A gaunt cat eating the remains of a garter snake looked up at me.

From under the table Leon dug out the Cheetos bag and unrolled one end of it. He took an obscenely orange fistful and ate it in one swallow, then pushed the bag at me. I took a couple myself, and as I watched Leon wipe the orange powder from his fingers onto his shirt, I did the same. The Cheetos were salty, and they collapsed into a soft mush when I held them on my tongue.

"I have something in the back of this book that might really interest you," Leon said. There was an expression behind his eyes that I could not read; the dark pupils seemed to dance. "But before I show you, I feel like I ought to explain a few things."

"Okay."

He seemed ever so grave. I made sure to look back at him with equal gravity, giving him the respectful attention he deserved.

"I feel as though I already know you, kind of . . . I mean, knew you before I introduced myself the other day. I've seen you out in the yard sometimes, from my window." He gestured toward the window near the bed, which was obscured by a bed sheet nailed up like a curtain. "I've read about you in the newspapers and seen you on all the local TV stations. You were big news for a few days. 'The child isolates of Bond Brook,' one story called you. That stuck in my head because I thought it was funny to use the word *isolates* as a noun."

"What's an isolate?" I asked.

"It's a person who is apart from the rest of society. I'm kind of an isolate myself."

I remembered Kevin calling him "Leonard the sicko." "Is being an isolate like being a sicko?" I asked.

Leon laughed again, a whinnying sound—the loudest sound I had ever heard come from him. "I guess you could say that. I guess some people might say I'm a sicko. Let them call me that if they want to. I'm used to it by now."

I looked at him, his thin frame, the faint dark circles under his eyes, and felt such a rush of empathy that I actually reached out and put a hand over his for a fraction of a second. "I'm sick too," I said. "I've been sick for a long time. Do you want to feel my lump?"

"Where is it?"

"Under my skirt. Near my hip bone."

"Maybe another time."

We looked at each other without saying a word for a minute. Leon licked his lips, and the half smile on his face was wistful. "Here," he said after a while, flipping ahead in his book of photos as if he'd only just remembered it. His hands were shaking a little. But he didn't seem scared—more excited than scared—and his smile spread. "Here's what I wanted to show you."

Glued to the page in front of me was a newspaper clipping with a lot of text and several black-and-white photos on it. "Is it from a movie book?" I asked, fastening my eyes on the perfect white oval of a woman's face, the perfect blackness of her eyes. Then I saw the way she smiled in the direction of the photographer, her head tossed back in a manner both challenging and coy, and knew at once that it was Mother. Below it, I recognized the photos of Orion and myself that I had seen on the news. "It's us," I said in wonderment.

Leon pointed to the boldfaced headline above all the pictures: THE CHILD ISOLATES OF BOND BROOK. "It goes on for two pages," he said. "This was a really good article. Probably the best one I found."

I turned the page slowly, a dunked-underwater noise rushing in my ears, and saw where the article continued on the other side. On the opposite page was another clipping, another headline: HEWITT SAYS, "I'M A GOOD MOM." Underneath was another photo of my mother, looking beguiling this time, her long hair tucked behind one ear and falling forward over her left eye in a peekabo bang like Veronica Lake. On the next page, and several pages after that, were more of the same: POLICE LOOK

INTO CHILD NEGLECT CASE. ISOLATE BOY, 9, RELEASED FROM HOSPITAL. HEWITT CHILDREN "GIFTED," SAYS DOC. BOND BROOK MOM UNDER WATCH. In each article, new photos of Mother appeared; she was the indisputable star of the story, even when the headlines concerned Orion or me. I kept turning pages, faster and faster, until there were no more pages left to turn. "We're famous," I said, trying to grasp the impact of the words as I said them.

"Locally, I guess you are. Not much happens around this part of Maine."

"How did these get in your book?"

"I cut them out and put them there. I have to admit that I cut out the first one just because of the photo. Loretta—your mother—is so intriguing. It's not often that I find people interesting-looking, present company excluded. Your mother has the kind of beauty not everyone might see—it might take a certain kind of lighting, a certain kind of angle—but if you know what to look for, there it is."

I smiled at this perfect description of Mother. Of course she was beautiful. Anyone who saw her, saw her for real, could see that. "And what about the pictures of me?"

"When I found out you were coming here—not that anyone tells me anything, but I do hear things—I started following the story more."

Leon took the book back from me, and I was so caught up in thought that I almost didn't notice. "That was nice of you," I said as Leon started looking at the pages himself. His hands, I saw, had stopped shaking.

"Thanks," he said. "You miss your mom, huh? I can tell."

"Yes."

"I'm sure she misses you, too. You wish you were still with her?"

"Yes," I said, and then I said it again. "Yes. Do you think that makes me bad?"

"Why would that make you bad?" Leon brushed his bangs off his forehead again, revealing his widow's peak, and looked me right in the eye. "I told you, I think you're very smart. A very smart and very pretty little girl. Even in the newspapers they say you and your brother are probably gifted."

"I don't know what that means," I said.

"It means," Leon said, "that you have gifts. And your brother has gifts. He's supposedly really good with puzzles. And he's been writing during his recovery—keeping a journal, I think. Pretty good for a nine-year-old."

I wondered what *my* gifts were. I hadn't done anything exceptional. I couldn't tie my own shoes yet—Aunt Bernadine had to do that for me every morning. I didn't know how to find my mother in the telephone directory. And I didn't know how to read my mother's cursive handwriting. I swallowed several times, trying to get the egg in my throat to go down.

"You look sad," Leon said. "What's the matter?"

"Mother wrote me a letter," I said. "But it's all in cursive, and I don't know how to read cursive yet." It was a disgraceful thing to have to admit.

"So you don't know what it says?"

Leon closed the photo book and considered me for several minutes. Once again I was reminded of Orion. "I could read it to you," he said. "I'll tell you what—it's getting late, so why don't you finish your Coke and go back to bed before someone notices you're gone. Here's what we can do. Let's meet in the yard

Monday afternoon—at the rock wall, where we met before—at about three thirty. Bring that letter from your mom, okay?"

"You wouldn't mind?"

"It would be my pleasure," he said. He straightened up and took my empty glass from me, and I stood up too. He walked over and opened the door. "Good night now, Asta," he said, laying his hand on my head for just a few seconds, leaving a tingle on my scalp. I felt like the recipient of a blessing.

"Good night."

"Make sure you're quiet going down those stairs. Don't wake your aunt up."

"I won't."

I had no trouble making promises to him already. That is what one does when one finally finds a friend.

A CARBON COPY

LEON WAS ON MY MIND as I walked to school the following Monday. The prospect of meeting with him in the afternoon and of hearing Mother's letter read aloud seemed to infuse the morning with such unnatural brightness that it was hard to see straight. Perhaps this is why I second-guessed my vision when I reached the top of the hill and noticed a different crossing guard on the curb.

A substitute wasn't unusual in and of itself; I had seen this other woman once before, on a morning when the usual crossing guard—the one with the owlish eyes and impertinent questions about *ornjoose*—had had the flu. What was unusual was that the substitute was drawing a small crowd that seemed to be in no hurry to cross the street. I was almost always one of the last children to be taken across the street, but now the children were lagging behind, risking tardiness to hear what this crossing-guard lady had to say.

"It took twenty years off my life, it did," she was saying as I approached. Seeing me, a fresh face in the group, she seemed all too glad to start over from the beginning: "I was just telling the kids that Miss Bonenfant, the crossing guard, passed on yesterday. Jumped right off the Memorial Bridge. I seen it happen with my own two eyes. I was driving by and I seen her climbing the security fence, and I put on the brake and says, 'Gladys! What are you doing?' She stared right at me and jumped. I ain't seen nothing like that, ever, and it took twenty years off my life."

"Did you see her after she hit bottom?" the oldest-looking girl in the group asked. "Was she all bloody?"

"Why'd she jump off a bridge?" another, less morbidly inclined child asked.

"She just lost hope," the substitute crossing-guard lady said, skirting the first question altogether.

I winced, not wanting to hear any more. Leon was completely erased from my thoughts as I recalled Miss Bonenfant's bright gaze, the thick French Canadian accent that so many of St. Germaine's older residents had, the odd persistence with which she had asked me meaningless questions, most of which colloquially ended with the word *there*: *It gonna rain today, you got the rain shoes there? Easter is coming, you gonna have the Easter-egg hunt there?* I always felt that she never liked my answers, which made me dread my brief interactions with her each morning. And now she was dead—*passed on*—from jumping off a bridge, on purpose. I had never heard of anyone doing such a thing before and couldn't imagine why anyone would want to.

I clasped my arms across my chest as I slowly crossed the street, looking up at the spring sky full of real clouds—somewhat less magical than the clouds I'd imagined on the ceiling of Mother's house, but pretty in their own right. I was baffled by what I'd just heard. Mother had always said that our earthly experiences didn't matter, for our real treasures would be found in heaven, but I liked the treasures I had here on earth, small though they may have been, and did not want to part with them before I absolutely had to. Out of habit, my hand searched for my lump. There seemed something very wrong and frightening about giving up hope the way the crossing-guard lady had.

I found Orion in our usual spot under the tree, feeling the same pleasant surprise I always felt when I laid eyes on him in the morning. Orion was growing on an almost weekly basis; sometimes, when I saw him on a Monday, I could have sworn he was bigger and heartier than he'd been the previous Friday. It scared me a little to see him gleaming with health, to note the new luster in his dark hair (which was falling into unruly waves again) and the chubbiness of his hands; these changes made less sense to me than his silence did. And how must I look to him? I had fattened up too, on Aunt Bernadine's starchy cooking, and almost didn't recognize myself when I brushed my teeth in the bathroom mirror each night before bed. My moonchild-round face had broadened, grown even rounder, and my dark eyes were hard to find; they were recessed in the swells of my cheeks like a couple of raisins pressed in a ball of dough. How was this person me?

I asked Orion if he had heard about the crossing-guard lady, and he shook his head no, so I told him the sad story of how she'd lost hope. I remembered as I was telling it that Orion didn't even know the crossing-guard lady since he always got a ride to school. He was staying on the other side of town, the side where Aunt Bernadine said the "swells" lived, the doctors and the lawyers—people who were disinclined to send their kids to school on the bus. The one time Orion had arrived later in the morning than I had, I had caught a glimpse of the man who drove him to and from school—a tall, straight-backed man whose head almost touched the car's roof. He tooted the horn twice before he drove away—his method of saying good-bye, I guessed—and Orion waved at him, which made me feel jealous in a way I couldn't quite account for. Jealous that my brother *communicated* with someone other than me.

"Anyway," I said, finishing the story about poor Miss Bonenfant, whose name I had never even known until the substitute told me, "she's *passed on* now."

Orion was a good listener; he always had been, even before his spell of silence took over, but now he couldn't correct me, couldn't chide me, couldn't tell me when I was stating the obvious or leaving out the most important part of a story. It gave me a narrative freedom I'd never had before. As he patched up our leaf wall, which inevitably lost some of its cover each day as dead leaves dropped off or bullies kicked away patches on their way home from school, a comfortable silence settled between us.

When the bell rang, I walked with Orion to where the fourth graders were lining up. Right before we separated, he showed me the face of his digital wristwatch, another recent acquisition, and then lifted up his finger. *Number one.*

"I don't know what you're trying to tell me," I said. "What's number one?"

But Orion only gave me a half smile—Orion, smiling!—and waved at me in the same way he'd waved at the doctor or lawyer who drove him to school. Sometimes he was mysterious just for the sake of being mysterious, I thought. I shrugged my shoulders, waved back, and joined my fellow second graders, who twittered with the news of the morning.

* * * * * * * * *

The children were eager to tell Miss Thibeau about the crossing-guard lady after the final bell had died down. "Miss Bonenfant jumped off a bridge!" shouted Ricky Trepanier, who was one of the more vocal boys in the class. "And Mrs. Lovejoy seen it happen!"

"Isn't killing yourself a mortal sin?" asked one of the girls who sat near the front. "Does that mean Miss Bonenfant's going to hell?"

The children pig-piled onto this idea, debating, protesting, their words writhing around and feeding off the speculation as though they'd never known such sustenance. Miss Thibeau shushed them. "It's a very sad thing," she said in a subdued voice that told us our excitement was not the order of the day. "Let's say a little prayer for her and her family."

We all bowed our heads while our teacher led us in prayer, but I wasn't concentrating on what she said; I was thinking that she hadn't answered the girl's question about hell. I knew that hell was a fiery place ruled over by a devil who had a tail shaped like an arrow and that everyone there became his servants; I tried to picture Miss Bonenfant among these hot, slaving people, standing off to the side and saying, "Did you have a good breakfast today there?" and waiting for new hellions to arrive so that she could bring them across safely.

"Amen," we said in one voice.

After that Miss Thibeau, with no sense of irony, assigned a group of children to craft a happy yellow sun out of brown paper and poster paints; this sun was to be used as a backdrop for the fifth graders' spring play. I tried not to think about Miss Bonenfant in hell and to concentrate on how much I enjoyed painting. Three of us worked on the inside of the circle, coloring the middle of the sun a bright lemony color, while three other children painted the outer points a subtly darker orange. There was some debate as to whether we should put a face on the sun or let the vibrant color speak for itself; a boy named Eric Small, who was considered a good artist, settled the issue by getting out the black paint and giving the sun two googly eyes and a grin. Everyone was pleased with the result, especially Miss Thibeau, who said that not even the fifth graders could have done as good a job and that we'd managed to do it with little mess. We shoved the sun in the corner of the room so that it could dry during the day.

Right before lunchtime, Miss Thibeau went to the back cupboard to get the cold lunches (she kept these locked up until it was time for lunch, as if we couldn't be trusted with them beforehand) and let out a wounded yelp. "Oh!" she said. "Look at this! Would you look at this!"

All the children gathered around to see what she was pointing at. I looked, too, and felt sick as I saw two small footprints on the outer edge of the sun and the smear of yellow paint that trailed on the floor beyond it. I remembered stepping over the sun to reach a book on the bookshelf during free reading time; I had thought my heel might have touched the edge of the wet paper, but I convinced myself I'd only imagined it. Looking down at my Buster Browns now, I saw a trace of yellow paint on the inside heel. With the side of my other shoe I discreetly began rubbing it off.

"Who stepped on this?" Miss Thibeau was beside herself. "I want to know *right now*. Whoever did this is going to have to repaint it. If I have to start checking the bottoms of your shoes for paint, I will!"

My classmates were all abuzz. A few of them had turned up their feet to see if any yellow paint could be seen on the soles of their shoes. I knew they wouldn't find any. My evidence destroyed, I kept my feet planted on the ground even as the accusations began to fly.

"I bet it was Philip," I heard someone say.

"Yeah, Philip!"

Philip, who was bigger than most of us and had a mysterious condition that required a special tutor to spirit him away for long intervals, looked down at the tops of his shoes but didn't show his soles. I felt a mixture of guilt at his having been singled out and relief that it hadn't been me. If Philip hadn't been around, the next likeliest target would have been Maria Sidelinger, who, with her thumb jammed in her mouth, was looking as nervous as the perpetrator herself. As long as these two scapegoats were present, it would be possible for me to stay under the radar.

Miss Thibeau, still quietly fuming but dropping the threat of a foot check—realizing, perhaps, that this might be taking things too far—got us in line for lunch. I felt too sick to eat, and the fact that Aunt Bernadine had put a sweaty and rancid-smelling macaroni and tuna salad in my thermos didn't help matters. I got up from my table and told the lunchroom attendant that I needed to use the bathroom, that it was an emergency. I slipped out and went back to my classroom.

Miss Thibeau was at her desk, eating something green and leafy out of a plastic container and drinking 7Up out of a can. In midchew, she turned her head to the doorway and saw me standing there. "Yes?" she said, swallowing. "Come in, Asta."

I approached her desk. It was the first time I had ever been alone in the classroom with her, and without the buffer of the other students and the diversion of schoolwork, the overhead lights hummed in a menacing way.

"I wanted to tell you that I'm the one who stepped on the sun," I said. "But I didn't do it on purpose. And I can repaint it if you want."

I waited for the punishment, the proverbial rap on the knuckles or box on the ears that children were always getting in the primer. Instead, Miss Thibeau averted her eyes and focused on her salad for what felt like forever. When she looked up again, her expression was hard to make heads or tails of. "Thanks for letting me know," she said. Her tone was gruff, or maybe she just hadn't swallowed her leafy green mouthful properly. "You can do the repainting after recess."

"Okay," I said.

"I've been meaning to tell you," Miss Thibeau said, "that your last two book reports have been very good. And your writing exercises, too. I liked that little story you wrote about the fairy and the lamb—the lamb who ran away and came back again? I've never seen a student pick up writing so quickly. I'd like to talk to your—is it your aunt?—about you sometime."

"Aunt Bernadine?" I must have looked horrified. "Why?"

"I was thinking of giving you extra writing assignments, and maybe some extra reading assignments since you tend to finish yours early," she said. "I have a feeling you could write some more lovely stories."

"Is that one of my gifts?"

Miss Thibeau smiled in a way I had never seen her smile before, with her lips still touching and deep dimples appearing in her cheeks. "Maybe so."

"Thanks," I said, my heart filling up with something akin to love for Miss Thibeau. It wasn't the same as the love I had for

Mother—I could never have been that disloyal—but I thought Miss Thibeau looked so beautiful, sitting at her desk with her fuzzy auburn hair unloosening itself from tortoiseshell barrettes, that I had a great impulse to give her a gift as nice as the one she'd given to me. "I wanted to tell you . . ." I said shyly, "I wanted to tell you . . . that I think you're a very good actress."

"A good what?"

"An actress," I said. "The way you stand in front of the classroom, and ask questions, and get everybody to answer back. Or when you say, 'Everyone take out your spelling books!' and everyone takes them out of their desks. It's very, very good. I think you should keep working at it."

"Why, thank you," she said. "I do my best."

I decided then that I would try to pick my nose a little less often in Miss Thibeau's class, and sing for real instead of mouthing the words when we learned new songs. If she could try her best, then perhaps it wouldn't kill me to do the same. It seemed the very least I could do.

* * * * * * * * *

After recess Miss Thibeau gave me Dixie cups filled with yellow and orange paint to cover my footprints while the rest of the students prepared to watch a filmstrip about nutrition and the four food groups. No explanation for my painting was given to the class—*It has come to my attention that Asta is the one who did this*, Miss Thibeau might have said—and I could feel the other students stealing curious, puzzled looks at me.

As I worked, I thought about the next story I could write for Miss Thibeau; the vaguest outline of it began to percolate in my mind. I knew it would be about a girl who had a dinosaur for a pet—maybe a dinosaur with a special talent, like dressing up as a vaudevillian and doing the soft shoe—and that something devastating would happen to it or to the girl. I had not gotten far in either my task or my imaginings when the classroom door creaked open. I looked up, expecting to see Ethan the helper, and was surprised when my eyes locked with my brother's.

Orion held his shoulders in a self-assured way that made him look bigger than he was—like a fifth grader, at least. When he saw that I was in the corner by myself, painting like mad, I recognized the look of respect on his face; rather than thinking I was being punished in some fashion, he clearly thought I had been singled out for some honor—*I was the girl who was so special, so talented, that she got to paint the sun by herself.* As soon as I saw that in his eyes, I began to believe it was the truth, and I preened a little over my work. Then I saw the big clock just above Orion's head, the little hand pointing to the one. *One o'clock.*

"This is Orion the helper," Miss Thibeau said. "Ethan is away on a family trip this week. Orion, your teacher tells me you're great with gadgets and can figure out this projector. I hope she's right. Ethan usually has to warm it up a little before it gets going."

Since when had Orion learned to use a projector? I wondered as the classroom lights went off. I divided my attention between watching Orion and painting, using the side of my brush to blend the new paint into the old without leaving any telltale streaks. The soundtrack started up before the picture did, causing a momentary scramble by Orion and Miss Thibeau, and as the first image appeared on the screen, Orion had to rewind the tape so that the audio and visual would be in sync.

"Some say you are what you eat," the narrator's voice said, "but what does that mean? Can a balanced diet lead to a balanced life?" The voice of the man narrating the film was so deep and full that it seemed as if he were speaking just to me, and this voice kept me company as I bent over my work. I couldn't help smiling as I heard each *beep* and glanced up to see the projector knob turning in Orion's capable hand.

* * * * * * * * *

When school let out, I walked home by myself, thinking of what I would say to Leon when I saw him. I usually enjoyed my solitary walks to and from school; I made it my business to find interesting, alternate routes home—*shortcuts*, I called them, though they weren't always shorter—that involved cutting through people's lawns and crawling on my hands and knees under bushes. The more rustic the route, the better. I often came home with burdocks in my hair and with runs in my tights from catching them on branches, but I almost always managed to look presentable by the time Aunt Bernadine came home.

Nearing the Lacombe house, I ran a hand through my hair, feeling for errant burrs or sticks or leaves. I didn't want to look silly when Leon saw me. I knew he would be waiting for me by the rock wall—the sanctuary—like he'd said. And there he was, a scarecrowlike figure with his hair standing on end, wearing the same baggy clothes I'd seen him in before and probing around the rocks with a long, gnarled stick. He had a bulky black object hanging from his neck; it looked heavy, like a small toaster oven, and I wondered if it would give his neck a crick.

"Hey, Asta," he said in his hoarse way when I'd almost caught up with him. Somehow, even though he hadn't turned around, he had sensed I was close.

"Hi, Leon," I said. "What's that around your neck?"

"This? This is my camera. It's what I take pictures with. I've got a great shot right here—you've got to come over and see this."

Obediently, I came and stood by him. He had lifted one end of a large rock and was holding it up. With his other hand he pointed to the longest worm I'd ever laid eyes on. "See how they're stuck together end to end?" Leon asked, and I realized this was not one worm but two. "That's called mating."

"It looks ugly," I said.

"It kind of does, doesn't it?" Leon placed the rock back over the two preoccupied worms with the gentleness of someone covering a baby with a blanket. "I just wanted you to see. It's not something you see every day, worms mating. Did you bring that letter you told me about?"

"It's in my book bag."

"Well, let's see it."

Leon took Mother's letter and skimmed through its pages. The corners of the paper flapped lightly, and I couldn't tell if this was due to his hands shaking or if there was an incipient afternoon breeze. "Sit down beside me and get comfortable," Leon said, indicating one of the flat rocks. "It will take me a few minutes to read all this."

"You can make out the cursive okay?"

"Of course. I'm a skilled reader of cursive."

I laughed a little, a delighted laugh; I laughed because this was the kind of thing Orion, the *talking* Orion, would have said. I sat on the rock next to Leon without hesitation. A few months before, being *comfortable* on such a hard, flat surface would have been impossible, as my bony bottom would have balked— but now I was all yielding flesh, capable of sitting any old place. For a minute—just for a minute—I wondered if my specialness had been compromised.

"Here goes. 'Dearest Orion and Asta,'" Leon began. "It's to both you and your brother."

Dearest Orion and Asta,

As you probably know by now, I haven't been able to come get you. I was in the hospital for a while, and now I'm in this place called Sandy Harbor. The name is somewhat deceptive, since it is neither sandy nor a harbor but a house owned by a woman whose name happens to be Sandy. If you ask me, that's too clever by half—a little too-too. There are eight other women staying here, and more on a list waiting to get in, from what I hear. If anyone wants my spot, they can have it! No, I don't love it here, but I have to admit this is preferable to being in prison, which might've been where I'd be writing you from if my doctor hadn't decided that I needed a different kind of care.

It's all because of that business with the spoon. Did you see that on the news? Poor dears, I hope it didn't frighten you. I was having a bad spell in the hospital and got the idea of trying to swallow the spoon that came with my breakfast grapefruit—I thought it would choke me and that in the long run everyone might be better off without me. It was a very small spoon, a demitasse spoon really. One of those silly nurses came in just as I was trying to get it to go down. Some people call me The Spoon Lady now. It's a very silly nickname—no poetry in it at all.

Leon drew in a deep breath, stopped reading, and looked at me. "Okay so far?" he said in an even gentler tone than his usual. "Do you want me to keep going?"

"Of course. Why wouldn't I?"
"Very well," said Leon. "Continuing."

A little birdie told me you've been taken in by families. Asta, I've been told you're staying with your father's sister, Bernadine. I always thought Bernadine was a cow—I don't mean to be rude, it's just that there's no other word for her. I only met her a couple of times, but a couple of times is a surfeit. Orion, I hear a doctor is putting you up. I hope to meet him sometime—I do love doctors—and no, not for their money, but for their <u>attentiveness</u>, their dedication to their field.

Since you're staying in separate homes, I want to remember to tell both of you to listen to what the grown-ups in your lives tell you to do, even when you know in your heart of hearts they're doing things all wrong. Now that you're outside, amongst people, you have to give in a little—you have to follow rules. Stupid ones, even. I would have liked to spare you that kind of stupidity, but there's no use crying over spilt milk.

If it makes you feel any better, I'm having to follow rules myself in this house. I'll give you an example. Sometimes I like to sit on the floor in the hall, curled up because that seems to be the thing to do: be perfectly still, curled inward. Sometimes when I sit on the floor like that, Betty, one of the women who helps run this place, tells me I ought to get up. "At least sit in the lounge and not on the floor," she says. "We don't act like that here, honey." (Betty is a black lady from the South. She's tough enough that she can get away with calling everyone "honey.") I always take umbrage at that because if

we can't act crazy here, why, I guess we can't act crazy
anywhere! And, really, people are always acting crazy
here—throwing things, shouting at people that aren't
even in the room.

I shouldn't complain. I am being cared for. I'm like
Persephone after she had been in Hades for a while and
gotten used to it. Just this morning I went to the kitchen
for breakfast and this one woman, Eileen, said, "Do
you know who you remind me of? You look like Judy
Garland . . . only not so perky." (She said this with a
mouthful of pancakes, of course—her manners aren't
what they should be. But it was odd that she could see
into me like that, to know my actress roots. There are
many people here like that, who have a deeper vision.)

I spend nights in my room alone, writing. This is not
the first letter I've written to you, but it is the first one
I've told myself I will mail. It comforts me sometimes to
think of you both, although when I picture you it's easier
to think of you as newborn babies. Isn't that strange? It's
not as though your infant years were especially happy for
me. Orion, when you were first born, I didn't even like
you that much, if you want to know the truth. It helped
that you napped a lot. You'd nap, and I'd nap right alongside you, with you on a little blanket that I'd folded up
into a square and put under you so you wouldn't ruin the
good bedspread if you decided to throw up. And I'd wake
up lying on my side and you'd look at me in that bug-
eyed way and after a few days I began to think, "We're
forming a truce here. We're going to be okay."

Now, Asta, by the time you came along, I had to do the
same darned thing all over again. More adjustments had

to be made. But that is life. And I am so fond of both of you, as it turns out.

I suppose I've gone on long enough for one letter. I did want you to know I am thinking of you, and I want you to think of me. Remember to do all your lessons and say your prayers. Don't watch too much TV. Three or four or five hours a day should be enough. If you play with other children, be careful not to share their combs or hats. And if you must talk to strangers, talk to good strangers. You'll know they're good by the look in their eyes.

> I love you both.
> Hugs and kisses,
> MOTHER

P.S. Orion and Asta, you are getting the exact same letter. I wrote it on carbon paper. Orion gets the original, and Asta gets the carbon copy.

"Wow," Leon said. He was fanning himself with the letter, unintentionally looking like Norma Shearer or Marion Davies getting the vapors. "That's a lot to take in. Did any of it even make sense to you?"

"Oh, yes, almost all of it! Thank you for reading to me."

I was sitting with my hands folded in my lap, staring down at the daub of yellow paint that was still on the side of my palm, just below my pinky finger. Leon continued to fan his face, slower now, more deliberatively. He regarded me for what seemed like several minutes.

"What are you thinking?" he asked.

The words popped out before I had thought them through. "I was thinking I'd like to . . . bury the letter."

"*Bury* it? Why?"

More certain of myself, I said, "So that a hundred years from now, if somebody digs it up, they'll know a lot about the Hewitts and what kind of family we were." I didn't have the word *posterity* in my vocabulary, but if I had, I would have used it: seven years old, and I was already concerned with matters of permanence.

"We can do that," Leon said. "Sure. We can do that. Where do you think would be a good place?"

"Right here would be good." I indicated a small patch of ground a few feet away, near my altar.

Leon took a penknife out of his pocket and knelt in the dirt. As he pared away at the dried mud, the camera lolled around on the end of its cord. "Tell me if you think this is deep enough," he said after a while. I knelt beside him and, after deciding that it was the perfect depth, tucked the letter, envelope and all, into its hidey-hole. I covered the letter with small fistfuls of the earth, a little bit at a time; I liked how some of the dirt slid through my fingers like sand, while some of it clumped like clay and stuck to my palms. Leon stepped back and watched me appraisingly.

"That would make a good picture," he said.

"You can take my photo if you want to. I don't mind." And I didn't mind; it seemed only fair, given his generosity in reading the letter and then helping me to bury it.

"Thanks," he said. "Just keep doing what you're doing. You don't even have to look at me." The camera snapped as I continued to pour the dirt with my hands. "These are going to be great," he said, stepping back even farther and shooting from different angles. "There's something intriguing about you that reminds me of your mom."

I felt flattered in spite of myself. Compliments were few and far between, but a comparison to Mother was worth a dozen of them. "Maybe it's my sickness?" I said.

Leon smiled. I had finished smoothing the last of the dirt, and Leon rewound the film and took the camera off. "Maybe," he said.

Impulsively, I burst out, "You're nice. Almost as nice as my brother."

"It's nice of you to say so. Maybe I'll meet him someday, too."

We were both on our feet again. A rotund bee—the first bee of spring—alighted on the altar, and I shrank away from it, officially losing, I was sure, whatever mystique Leon had seen in me. "Stupid old bumblebee," Leon said, waving it away, then watching it amble off to a dandelion bed in the next door neighbor's yard.

There was an awkward pause.

"I guess I should go inside now," I said.

"Wait. I wanted to ask you something. When I was taking your picture just now, I got this idea. I need to do a new photo series for class . . . I've been working with the idea of crime-scene photos—taking pictures at places where bad things happened—but there's not much crime to speak of in St. Germaine. I mean, not unless you count kids toilet-papering the cemetery or some guy getting ticked off and shooting his neighbor's dog. But I was thinking I'd like to go see the house you lived in, the house in Bond Brook that was in all the papers, and maybe take some photos. And you could come, too. I could photograph you by the house and it'd be like a sole-survivor concept, kind of. A shipwrecked girl beside the wreck of a ship." He said this all in one breath.

"But I'm not a sole survivor," I said. "And my house isn't a wreck!"

"That's not what I meant. I just thought it would be a good idea. A photogenic old house . . . and a photogenic kid."

If I had looked rather dazed listening to Mother's letter, I must have looked flabbergasted now. "I don't even know how to get there."

"I could drive us. Bond Brook's not even an hour away."

"I don't think Aunt Bernadine would want me to go to Bond Brook."

"Does she have to know?" Leon asked, and he smiled so that his eyes crinkled up and his irises all but disappeared. "We could keep it just between us. It would be better that way, anyway. And we'd both get something out of it—I'd get my project done, and you'd get to go to your house again. Don't you think it'd be nice to see your house?"

"Yes," I admitted.

"And you could stand spending one afternoon with me, couldn't you, Asta?"

I nodded.

"Let's do it tomorrow," Leon said, and he told me his plan: around twelve thirty, I was to tell the school nurse I was sick to my stomach and wanted to go home early. "I can borrow my cousin's car and wait for you in the parking lot," he said. "If you live within walking distance from school, they'll let you go home by yourself. I went to St. Germaine Elementary. I know how they operate."

I smiled to think of Leon that young. This air of intrigue gave me permission to go along with his scheme. "Okay," I said. "I can try it."

Leon stuck out his hand; this time I knew enough to shake it. He squeezed my hand tightly before letting it go, so tightly that I felt as if it were still being held even after it had been dropped. "Go back inside now," he said, "before somebody sees us."

"What would be wrong with somebody seeing us?"

"People get all kinds of dumb ideas."

"Oh," I said and nodded. I had no sense of what he was talking about, but I didn't want to appear ignorant, so I picked up my book bag and turned back toward the house.

"See you tomorrow!" Leon called after me.

I went through the backyard, sneaking a parting glance at Leon before I turned the corner of the house. In the time it had taken me to cross the yard, Leon's attention had turned elsewhere; instead of staring after me, the departing figure, as a hero in a movie might have done, he'd gone back to lifting rocks. Then he was standing up and cupping his hand in front of him, and though I was too far away to see what he was holding, I was certain it was an insect.

THE EMPTY STAGE

CONVINCING THE SCHOOL NURSE to let me go home early proved harder than I'd been led to believe.

First I had to convince Miss Thibeau that I was sick and needed to see the nurse; I had to clutch my stomach and double over in order to get her attention, and while part of me thrilled at the efficacy of my performance, the other part felt guilty about taking advantage of my teacher's newfound sympathy. In the school clinic I had to act the whole thing out all over again, telling the nurse I was too sick to make it through the rest of the day, citing stomach pains, a headache—nebulous ailments that I hoped would sound impressive when totaled up. I explained that Aunt Bernadine had the day off from work and would be there to meet me when I got home; however, the nurse insisted on calling the Lacombe house to make sure this was all right. "She must be in the garden," I said when the nurse told me that no one was picking up. (This was another lie. There was no garden at the Lacombe house.) I told her I'd have my aunt call her as soon as I got home, thus finagling my way out during one of the nurse's weaker moments.

Once outside, I realized Leon hadn't told me what color or model his cousin's car was, and there were at least twenty different ones in the parking lot. I had to pause, car by car, and look through each driver's window to see if Leon was in there; I had already peered through the windows of a tomato-red truck, a big brown Oldsmobile, and a silver punch buggy when I heard Leon say, "Pssst. Over here."

He was craning out the window of a white car about two rows from where I was standing. I saw that he had his camera around his neck. "You made it. I was afraid you might not come."

"I said I would."

"I know you did." He opened the passenger door for me. "Get in. Sorry about the mess."

There were empty Coke cans on the seat and floor, along with crumpled-up bags that smelled of grease and fast food, but happily—cozily—there was still enough room for me. As Leon backed out of the parking lot and turned onto Eastern Avenue, the vibrating hum of the engine and the wind fluting through the open window made a nice complement to the Coke cans rolling around my feet, sounding like a timpani. I couldn't believe I was riding in a car to Bond Brook—much less in the *front seat!*—with the upstairs tenant. Days earlier, it would have been unimaginable, but now it felt like a matter of course. It was turning into a bright afternoon, unseasonably warm, and since Leon continued to drive with the windows down, I stuck my arm out, spreading my fingers to feel the air moving against them.

"Careful," he said. "If a truck came by real close it'd rip your hand right off. Then your arm would just be a—a stump."

"A stump?"

"Well . . . a flipper, maybe."

This made me laugh and laugh. I would've laughed at just about anything then. I was giddy not only at the prospect of seeing my house in Bond Brook but also because what we were doing had a whiff of the illicit about it. Leon's hands seemed whiter than usual as he gripped the steering wheel, and my heart was banging along at twice the usual rate. We were in collusion. Someone and I were a *we*. Aside from those brief, wordless mornings with Orion before classes, I hadn't been part of a *we* in a long time.

While driving, Leon asked me about myself and the kind of life I'd had in Bond Brook. Once again it occurred to me how much I liked the way he spoke to me, not changing the cadence of his voice to make it more singsongy or speaking more loudly than normal the way some grown-ups do when talking to children. I told him all about Orion and how we amused ourselves when Mother was at work; I told him about Mother and the games she would devise for the three of us when she was in high spirits. I told him about our movies. I found myself telling him about one reenactment of *Way Down East*, the famous silent movie directed by D. W. Griffith. In our version, Mother had played Anna Moore, while I took the part of "Susceptible" Sanderson, the playboy who tricks Anna into a sham marriage, and Orion was the decent chap who rescues her from a waterfall. "We had to put Mother on an ice floe," I said, "but we didn't have any ice, so we used a piece of Styrofoam that we put on the bathroom floor, and we scraped out some icy bits from the inside of the freezer and put them on top of that. Mother said it helped her to think cold thoughts."

When I felt I had talked enough, I asked Leon about his family—having remembered (from the "Manners" unit in the primer) that when someone asks you about yourself, it is polite to ask them a question in turn: "Do you have a mom or a brother?"

Leon responded with a sound that was not quite a laugh. "I have parents. They're okay. I think I embarrass them sometimes, but . . . they're okay. You already know about my brother. I had a half sister who died when she was three days old."

"Did that make you sad?"

"I never felt enough of a connection to her to feel sad."

I couldn't help comparing this attitude with the way I felt about Orion. My connection to him was so deep that I couldn't fathom growing up without him. I couldn't imagine not sharing my secrets with him. Earlier that morning, on the playground before the first bell rang, I had told how and why Leon had come to know our names, how he kept articles about Mother glued in one of his books. I also told him that Leon was taking me to see our house in Bond Brook. "Maybe you could get out of school early too and come with us," I'd said, the idea coming to me in a flash. "Leon said he'd like to meet you someday. He could take pictures of us together! He just needs good pictures for his school *portfolio*." But Orion, who often didn't respond with much more than a nod or a shake of his head, had given an eloquent eye roll at this proposition and covered his face with his hands. He was terribly camera shy.

"What about friends?" I asked Leon. "Do you have any of those?"

"I don't have any of those. None that matter."

"Not even Deanna?"

Leon looked away from the wheel to give me a brief sidelong glance. "I haven't seen her in years. And she was just the daughter of a guy my dad knows—kind of young to be my friend."

"But I'm your friend, aren't I?"

"Sure," he said. "Sure you are."

I covered my creeping grin behind my hand so he couldn't see how pleased I was.

Keeping my arm inside the car, I looked out the window at all the houses we passed. I hadn't seen much of residential St. Germaine; although I was now ostensibly part of the outside world, Aunt Bernadine had never had time to take me sight-seeing, so I had not viewed much beyond the route from the Lacombe house to school. I wondered if Orion was staying in any of the houses we passed. I pictured him sitting with the tall doctor and a faceless woman, a faux mother and father, with their heads bowed over their food and the only sound the clink of their forks against the family's good china. (Never mind that it was much too early for dinner.)

Just outside of St. Germaine was farmland, where strip malls and fast-food restaurants were replaced by dilapidated barns and houses with steeply pitched or sunken roofs. A field of sleeping cows swept past the window. And then, as we got closer to Bond Brook, the air began to change—a saltwater smell replaced the fragrant manure—and I felt this was a change I should have recognized, but didn't. Smells from the outside had so seldom penetrated the sealed-up, tar-papered windows at Mother's house.

We drove past a house that looked familiar, and it wasn't until we'd passed it that I recognized it as Crazy Carl's General Store. "I know that place," I said nostalgically, as though Orion's and my encounter with the general store had happened years earlier, when I was a much younger child. We neared my house. I might not have recognized *it* if Leon hadn't slowed down and turned into the dirt driveway. Unlike the general store, there were no

OPEN signs, no advertisements for NIGHT CRAWLERS, to identify it. The little Cape Cod–style house was pretty—much sweeter and prettier than it had looked in the newspaper photos—and for the first time I noticed that our windows had decorative shutters painted a shade of green that Mother would have called *eau de nil*. "Is that it? It is, isn't it?" I said to Leon. "That's where we live."

I related to Leon the circumstances surrounding the morning Orion and I had left the house for the first time. "That's the only other time I ever saw the outside of it," I said.

As we walked toward the house, Leon's camera bouncing at the end of its tether, he asked if I could show him the exit we'd used. I led him around to the back until I found the small door, a door not much bigger than I was tall—a grown-up would have to hunch to use it. It hadn't seemed that small when Orion and I had passed through, I assured him.

"Looks like this door goes through a little shed," Leon said. "Either that or this was somebody's private entrance a long time ago."

"I don't know. We never used it. The passageway to the stairs was all boarded up."

Leon took a few pictures of the door, then asked if I'd stand in front of it for a few additional shots. I leaned against it, crossed one ankle in front of the other, and tried to take on the look of a shipwrecked person. Then I tried peering out from under my bangs and looking sideways, as Mother had once recommended, imitating poses from the Big Movie Book. By the time I had taken on Mary Pickford's attitude in the still from her movie *Sparrows*, complete with her outstretched arms and rapturous expression upon rescuing an orphan from an evil baby farmer,

Leon was smiling—but his eyes didn't quite match up with the smile. "You should just be yourself," he said. "I think that would make a stronger picture."

It didn't seem as if it would be a great deal of fun to be *myself*. Hurt, I said, "I don't know what you mean."

"Just think about being Asta. Be the seven-year-old girl that you are, standing outside your house."

I tried to think about what made me uniquely Asta—what made me uniquely seven years old—and thought about myself out in the Lacombes' backyard, reciting the Magnificat: *For, behold, from henceforth all generations shall call me blessed.* I pictured Mother and Orion sitting in white lawn chairs, watching me and applauding.

"Better," Leon said, and the flashbulb went off. Then, as if it were a matter of course, Leon came over and lightly patted the crown of my head.

Shyly, I said, "Orion and I never spent any time out here, you know."

"I know that," Leon said, "but I don't know if we can get inside the house."

"We could try," I said. "It's much nicer on the inside."

Leon pushed on the small door and found it shut fast. "Let's go back around to the front," he said. We tramped through the backyard, snapping twigs underfoot and ducking under a bush I had never been aware of—Leon said he thought it was a lilac tree, and that the lilacs would be coming soon—and along the footpath to the front door. Mother's dead bolts had been removed. Leon rattled the doorknob, and when it proved uncooperative, he told me to stay put while he got something out of his car. While I waited for him I admired the brass knocker on our front door and even tried it once, just to hear what it sounded like; it seemed a shame to have a house with such a fine brass knocker when we had never had any guests come by and knock.

Leon came back with a tool in his hand—it was a torque wrench, he said—and he began attacking the lock with this tool and a long, thin piece of metal. He did this with a jeweler's loving precision, as if it were an art for which he had been specially trained. When he got the door open, he stepped aside so that I could be the first to enter the house.

At first glance, all was in order. The long green carpet stretched before me like a mossy bridge from the doorway to the living room. The uncarpeted staircase inclined upward as it always had. I ventured farther down the hallway, looking for the Victorian hall tree, an object of which Mother was especially proud. This hall tree had a beveled mirror in its center and what Mother said was a "petticoat mirror" at the bottom, to check the hem of one's dress. But the grand object was gone, and the corner of moss-green carpet on which it had stood was bunched away from the wall, revealing a freckled linoleum floor and a scattering of dust bunnies.

"That's strange. There used to be a piece of furniture here," I said.

Leon started to respond, but I was already in the living room, looking for more changes. Instead of the sanctum I remembered, with the fainting couch and matching armchairs and the portrait of Mother, I saw a partially empty room. The fireplace was still there, along with an old hassock, a couple of mismatched chairs, and a side table with scratches down the front. A few pieces of bric-a-brac remained on the mantel and on a corner shelf.

"This is our living room. There used to be a fainting couch over there. I used to do my homework on it and look at my mother's picture, which hung right there," I said, pointing at the bare wall. "I don't know where our things went, do you?"

"Maybe someone put them in storage." Leon seemed unconcerned. He was fiddling with his camera again. "It's a nice room. I can see why you would have used it for a study. And that's a great old fireplace. Would you mind sitting in front of it for a picture?"

Leon's response did not offer the reassurance I was looking for. Still perturbed by the question of what might have happened to our belongings, of who might have violated our space, my enthusiasm for posing had waned a little, but there was no point in making Leon suffer for that. I sat down on the brick hearth and smoothed my skirt over my knees. "What do you want me to think about this time?"

"Nothing. You don't even have to smile. Just look at this spot right here on the camera, and I'll start snapping away." He took the first picture, then another and another: *Click-click-click-click-click.* "Did you ever light fires in this fireplace? To keep warm?"

"Mother burned our toys in it once," I said. "I don't remember any other time."

"What else did you and your brother do in this room besides study?"

"We mostly spent time in Orion's room. Orion didn't use this room much at all. He didn't come down much in those last days. He had to stay in bed a lot."

"Could you show me his room?"

Click-click-click-click-click.

"It's upstairs."

"I guess it makes sense for you to show me the rest of the downstairs first."

"I'll show you the kitchen next," I said. "I hope nothing's missing from there." In the kitchen I found that my vision was still impaired by the flash of the camera; I squinted, trying to see things as best as I could. The only item I couldn't account for was an antique spice rack. The nail from which it had hung was all that remained. I pointed out the approximate spot on the kitchen floor where Orion had gotten his magic pickle-juice treatment, briefly recounting the story to Leon, who seemed fascinated. "Was he cured?" he asked.

"Of course," I said.

"Maybe you should try doing magic to get him to talk again." With his expressionless eyes and his soft, hoarse voice, I couldn't tell if he meant this to be funny or not.

"Maybe," I said. "I hadn't thought of that."

Before we left the kitchen, Leon snapped several pictures of me crouching under the table; since the table was so big and I was so small, he said, this would give me a waifish quality. (I made a mental note to find out what *waifish* meant later on, when I could get my hands on Kevin and Wendell's dictionary; I had a hunch it might be something good to eat.)

I took Leon to the rooms on the second floor, first showing him my mother's room, now bereft of its bureau; untroubled by this loss, Leon homed in on the hole in the closet floor, which he photographed in a rapid series of shots. He asked me if I'd be willing to lower myself onto the stairwell and be photographed from above, in the darkness, but when I hesitated, he said, "Never mind. I don't want you to get scared."

"I don't think I want to go in there again."

"I understand." Leon's tone was infinitely gentle. "Why don't you show me your brother's room instead?"

In some ways Orion's room seemed the most transformed of all. Even though his narrow cot still stood there, and the rabbit-eared TV, someone had torn the tar paper off his window—the window he'd been so eager to see out!—so that a clear light bounced off the opposite wall. I could hear bird calls outside—the descending *tee-urr* of the cardinals and the high-pitched, energetic *chips* of the chimney swifts, so close that they seemed to be in the room with us.

"That's the TV over there," I said, pointing. "We'd sit on the bed or put cushions on the floor when we watched it. It's a black-and-white TV. I never saw a color one till I got sent to Aunt Bernadine's. I don't get to watch the color TV much anyway—the boys are always watching it, or Aunt Bernadine after she gets home. She watches nighttime soap operas. One time I got thirsty after I'd gone to bed and I came downstairs for a glass of water and Aunt Bernadine was watching this show where a woman was in a burning building. Maybe she was just an actress, I don't know. But the woman was screaming. She was screaming really loudly."

"It's okay, Asta," Leon said.

Did he think I was about to cry? Perhaps he hoped tears would come as he snapped my picture—snapped a whole succession of pictures—while I pointed to the TV and then looked, almost furtively, back in the direction of the window. For several seconds my eyes burned from a combination of the unexpected afternoon sunlight and the flash of Leon's camera.

"Don't be sad about the stuff that isn't here," Leon said. "It didn't get up and walk off by itself. Like I said, somebody probably put it in storage."

"It's not just *stuff*. I was thinking about my brother. The good times we had here."

"I know," Leon said, and for some reason this simple statement comforted me. I believed Leon's sincerity. I believed he really did understand that I'd been happy at home, in a way that other people couldn't understand. They didn't know the magical things I had known. "That was our tent," I said, pointing to the bundle at the foot of Orion's cot. "We made wishes under there, and said prayers, and cast spells."

"Would you show me?" Leon asked.

I picked up the afghan, shook it out, and said, "You have to get on the bed with me to hold up the other side. That's what makes it a tent."

We sat on the cot. When Orion and I sat on the cot together, the mattress stayed level, for our weights were comparable, but when Leon sat on it, the mattress dipped on his end. "You sit across from me, like this," I said, "and pull your end of the afghan over your head, like I'm doing."

Leon did so, and I looked at him in the sudden dark, interested in the way the shadows made his nose seem longer and his eye sockets deeper. "Hear ye, hear ye," I said. Then I stopped, looking at him apologetically.

"What?"

"I don't remember what line comes next," I admitted. "But we used to say *something*."

"The tent is very pretty with the little holes of light."

"Those are the stars," I informed him.

"Oh, right. The stars."

He snapped my picture, just once. Then he dropped the camera, and it made a thud as it hit his bony sternum and then floundered on the end of its cord. I flinched—it sounded as if it had hurt—but Leon looked as though he hadn't felt a thing.

"I think I've seen this place before," he said.

Even in the darkness of the tent, I could see a fearful look glazing over his features. "I've been here before. I've been here."

"But you couldn't have," I said. "You—" I stopped. Leon leaned toward me, looking for a moment as if he were going to remove something from my eye—a sleepy seed or a loose eyelash. Then he went stiff as a poker, jerked once, and fell sideways off the cot and onto the floor.

I scrambled off the cot and dropped to my knees beside him. "Leon?" I said. He was lying on his back, and his shirt had ridden up, exposing his white stomach, which—I was embarrassed to see—had fuzzy, dark hairs all over it. I pulled his shirt down so that he was decent again. His eyelashes fluttered, and his eyes rolled back in his head as if he were searching for something way, way up in the top of his skull; I thought at once of Orion and his trances. "Are you seeing anything?" I asked eagerly, leaning in closer. "Do you see yourself walking down a green hill?"

I half expected him to tell me to be quiet—if he was as much like Orion as I thought he was, he wouldn't appreciate having his concentration interfered with. But his eyes just rolled farther up, until there was nothing but white, and his arms and legs began to jerk and vibrate in a way that let me know that there was something very wrong happening to him—that whatever was happening was not good, not good at all.

"I'll get help," I said when he began to cough. "I'll get somebody. You stay there!"

I didn't have a plan when I said those words, but once I flew down the stairs and threw the front door open, I knew where to run—to Crazy Carl's. Someone was bound to be there. Even if it was the woman with the plaid pants and the kerchief on her head, who'd been so displeased when I ate one of her cupcakes, I knew she'd be better than no one at all.

In the deep snow, in Orion's and my weaker state, the trek to Crazy Carl's had seemed a long march. But I was stronger now, faster, and the ground was no longer covered with snow and ice. The walk was really not much farther than my daily walk to school, and when I sprinted as I was sprinting now—running as if I were possessed—it seemed half the length.

I reached the parking lot of Crazy Carl's and reeled the last few yards until I reached the door, my body pitching itself in with the last of my strength. I didn't even hear the bell tinkle overhead. The woman whom Orion and I had spoken to was not behind the counter, after all; a bald old string bean of a man was there instead, sitting spread-legged on a stool. "Afternoon," he said.

I could only stand there, too winded to speak. A froggy sound came out of me. Feeling rather desperate, I looked all around, and in a disconnected way I noticed how small the shop really was; instead of the majestic food emporium I remembered, this was just a dingy general store—nothing like the big supermarket in St. Germaine, which sold not only groceries but also beauty products, toys, and seasonal items like snow shovels. It was funny how much my perspective had changed in just a few short months.

"A man fell down," I heard myself say. "He's having a fit in the house down the street."

The man was already off his stool, and he bellowed a name—"Ruth!"—toward the back of the store. The woman Orion and I had met bustled out, her pants fabric rustling as her thighs brushed together, and I braced myself for whatever lecture she had for me. I was strong enough to handle it now. I could apologize for the cupcake. But it soon became apparent, from the woman's look of concern, that she didn't remember our earlier meeting at all.

"I'll call an ambulance," the old string bean of a man said, rubbing the top of his bald head, then digging his fingernails deep into the short white hairs at the nape of his neck. He disappeared down one of the shop aisles. The woman pulled out the stool for me—it made a scraping noise along the floor—and told me to sit with the same masterful sternness with which one might speak to a dog.

I sat.

"Now breathe," she said, and I did, feeling the pounding in my head begin to clear as I was able to take more and more air into my lungs. She gave me a Dixie cup filled with clear, cold water. I drank from it. "Now tell me," she said, in that flat voice that I'd found so off-putting when I'd first encountered her, "exactly what happened, and what you were doing in that house down the street."

"It's *my* house," I said. I told her what had happened, though perhaps not with the degree of exactitude she'd demanded. I told her of Leon, his camera, the strange way he had moved under the afghan tent. The way his eyes had looked just before he'd gone stiff as a poker. "I think maybe I did it to him," I said, tearing up despite my efforts not to. "I think I did something to make him sick." My voice sounded as if it were coming from someone else.

As I was talking, my eyes traveled behind the counter, where packs of cigarettes and tins of chewing tobacco were kept. On the floor, leaning against the wall, were a couple of framed pictures.

There was a painting of a girl drinking from a water fountain, standing on her toes to reach the jet of water. Behind it, half visible, was part of a face—a dark eye and a bright pink cheek framed by a fall of white tulle. The dark eye seemed to speak to me. I realized that I had stopped talking and was now simply looking.

"Where did you get that picture?" I asked.

"What?" the woman asked, turning around. "That? Don't mind that. Keep telling me your story. The police'll be here any minute."

"Please. I want to see the woman's face."

I could hear an ambulance wailing now, louder and louder, and another set of sirens right behind that.

The woman moved the picture of the little girl aside to show me the portrait that had been half covered. "I bought it for the frame," she said with a strange combination of apology and defiance. "We were going to put an old picture of the store in it and hang it right here. The frame alone is worth about a hundred dollars."

"She's mine," I whispered. "The woman in the picture. She's mine."

* * * * * * * * *

This is what I learned after the fact: The EMTs who went to our house found Leon sitting up straight on the floor, dazed and uncertain of his whereabouts. The lady police officer who came to pick me up at the store was filled with assurances that he would get the medical attention he needed. As we began the journey back to St. Germaine, she had one final comment on the subject. "It must have been scary, seeing that," she said. "Epileptic seizures aren't pretty."

The word *seizure* seemed slippery, and *epileptic* seemed loaded and overripe, with its juicy plosives; I didn't feel right hearing them. I ignored what she said and looked out the car window. It was still daylight out, but the sun had lost a lot of its midday brightness. At least I would make it back in time to wash up for dinner before Aunt Bernadine got home from work, I thought.

"Tired?" the lady police officer asked. "You can put the seat back and go to sleep if you want."

"I'm all right," I said, although I *was* tired. "I was just thinking."

"About your friend?"

"Kind of." I was thinking how sickness seemed to follow me and rub off on everyone with whom I came in contact; the sickness had gotten to Leon, and it had invaded my home— the missing belongings, innocents all, had fallen victim to the outside world. I told the lady police officer about how things were different at my house, and she shrugged as if this were an inconsequential detail. "Whoever's in charge of the house now put some of the stuff up for auction," she said. "Some of it got bought up by antique dealers from New York. I heard a local doctor bought a lot of it—Dr. Van Somebody."

I shifted in my seat and adjusted the portrait of my mother— now held only by its matting, as the woman at Crazy Carl's General Store had liberated it from its frame before giving it to me. I held it protectively between my legs as though someone might try to pry it away.

The lady officer took a long swig of the beverage she was drinking, belched quietly, and offered the bottle to me. I shook my head. "You've just got to believe that everything will work out for the best," she said as if reading my mind. "It can't hurt to hope. Right, kiddo?"

As we pulled into the Lacombes' driveway, I saw Kevin and Wendell and a neighbor boy playing Wiffle ball in the backyard. Seeing the police car, they froze in their places and stared at us. Then the front door banged open and Aunt Bernadine came running out, practically hopping up and down with agitation. Why was Aunt Bernadine home already? She was yelling at the top of her lungs, and it took me a minute to realize she wasn't yelling at me but at the lady police officer, who was getting out of the car. "Did you get *him*?" I heard her ask. "What about *him*?"

The boys had come closer to us, presumably so they could take in every last word. Kevin even had a shadow of a smile on his face.

The lady police officer spoke quietly to Aunt Bernadine, whose cheeks got redder and redder. Eventually, she opened the car door and looked at me, then at the unframed portrait I was holding, and up at my face again. "*What* were you thinking, sneaking away from school like that?" she said. "Do you have any idea how crazy you've made me? I've been home since two o'clock. The school nurse called me a couple of hours ago to see if you'd gotten home all right, and here I am wondering what's happened to you all this time. And it's just as I suspected—nothing good! It's enough to make me *sick*."

Everything happened very quickly after that. The lady police officer left, I was ordered inside, and Aunt Bernadine ran a hot bath for me and made me get in it right away. I didn't know why—I was neither cold nor particularly dirty. While I stirred under the bathwater, noticing how my knees looked grayish and magnified, I could hear Aunt Bernadine on the hall phone. She was making a succession of phone calls to people I didn't know, raging as she recounted the story of how I'd come home with a police escort after traipsing around with the "no-good, crazy" upstairs boarder, who'd been carted away after having *conniptions*. "And to top it all off, she brought back this *picture*," she said, "of that crazy woman. Can you believe it?" The portrait now leaned against my bedroom night table as if awaiting a punishment that would inevitably be carried out once Aunt Bernadine had finished making her calls. "You can't trust anyone around little kids nowadays," she said into the phone. I could hear her pacing; I imagined her going back and forth until the phone cord was in knots.

Finally, she hung up the phone and stood in the bathroom doorway. Naked in the tub, I curled up in a ball to cover myself. I didn't know what to make of the strange expression on Aunt Bernadine's face—that look of piety alloyed with conviction. "I'm only looking out for you, you know," she said. "I could have told you he wasn't normal. A boy his age hanging around a seven-year-old girl! He didn't try anything funny, did he?"

"I don't think so," I said.

"What on earth gave you the idea to go to Bond Brook?"

"He thought of it," I said. "He wanted to take pictures."

"*He* thought of it. Of course *he* thought of it," Aunt Bernadine said. "He's not coming back here, that's for sure. Let his parents deal with him. I can't believe he took you back to that house just when you were starting to forget about things. That mute brother of yours—I bet he's forgotten he ever lived there."

"He hasn't," I said, so vehemently that the water rippled around me. "Neither of us will. Not ever."

Aunt Bernadine stood with her hands on her hips, looking down at me. She shook her head. Her face was beginning to take on a new look, one that seemed almost sad.

Lacombe house to the room that had been Leon's. The door was unlocked, at least for the time being; the only sign that anyone had ever lived there was a trash bag that Aunt Bernadine and the boys had neglected to throw out. The bag had the pungent smell of rotted fruit, which threatened to overtake the smell that still clung to the walls; any day now Pam would complain about the fetid odor wafting down the hall.

It would be a while longer yet, I guessed, before Aunt Bernadine would remember to lock the door. In the meantime, I liked sitting in the gutted, stripped-down space of my only friend's room and re-creating our last moments together. Almost everyone I'd met in the outside world eventually gave me that much: the dubious gift of empty spaces.

* * * * * * * * *

For the first week or two after the Leon incident, I assumed I'd be subject to more of Kevin's and Wendell's taunts and punishments. I imagined Aunt Bernadine giving me the silent treatment and the evil eye, slopping dinner on my plate with more force than necessary, as though distaste could be measured in serving spoons. But instead, everyone gave me a wider berth. Sometimes I'd catch Wendell pulling down his lower eyelids and pugging his nose, trying to scare me, but even this didn't have the same bite, the same bad intent, it'd had before.

Orion's silence during this time felt especially significant, even though I knew that his refusal to speak had nothing to do with me. As much as I wanted to talk to him, to hear his voice, his silence meant that he couldn't ask me how my outing with Leon had gone, and I was more than happy not to volunteer that information. As more days passed and Leon seemed farther and farther away, I realized I had made a mistake in comparing him to Orion. Worse than that, I had betrayed my brother— diminished him, displaced him. One morning, when we were working under our tree, I came as close as I could to expressing this. "I did something bad," I said to him, looking him in the eye. "I should never have tried to make another friend." He looked right back at me and cocked his head. He leaned in closer, mouth slightly open, his breath smelling sweet—maple-syrupy.

I waited.

And then this noise came from the back of his throat: *Nynnnnhhhh*.

I took it to be sympathetic—forgiving, even—though I couldn't be sure. "Thanks," I said, and he nodded back. Sometimes such exchanges were enough. It was amazing how much mileage I could get from the briefest of his acknowledgments; it was amazing where mercy could be found.

But on other days mercy was scarce. Just a few mornings later, a couple of weeks after Leon's departure, I reached the school playground and saw that Orion was not in our usual spot by the tree. Nor was he anywhere else on the playground, I concluded after circling the grounds several times. On playground duty was Mrs. Stinchfield, teacher of the big fifth graders, and I went up to her and asked if she'd seen my brother. "I don't think I know who he is," she said brightly when I gave her his name. "Sorry!"

It was a windy, bleak morning, and I sat alone. Our leaves quivered against the chain-link fence; the wind spat some of them out, pummeled the dry leaves to dust. I watched the cars go by through the peepholes in our mulchy wall. I had known how much I valued my mornings with Orion, but I had not realized until that moment how much I depended on them for my well-being. Not even 8:00 AM, and my day was as good as ruined!

My morning lessons were in vain, for I spent the entire time wondering why Orion hadn't shown up and envisioning dire predicaments—had the car that was driven by the tall doctor crashed into a telephone pole? Were they both in the hospital, getting their ribs bandaged? Had I heard any distant ambulance sirens that morning? Sitting at my school desk, I couldn't even remember.

"Asta, are you paying attention? I asked you a question." Miss Thibeau stopped short in the middle of a lesson on (I think) the metric system.

"Yes, Miss Thibeau. I'm paying attention."

"Then what is the answer?"

"Um," I bleated.

Stacey Cherry, a girl who had emerged as one of the teacher's pets despite the fact that she couldn't read or write anywhere near my level, giggled behind her hand.

Miss Thibeau looked pointedly at me. "I would like you to stop staring out the window and daydreaming. What could possibly be so interesting out there?"

Unable to help myself, I glanced out the window again, seeking out an answer. Rain was now coming down in sheets. It looked like the kind of cold, hard rain that would hurt when it touched you. I really *didn't* know what was so interesting out there. Without my brother, what was outside for me now?

The next morning, after I'd had a fretful night of interrupted sleep, Orion was still not at the playground. In the back of my mind I had feared this would be the case, and now that it had come to fruition, something had to be done. After the first bell rang and the second-grade classes were let inside, I sneaked up to the floor where the fourth-grade classes were held.

I had never had any contact with Orion's teacher, but I knew she was called Sister Louise Marie, and in her nun's habit she was easy enough to spot as she stood outside her door, ushering in her students. A much older lady than Miss Thibeau, she cocked her head to hear me better when I asked if she knew why Orion Hewitt wasn't in school today. "His dad called him in sick, dear," she said. "He probably has that flu that's going around." As if to underscore this point, one of the children filing by sneezed zestily without bothering to cover his mouth.

His *dad*? I thought. Who was his dad? The doctor? Surely she'd made a mistake, but Sister Louise Marie seemed like a nice old lady, not someone I should correct. I thanked her and went back downstairs to Miss Thibeau's room, where the rest of the class had already taken their seats.

"I was wondering where you were," Miss Thibeau said as I came in. "I knew you weren't absent. I saw you earlier in your little spot you like so much."

I thought my classmates might laugh at the way she emphasized the words *little spot*, as though there were something ridiculous about my place under the tree, but only one or two did.

"I got lost," I said, slipping into my seat. "I got lost on the wrong floor." And I smiled at her. At least I tried to, but my lip twitched and then stuck to my upper teeth in a way that must have looked unpleasant. (It was deflating to think I was losing so much ground with my teacher, so quickly.) Miss Thibeau sighed and took her attendance book from her desk. "Hewitt, Asta," she murmured, finding my name and checking it off with a pencil.

Hewitt, Asta, I mouthed to myself without making a sound. Hearing my first and last names transposed made me think, fleetingly, of the telephone directory, with all those listings of other Hewitts in it; somewhere in that book, perhaps, was a listing for the doctor who drove Orion to and from school—the one person who might know of his condition. But I didn't even know his name.

* * * * * * * * *

Later that afternoon I was back at Aunt Bernadine's house, in my room, constructing new paper-doll dresses from scraps of gift wrap. I felt at ease knowing Kevin and Wendell were outside, caught up in yet another game of Wiffle ball. Every now and then one of their voices penetrated my bedroom window ("Cut it *out*, losah!"), along with a crack of the bat.

There was a rap on the front door. Not loud, but decisive enough. It might be one of the older neighborhood children selling magazine subscriptions, I thought; as of late they had descended like locusts, but Aunt Bernadine had already ordered her *TV Guide* and *Good Housekeeping* from Wendell. Warily, I looked down the stairs. The front door was open to let in some of the warm spring air through the screen. I was prepared to run in the other direction at the sight of an unfamiliar face.

But the figure at the door was far from unfamiliar. Orion, of all people, stood on the other side of the screen, shifting his weight from one foot to the other.

Sometimes, when you see someone you know in an unexpected place, it takes a moment to recognize him, to reconcile the known with the unknown. The only thing more surprising than seeing Orion materialize in my classroom a few weeks before was seeing him here, on Aunt Bernadine's stoop. He looked a veritable picture of health—not like a victim of the flu at all. "Come in" was all I could say—idiotically, since it came out in a whisper—and I stormed down the stairs, landing so hard from the bottom step that my ankles stung. I couldn't speak again for a moment. When I could, I said, "Come in!" again, louder this time, and threw the screen door wide open.

Orion shook his head. He continued his little shuffle on the stoop, glancing over his shoulder, and I saw there was a blue car idling in front of the house and that the doctor was behind the wheel, watching us with an unreadable expression. He waved at me when I looked his way. Embarrassed, deferential, I dropped my gaze and pretended I hadn't seen him.

"Why can't you come in?" I asked. "Why haven't you been in school?"

A sound came from Orion, more from his stomach than from his throat. I saw his vocal chords tense and his Adam's apple move, as if he were trying to form a word. "Muh," he said at last in a voice like gravel. "Mudder."

"Mother!" I exclaimed. "That's good! You can talk! But what about Mother? Is she all right?"

Orion sighed, but his expression was patient—the preternaturally calm patience of one who'd grown used to being misunderstood. He reached into the pocket of his hooded sweatshirt, pulled out a small memo pad and the stub of an old pencil, and began scratching something down. When he was done writing, he handed the pad to me.

I looked down at what he had written, in his characteristic printing, with the lines broken off at odd places:

Come for a ride with Dr Vanderwide
and me. Dr V is the man I'm staying with right
now. See him over there waiting
in the blue Lincoln? He will take us out
to see Mother. We will be back by six.

I couldn't have been thrown for a bigger loop if Orion had told me we were about to ascend into heaven. I felt different emotions—pure excitement, on the one hand, and terror on the other as I thought of my disastrous excursion with Leon and what it had cost me, what it had cost both of us. But since Orion was making the invitation and Mother was involved, I didn't see how I could refuse.

I would have given just about anything to see Mother.

"You aren't kidding, are you?" I couldn't help asking Orion.

He raised his eyebrows and shook his head soberly. His eyes shone black behind his glasses, with no hint of irony in them.

"All right, I'll come. But I'd better leave a note for Aunt Bernadine." I did not want to waste time telling Kevin or Wendell where I was going because they might try to waylay me, prevent me from going, or, worse still, say something snide to Orion's face: *So you're Medusa's brother, huh? The boy who doesn't talk?*

"Wait right here for a second," I said, still holding my brother's memo pad while I went into the kitchen and sought out a good pen. I racked my brain for the appropriate thing to write. I began writing words down, pausing only to remember how Orion had spelled the surname *Vanderwide* in *his* note, until I had composed the following:

I AM OUT FOR A DRIVE WITH MY BROTHER AND
DR. VANDERWIDE WHO HE IS STAYING WITH. I

WILL BE HOME BY 6 SINCERELY, ASTA HEWITT

I tore off the sheet of paper and left it in the center of the table, where it could not be missed. It was a craftily written communiqué, I thought, omitting any mention of Mother but including a mention of the doctor, whom Aunt Bernadine had once called a "muckety-muck" with envy in her voice.

I thought of Mother's matted bridal portrait, still leaning against my night table upstairs. Impromptu though this visit to Mother was, I did not want to greet her empty-handed, and I wondered if I could bring it with me as an offering; maybe she would view it in the same spirit as she would a present, something I'd picked out specially for her. "Be right back," I said to Orion through the door. "I have to get something from my room."

Upstairs, I hastily wrapped Mother's portrait in a bed sheet. By the time I came back downstairs Orion was sitting on the stoop, inspecting the first sign of a jack-in-the-pulpit that sprouted from the ground below the railing. He scarcely looked at me as I came out, but he did raise an eyebrow at the sight of my bundle.

"It's something for Mother," I said. "A surprise."

As I came down from the stoop (being careful not to let the portrait trip me up), the driver of the Lincoln Continental—Dr. Vanderwide—rolled down his window. "Hello! Do you need help with your package?" he said, and before I could answer he unwound his body from behind the steering wheel and took it from my hands. "I can put this in the trunk for you," he said, and did so without even asking what *this* was. I appreciated his discretion. He was even taller than I'd thought—taller than Leon, I was almost sure—and he had neatly clipped iron-gray hair, with a bald patch in the back that was about the size of my palm. He had a long upper lip, and his mouth turned up at the corners in what I thought might be a good-humored way. I made an effort to smile back at him.

"I'm Asta."

"It's awfully nice to meet you. I'm Peter Vanderwide," he said. "My wife and I are the ones taking care of Orion for the time being."

"Are you a doctor?"

"An ophthalmologist, actually—an eye doctor. But you don't have to call me Doctor if you don't want to. You can call me Peter."

I looked him up and down, taking him in—his long face, his clear eyes. "I think I'd like to call you Doctor," I said.

"That's fine," he said, opening the car's back door for me. "Go on, scoot in back. Orion, sit next to your sister."

Orion furrowed his brow.

"Sure I'm sure," the doctor replied as though my brother had questioned him out loud. "Everyone will think I'm your private chauffeur." He gave a laugh. "I'm a poet and I don't know it."

The memo pad and pencil stub came out of Orion's pocket again. On a fresh page he wrote, "But your feet show it. They're Longfellows," and held it up for the doctor to see.

I gathered this was a joke between them (though, frankly, I didn't get it; I hadn't a clue what a Longfellow was). Crawling into the backseat, I found it upholstered in leather so new it squeaked, and Orion squeaked right up close to me. From this proximity I could smell his freshly laundered sweatshirt and a shampoo that smelled of tart green apples.

"Seat belts, please," Dr. Vanderwide said. "Precious cargo."

I was thrown off by that, for neither Aunt Bernadine nor

Miss Shelton had ever asked me to put on a seat belt before. Orion helped me pull the belt over my lap and showed me how to insert the buckle.

"Orion, did you tell your sister about where we're going?" the doctor asked.

"Nuh-uh."

"All he said was *Mother*," I said, "but he wrote me a note."

The doctor chuckled. "Orion, *really*. Aren't you going to talk for your sister?" And then, to me, "He *is* talking now, you know—he's just gotten lazy. But it's such an interesting story— how Orion found his voice again."

Orion shrugged and pushed his glasses up on his nose. But his half smile told me that what the doctor had said was true.

As we rode through downtown St. Germaine, Dr. Vanderwide recounted the past two days' events for me. Orion had woken a couple mornings ago to the blare of his alarm clock, sat up in bed, and shouted, "Knock it off!" Not only was this the first thing he had said in weeks, but he had never in his life said anything quite that rude, either to a person or to an appliance. He shut off the alarm, went downstairs to the kitchen, where the doctor and his wife were eating Shredded Wheat, and remarked, "One of these days I want to try the kind that have frosting on one side. Don't you think those would taste better?" Dr. Vanderwide dropped his spoon into his cereal bowl. (I could picture it—his blue eyes bugging out with astonishment, the milk splashing onto his purple necktie.) Then Orion had said, "Do you think I could stay home from school today, Dr. V? All we're doing is memorizing the fifty states and capitals, and I already knew all of those when I was four."

Dr. Vanderwide's wife asked what he wanted to do with his time if he took the day off from school. "I want to stay home and read out loud," he said. "I think *Great Expectations* would be much more enjoyable read aloud."

Thus it was decided that Orion would stay home from school that day, and the doctor canceled his own appointments for the next forty-eight hours; he listened to Orion read aloud until his voice was a croak in danger of being extinguished again. Orion stayed up that night finishing the book silently and slept in late the following morning. When he woke up at midmorning (and discovered a new, unopened box of Frosted Shredded Wheat waiting for him on the table), Orion rather formally handed the doctor a note that had been written on a torn page from his spiral-bound notebook and waited for him to read it:

> The next person
> I talk to should be Mother. I will save my voice until
> I can see her. This isn't meant to be rude. It's just
> how she would want it. Maybe you can
> help me with this?

So Dr. Vanderwide made a series of telephone calls, eventually speaking to the woman who owned Sandy Harbor, and then to my mother, who laughed as the doctor told her Orion's story—sometimes even at parts that weren't meant to be funny, Dr. Vanderwide said—and when he had finished, she'd said, "Orion has always been the least talkative of my two children. I'm not surprised he took a vacation from talking. I'm sure it was a lovely respite for him."

Then Mother had spoken to Orion, and after that, an afternoon visit was set up. The owner of Sandy Harbor said she thought Mother was *ready* for such a visit. To hear Dr. Vanderwide tell it, Mother was more than ready—her delighted shrieking upon hearing of the proposed visit could be heard even when he held the receiver away from his ear.

"I'm sure she was just excited knowing she'd see Orion," I said. "She always liked him best. She used to go through Morning Recitations with him, and she told him a lot of things she didn't tell me."

"She said she wanted to see you too," the doctor said. "Why do you think we came and got you?"

"She wanted to see me? Really and truly?"

Out of the corner of my eye, I saw Orion nod in the affirmative.

"I've tried calling on the phone a couple of times, to try to arrange get-togethers between you and your brother. Your aunt said she would get back to me."

"She never even told me you called."

The doctor winced as though a sharp pain had flared up somewhere. "I'm sure she has her reasons," he said, "whatever they may be. Anyway. What's important is that the lady at Sandy Harbor said your mother could have company today, so long as we arrive at four. I hate to think of what might happen if we got there at three-fifty-eight or three-fifty-nine, don't you? But we won't—we're going to get there right on time."

I couldn't help sighing at this satisfying development. I settled back against the leather seats while Orion looked out his window, watching some construction workers who were engaged in the interesting business of digging a hole under a sidewalk. Dr. Vanderwide asked if anyone felt like singing, and he turned on the car radio. A female voice came warbling out of the speakers, and Dr. Vanderwide said, "That's Dolly Parton!" betraying the kind of excitement grown-ups usually reserve for more serious things, and turned the volume up. He sang along with the music in an enthusiastic if not entirely melodic voice: *Here you come again, lookin' better than a body has a right to* . . . To keep him company, Orion and I swayed in the backseat, and I hummed the chorus—or a series of notes that sounded something like it. A warm buzzing sound came out of Orion as he tried to hum too. I could not help thinking of how different this was from the last time I'd been in a car with Orion, listening to the squad-car radio just before being separated—and of how much better it was to be together again, singing all the way to where Mother was.

* * * * * * * * *

After a straight path down an isolated stretch of road, we made a sharp turn and ended up in a parking lot. An expanse of lawn began where the lot ended, and at the top of a hill, past the beginnings of a flower garden and a still-fallow vegetable garden, were two brown houses connected by a walkway. On the exterior, these were somber, unremarkable-looking houses; no one would have guessed they housed a woman as singular as my mother.

Dr. Vanderwide, still in chauffeur mode, helped me out of the Lincoln. He was moving more slowly now, his movements less spry, and his voice was gentler—he now had the kind of voice that Mrs. Mello, the school librarian, expected us to use. "That brown house on the right," he said, pointing, "is called Mama Bear. The bigger one on the left is Papa Bear. What do you think of that?"

"Why do they call them that?" I asked. "They don't look like bears at all."

"If you use your imagination, they look like two brown bears sitting side by side, don't you think? Some residents gave them those nicknames a long time ago, when the place was first set up."

Dr. Vanderwide led us along the footpath up the hill, from which I had a better view of the gardens and the thickets of trees enclosing the property. I was already plotting what I might do if Sandy Harbor were mine—if Mother and Orion and I moved in and made it our permanent home. If I lived at Sandy Harbor, I thought, I would make a tree house in those wooded areas and spend time in it whenever I got tired of being in Mama Bear or Papa Bear. I would come down sometimes and work in the garden, pulling up carrots and beets while making up movies about a farm girl in a sunbonnet—the sunbonnet was a *very* important detail, and it had to be calico.

Up past a thicket, a clear yet distant female voice rang out as if proffering an answer instead of asking a question: "Did you know that when I was born," the voice said, "I was as black as the ace of spades."

"Who's that?" I whispered.

Orion put a finger to his lips.

A picnic table sat at the top of the hill. A gaggle of women trickled out the back door of one of the houses and lit upon the table one by one. The biggest of the women, the one who'd waddled out first, went on talking in such an inflected way that I knew she meant to be overheard—desired it, even. "My father's reaction was priceless," she was saying. "He was a Southerner, and when he saw how dark I was he shot a hole in the ceiling that was so big we had to get it patched! It was a good thing I lightened up; otherwise we would have had *problems*."

"Eileen, you've got problems now," a black lady with a short, neat afro said. The other women laughed in a bawdy chorus, one laugh triggering a volley of others: *bwah-hah-hah.*

Every inch of me craned to find my mother among the women. She didn't seem to be present. Then there she was—sitting on the corner of the bench with her shoulders thrown back. Smiling, if not laughing, with the other ladies. Even from that distance I could see her toss her head back and curl her lip in a way I recognized well.

"Hmph!" I heard her say—more quietly than the big lady, but not by much. "What do you mean, you lightened up?"

"Why, Loretta, you know what I mean! I got lighter and lighter till I was almost as light as you!"

I had an urge to duck behind Dr. Vanderwide before Mother could see me—realizing that maybe I should have freshened my outfit or at least combed my hair before making this trip—but it was too late for that now. Even though Mother was caught up in the conversation, it would only be a matter of time before she noticed the three of us soldiering up the hill.

I sneaked a look at the black woman who seemed to be in charge; she was handing out single cigarettes to each of the women. I wondered if this was the Betty my mother had mentioned in her letter. "Your father sounds like an ignorant man," she said, passing a cigarette to Eileen. Then she gave one to my mother.

"Not ignorant, *intolerant,*" my mother said, now raising her voice so that (to use her own patois) she could be heard in the cheap seats. "All men have things they can't tolerate. My husband, for example, had musical intolerance. He could never have even the slightest hint of music in the morning; if you sing before 9:00 AM, someone close to you will die, and that's a known fact—but still I tried to buck it. He'd put his face flat into the pillow and *moan* in protest."

"With the way you sing? I don't wonder," the black woman who might have been Betty teased. She was now lighting everyone's cigarette, going from one woman to the next like an acolyte lighting a row of church candles. My mother didn't answer, but she gave a little nod of thanks when it was her turn. Her long black hair hung partly over her face. I couldn't tell what she was thinking, if she was thinking anything at all, as she adjusted the cigarette between her lips and cupped her hand around it to keep the wind from snuffing out the match.

We were close now, very close. Dr. Vanderwide coughed a little. Whether he did this on purpose as a way of announcing our presence or was overcome by the smoke, I couldn't tell; it alerted Betty, however, and she was the first to see us. Then there was a collective rustle of interest among the women, and one or two of them suppressed a giggle.

"There they are," Betty said as if she had been waiting all day. "Your visitors, Loretta."

Mother, who had just taken the first drag off her cigarette, got down from the picnic table and slowly straightened up. Her face signaled incomprehension as she looked from Orion to me to the doctor. She was wearing the type of sandals she called *thongs* and one of her old summer dresses, neither of which was quite in season; the dress was thin and exuberantly flowered, with useless belt loops hanging where a sash had once been. She attempted to push the dark hair out of her eyes and stared at us, hard.

"Don't you recognize us?" Orion spoke up. I jumped at the sound of his voice. It was rusty, out of practice, but the syllables were clear, and there was no mistaking his words.

My mother came to life, as if someone had plugged her in, and her frown stretched into a faint smile. She lifted her arms like someone about to signal an airplane; her bell sleeves slid down around her bony white elbows. "Of course I recognize you," she said. "You're my children." Then her arms fell back at her sides, as if she'd come unplugged again. Orion nudged me, and before I had much to say in the matter we were trotting toward the picnic table, leaving the doctor a few paces behind.

When we were close enough for her to reach out and grab, she dropped the cigarette in the grass and enfolded Orion and me in her arms as if she wanted to tuck us into her body for good. "Here you are," she breathed. She felt different, softer, from what I remembered. Even her smell was different. She smelled like an animal. She could have been anyone's mother, a wolf's or a fox's, as easily as mine.

"These are my children," she said in a murmur against the tops of our heads, as if saying it to herself and us only. "My children."

"I'm glad to see you," Orion said.

"Look at that. Them kids're so homely they're almost cute," someone commented. Another of the women, a wide-eyed, age-less-looking wraith with a bowl haircut, had crept forward until she was within reaching distance, and I saw that she was sur-reptitiously touching Orion's hair. "So soft. So soft," she crooned under her breath until Betty intervened and made her sit down again.

The wind rippled across the hillside. Mother, Orion, and I squinted and huddled closer together. All the women save for Betty were looking at us with hawkish interest now, puffing their cigarettes and squinting. Eileen, the big woman, took in a huge lungful of smoke and voluptuously blew it out in our direction.

My mother tried to speak, but she seemed to have a little of Orion's affliction—her words were mushy, her vowels and consonants colliding into one another, until Betty came to her rescue. "I'm Betty, one of the house mothers," she said, and she shook Orion's and my hand. Her own hand was brown, with immaculate white fingernails, and as she told us the names of the other ladies—most of whom didn't bother to nod or say hello as they were introduced—I obsessed over whether or not I had shaken her hand the right way; I had never shaken anyone's hand before except Leon's, and his had looked and felt so different. "I know your mother's been looking forward to seeing you," she said.

"Is Mother all right?" Orion asked in a low voice. "I mean . . . has she been all right?"

"She's doing just fine. Don't you worry."

I felt as if there were a veil draped over this exchange that I couldn't see through, and it frustrated me. Dr. Vanderwide was now speaking in a quiet way to Mother, his blue eyes fixed alertly and kindly on her. I heard Mother say, "His glasses look beautiful. I never knew he couldn't see well. I knew he liked to sit right up close to the TV set, but children do that, you know. You don't suppose it was the TV that damaged his eyes?"

"Oh, I doubt that," Dr. Vanderwide said. He said it in a very reassuring way, as a good doctor should.

"He always saw magical things. Now he'll see twice as many. He's a most exceptional boy."

"That he is."

I wondered when Mother would say something about me—something about me being exceptional too. But Betty preempted whatever she was about to say by thundering the words "Time's up, ladies!"—and one by one the women reluctantly got up from the picnic table. A few of those who were wearing shoes ground their cigarettes out with their heels. They began dawdling and shuffling back to the door from which they'd exited.

"Can we go in too, Mother?" Orion asked.

My mother passed the question on to Betty. "They can, can't they?"

"Of course," Betty said.

"Come on, Charlie. 'At's a good dog," I heard the woman with the bowl haircut say, falling in line behind the others and treating her hair to hard, evenly dispersed little pats from the heel of her hand.

"She must have an invisible dog," Orion whispered to me.

"It's not polite to whisper, children," Betty said over her shoulder.

"Sorry," Orion and I said, chastened.

We were the last to go inside. Betty took our coats from us. Then she turned to Dr. Vanderwide. For a few moments the two grown-ups engaged in small talk, their voices a bit higher and more lilting than they'd been moments before. Orion and I stood on the sidelines, too young to participate in this patter and politesse.

I watched Orion's eyes rove to every corner of the room, taking in every detail. "It's different from what I expected. I thought it was going to be like a hospital on the inside," he whispered to me, already forgetting Betty's admonition. "You know . . . white and clean." I didn't tell him I had been too busy conjuring up a tree house to give much thought to what the inside would look like. The place had the feel of a cottage or a lodge, with hardwood floors and high-beamed ceilings. The hallway had overflowing bookshelves, and on the walls were tacked-up drawings and poems that appeared to have been rendered by children. I paused to look at a drawing of a rainbow; above it, in red crayon bubble letters, someone had written the words

NO MATTER HOW HARD IT IS, NEVER FORGET
DON'T GIVE UP AND DON'T YOU QUIT!

At the bottom of the drawing, I saw "by Jo Ann" written in smaller bubble letters. My mother, I thought, would probably have something scathing to say about this attempt at verse; I could see Orion wrinkling his nose at it already. But Dr. Vanderwide said, "It's good to have a creative outlet—writing, drawing. Do you do art therapy here?"

"We do," Betty said, "although we call it recreation, not therapy. Most of the residents seem to get something out of it."

I saw my mother make a face that looked very much like Orion's. It was the most familiar thing I had seen from her thus far, and I found it encouraging. I had to bite my lower lip to keep from laughing, for Betty was all business, continuing her muted talk with the doctor, unaware of my mother's insubordination. Then Betty was striding down the hall, urging us to follow. "I'll show you your mother's room down here. You have gifts for the children, don't you, Loretta?"

"Yes," my mother said. The *s* had a little hiss to it.

It was strange to have this woman talking for my mother; I got the feeling that Mother didn't like it much. The mention of gifts reminded me of Mother's portrait, still in the trunk of Dr. Vanderwide's car. I went over to his elbow and whispered to him, and he nodded and cleared his throat again. "Asta has reminded me that I left something in my car," he said. "Go on ahead and show the children around while I go get it."

His departure was punctuated by a wail that issued from one of the rooms to our left. A short, moon-faced woman was framed in the kitchen doorway, hollering as if someone or something were pecking out her liver. Upraised in one of her hands, twirling in the air like a baton, was a wooden spoon liberally coated in what might have been cake batter. "That's just April," Betty said. "And that's Sandy with her. Sandy's the one who owns this place."

The woman named Sandy leaned against the kitchen counter. She smiled at us neutrally, revealing a brown spot on a front tooth. "Don't mind April," she said. "She's just excited. April, honey, put the spoon down before you make a mess, y'hear me?"

Mother, perhaps feeling the tension transmitting from Orion to me and back again, put a hand on top of each of our heads, and I felt a rush of love for her, for her protectiveness. "Nice to meet you!" Sandy called after us as we started back down the hall, but she seemed far away already—the farther, the better. I didn't know what I would do if the hobgoblin-like woman named April came after me with that dirty spoon. Mother kept her hands on us until we were well past the kitchen and approaching the door to her room. Betty followed us.

"Here it is—the place where they've kept me hidden all this time," she said with mock grandeur, gesturing inside. "This is what I see when I go to sleep at night and what I wake up to in the mornings. Now you can picture it too, when you think of me."

In Mother's room were a twin bed, a dresser, and an old roll-top desk whose top had long ago gotten stuck in midroll. Her dresser had nothing on it except a hairbrush, a toothbrush, and a small bottle of hand lotion. The walls were bare. I wondered how she could stand to live that way; it was so unlike her not to be surrounded by paintings or pictures. I was glad I had brought the bridal portrait along. It would give her something to look at just before nodding off to sleep at night. It would give her something to wake up to in the mornings.

Orion and I sat on her bed while Mother knelt and tugged at a wooden drawer that was built into the bottom of the bed. Betty was silently watching us from the doorway, her arms folded across her chest.

Mother's drawer came open at last. "I've made a couple of things for you both. Remember, it's the thought that counts. You first," she said, turning to me.

I was first! Would wonders never cease? "Close your eyes and put out your hands," she said. I felt something in my palms, and when I opened my eyes there were two bracelets of brilliant colors; one was electric pink and emerald green, and the other was midnight blue with alternating rows of gold, both made of plastic beads strung on a piece of elastic that knotted in a circle.

"They're beautiful," I said. *Delicious* might have been a better word. The beads looked so much like hard candy that I wanted to put them in my mouth, but I showed restraint and put them on my wrist instead, holding my bejeweled arm out for Mother to see.

"I picked the colors out myself," Mother said. "I picked green because that's a calm color, and I picked pink because it's the color of the fairies. I don't think it can hurt to have a few calm fairies around you—it's a nice variation on the usual flighty ones, isn't it? The blue and the gold—well, that's just regal."

Next was Orion's turn. While he closed his eyes, she placed a new model airplane, about six inches long, into his open palms. I murmured in approval before Orion had even seen it.

"Now I must admit," Mother said, "that I didn't make this myself—Sandy's husband does them in his spare time, and he gave me this one when he heard how much you liked them. It came from a kit."

Orion didn't say anything, but he didn't need to—he appeared transported for a moment. His face, already pink, positively reddened with gratitude at the sight of his present.

"So that's that," Mother said, giving the drawer a shove so that it slammed shut. "I'll show you the rest of the place. It's not so much to look at, but I'll show you. Orion, my darling, do you want to take your plane with you or leave it on the bed for now?"

"Take it with me," Orion said.

Dr. Vanderwide appeared in the doorway then. Handing the bundle off to Betty, he murmured something unintelligible before disappearing again down the hall. "What's this you sent the doctor out to get?" Mother asked. "Is it for *me*?"

"It's nothing much," I said, convinced all at once of the inferiority of my gift, but Mother was already unswaddling the portrait. Having removed the covering, she turned it right side up and studied the bridal portrait with pursed lips. "Who is *this* exquisite creature?" she asked.

"It's you!" Orion said, clapping his hands.

"Of course it's me," she said, holding it out for Betty to see. "Oh, heavens, see how my eyes look almost crossed? I remember not knowing if I was supposed to look at the photographer or off to the side. I tried looking sideways, thinking this would give me a more mysterious look, but one eye strayed back." She propped it up on top of her dresser and patted it once like an old friend. "Thank you, Pork Chop," she said to me. "How very thoughtful you are."

Orion clutched the plane to his chest and I caressed my beads as we continued down the hall past other doorways, other rooms

that looked like Mother's. Betty followed from a respectful distance, walking softly in her thick-soled nurse's shoes. Women
looked up as we passed their doors. Some of the women's eyes
held accusations in them. Most were simply blank. One thin
blonde lady was sitting at her desk, writing something—a letter,
I supposed. Another lay on her stomach on her bed, breathing
heavily through her mouth and reading a fat pink paperback.
The farther down the hall we got, the closer we came to a comforting TV noise and the welcome (if incongruous) predictabil-
ity of a laugh track. "That's the den," Betty said as we arrived at
a big room. To our surprise we saw Dr. Vanderwide sitting on
one of the den's two long couches, absorbed in a program.

"I was wondering where he went," Orion said, and the doctor—perhaps not as absorbed as he seemed, after all—waved to
us as we passed. My mother waved back. We passed another
large room that looked like a workshop area, with benches and
easels and shelves lined with color-coordinated storage bins;
it reminded me of my classroom at school, but less convincing, somehow—like a studio-set art room and not an art room
itself. "That's where we do our so-called recreation," Mother
said. "And down here's the kitchen—we walked past it already.
Through there's the dining room, where we have all our meals.
Come in and I'll give you some juice. Can I give them some
juice, Betty?"

"I don't see why not," Betty said.

"It's very good juice," Mother said in an affirming way, as
though the juice were not only tasty but also chockful of vir-
tue. "I've drunk it myself. It's not the least bit tainted with
anything."

The dining room had a checkerboard floor, a few round tables
surrounded by metal folding chairs, and one lonely-looking

refrigerator with a padlocked door. At a table near the entrance, the woman named Sandy was sitting in front of another woman who looked to be about my mother's age. Sandy's companion had a covered dinner tray in front of her, and as we brushed past, the woman lifted its lid, and steam that had turned to liquid rolled down the inside of it in a profusion; broccoli, my nose registered—I'd have known that medicinal smell anywhere.

"She has to eat early because of the medicines she takes," my mother said in a stage whisper. "Otherwise she's liable to go ape! She has poisons in her blood, and the medicines take them out . . . but the poisons always come back."

"It's not polite to whisper," I whispered back.

"Well, that rule doesn't go for me. I'm a grown-up. Aren't I lucky?" my mother said. She stopped at a table near the back of the room. "We'll sit here," she said. "I *always* sit here."

Orion and I pulled out chairs and sat.

Mother and Betty went over to the refrigerator, and after Betty had unlocked it, Mother deliberated at the open door for a while. She seemed greatly conflicted as she considered the options. While we waited for her to come back, I scooted my chair a little closer to Orion's and took his hand, a damp and solid little thing, and wrapped it around my own.

Mother came back with three small cans of pineapple juice. She had also brought paper-wrapped straws, which she must have gotten from one of the cupboards. Orion put his plane down in front of him like a place setting so that he could still see it while we drank our juice. We unwrapped our straws with great ceremony, and Mother leaned over and flipped the tops off our cans. "That makes me feel motherly," she confided.

It was peculiar to be sitting across a table from Mother in a strange place. (There was, however, something familiar about the presence of cans.) Betty stopped by our table, hands on hips, but did not take a seat. "What do you think of our humble dining room?" she asked.

"It's like the school cafeteria," Orion said. "Straws and everything."

"It is, isn't it? Do you take hot lunch at school?"

I shook my head. "Cold," I said.

"I have hot sometimes," Orion said. "Asta and I have different lunch periods. I try to get hot lunch if there's going to be pizza."

"And do you both like it there? At school?"

Orion and I looked at each other. "I don't know," I said and instantly hated myself for this diffident answer. I had opinions about school, but now Mother, who was obviously listening, would get the impression that I didn't.

"You probably will, in time," Betty said. She was already looking away from us, at the women on the other side of the room. "I'm going to see what Sandy and Naomi are up to," she said. "I'll be right over there if you need me." I glanced over to see for myself what the women were up to and locked eyes with Naomi, who was pulling a chunk of cartilage off a chicken wing. I looked away.

Mother drank her juice without saying much at first, the hollows under her cheekbones becoming more prominent as she sucked from the straw. She was thinner than she'd been when I'd last seen her; her wrists, under the billowy sleeves, were only slightly bigger than mine. We drank and looked at each other, the three of us, and put our cans down and picked them up again. "In the evenings, after dinner," my mother said, as if weighing each word, "people play cards in here. I've never liked cards."

"Me neither," I said loyally, forgetting all about the few games of crazy eights I'd played at Miss Shelton's house.

"I'm too big for this place. I oughta bust out of this joint," my mother said, sounding like Jimmy Cagney. "That's me, the big fish busting out of its small pond."

"I know," I said, giggling both at the image and at her impression.

"Do you know the story of Germaine Cousin?" My mother, who was stirring her juice with her straw, slipped back into her normal voice. "Of the girl who your school is named for, that is?"

I was stumped. After a beat, Orion said, "Germaine was a saint, wasn't she?"

My mother looked at Orion and smiled what I thought was a private smile. "I'll tell you," she said. She reached over and took Orion's other hand in hers, then took my free hand as well so that we were linked, the three of us, in the story.

"Germaine Cousin was a girl who lived in France a long time ago. She suffered from a disease called scrofula, which was just as ugly as it sounds—it used to be called the King's Evil in the Middle Ages. It made lumps form in your neck until you looked like you had swallowed a basketball."

"It sounds a little like the plague," Orion said.

Mother was looking from me to Orion, gauging our reactions. "Scrofula's not as fast acting. It doesn't kill you right away. To top it off, Germaine had a deformed hand—she had *all* the fun, didn't she? Her family, thinking her a discredit to them, made her sleep in a cupboard under the stairs, which I'm sure was a tight fit. When she wasn't holed up in there she was doing chores or being a shepherdess—I don't know what shepherdesses *do*, exactly, but I guess they watch sheep at least part of the time."

"They carry a crook," Orion offered.

My mother's eyes glittered with annoyance. She didn't like being interrupted. "Germaine was a shepherdess, like I said, and because of that some people called her 'The Girl with a Sheep' or 'The Girl with a Watchdog.' In light of her appearance, she could have been called so many worse things. One day the other villagers accused her of smuggling a stolen loaf of bread in her apron—but she hadn't stolen anything and was only being accused of it because she was so strange and ugly—so she dropped her apron to show that she hadn't hidden a loaf of bread in it at all; instead, hundreds of fresh flowers fell from the folds of the cloth. After that, some people referred to her as 'The Girl with Flowers in Her Apron.'"

That's nice, I thought; *I would like to be called that.* But I didn't say it for fear of sounding trite.

"I almost don't want to tell you the ending of the story, it's so sad." My mother gave a demure downward glance at her juice can.

"Go ahead," Orion said.

"You mustn't stop now," I said.

"It's sad but not sad at the same time. You see, the poor girl was found dead when she was still very young—scrofula got to her eventually, or maybe she'd received a bad thrashing; it was never very clear—so she was put in a pauper's grave. When the grave was accidentally dug up years later, her body was found without a mark on it—the bones in her hand were made good again, and her neck was smooth. I believe it was then that she was declared a saint. You see, there's a happy ending to it after all! It's a funny name for a school, though—Germaine Cousin."

"I like it," I said.

"Good. I thought you might."

My mother was wise. Even though I hadn't shared my feelings about school, she understood that I had occasional reservations about it; she knew this story would help me like it a little more. She smiled at me in the same way she had smiled at Orion before and dropped our hands to pick up her juice can. She finished it off with a noisy, tortured, agonized slurp. Orion and I followed suit, Orion holding out the sucking sound the longest.

"How are you doing over here?" Betty asked, reappearing at the table. "Catching up?"

"Oh, yes, on all kinds of lovely things," Mother said.

"Sandy said Naomi's getting distracted," Betty said in a lower voice. "It might be better if you and the children went to the den. Your doctor friend's in there."

"Fine," my mother said. "We're finished in here anyway." She pushed back from the table, leaving the cans behind. "Imagine," Mother said as we strode back down the hall, "we were *distracting* her! We should take that as a compliment!"

We veered to the right into the den. Dr. Vanderwide was still stationed on one couch, and an older, white-haired lady was on the couch opposite, wrapped up in a blanket and staring open-mouthed at the TV. I felt as if we were encroaching on her territory, stepping into her parlor uninvited, but she didn't even look at us as we came in, and Dr. Vanderwide motioned for us to sit next to him. The three of us lowered ourselves as unobtrusively as possible.

I Dream of Jeannie was playing. The titular genie, who was decked out in a gauzy pink costume, had turned a man into a poodle, with hilarious results: the man called Master had gone to the pound to rescue the poodle-man but had gotten mixed up and taken home a Great Dane instead. Every time the laugh track fired off, the woman on the couch across from us added her own laugh a few beats too late—her mouth fell open a little wider and her whole body shook, but no sound came out. About halfway through the episode, she got up and left, sighing and gimping along as though she were doing a terrible chore. Dr. Vanderwide moved to the other couch, giving us more room to spread out.

It was just the three of us again—Orion a warm, solid figure on my far left and Mother between us, her elbows propped on her knees and her chin in her hands, her smile deepening as Jeannie became more and more flustered.

"The only thing I'm going to miss about this place when I leave," Mother said, to no one in particular, "is this TV set. The picture quality's better than what we have at home."

"When are you leaving?" Orion asked.

My mother looked foggy for a minute, then regained a bit of her effulgence. She shook her head from side to side in a way that I sometimes did when I had a bad dream—a lucid dream— and wanted to wake from it. "I don't know. Soon, I hope," she said and looked back at the TV screen. "Watching this TV, you could almost think you're at the cinema. Say—do you know what I'd like to do more than anything in the world?"

"What?"

"I'd love to take you children to a movie. There's a theater in the town square. Have you been down there? There's a bank, and a post office, and a couple of boutiques, and there's the the-ater, which is one of the oldest buildings in town. You don't see too many like it anymore. It was done in a Greek Revival style, with marble and granite columns on either side of the marquee. And the marquee is always illuminated—always."

"What is it like on the inside?" I asked.

"Let's see," my mother said. "There's movie posters on every wall and a ticket booth in the corner—right over there—" she said, pointing to an imagined spot in the distance, "and across the lobby there's a concessions stand where popcorn pops, and the whole place seems to bathe in a buttery light."

Beyond us, in the hall, the large, outspoken woman we'd seen outside—Eileen—was lumbering past. I couldn't imagine what had transpired between her smoking break and now, but Eileen seemed different—she was breathing heavily and muttering with each step she took, and her broad face was florid with exertion. She didn't seem to know, or care, that anyone was watching her. I looked away, holding my breath until she had passed by.

My mother got up and switched off the TV. The silhouette of Jeannie lingered on the screen for a split second after the color had drained out.

"Betty!" my mother called out. "Betty! We want to go to the movies!"

Betty appeared in the doorway, looking nonplussed. "You want to what?"

"We want to go to the movies," I said, emboldened by my mother. "Can we, Betty? Can we?"

"It's close enough that we could walk," my mother cajoled. "And there's plenty of time. All the time in the world!"

"Maybe some other time," Betty said. She hurried down the hall after Eileen.

My mother reached out for us and whispered, "Sit closer to me, children. Sit closer." She put an arm around each of us, pulling us in. My head went into her armpit, Orion's into the curve of her neck

"Let's pretend we're at the movies," Mother said. "We're standing in front of the ticket counter, buying tickets. There's an old lady behind the counter, licking her fingers, thumbing off four tickets—one for each of you, and one for me, and one for the good doctor over there."

I closed my eyes, and after a while, the uniformed old lady appeared in my mind. "I see her!" I said. "She's asking us if you're our mother."

"Why yes, I am—thank you for asking!" my mother cried out. "These two are my children. Asta and Orion." She stroked my hair as she said my name.

"I'd like to go over to where they make the popcorn," Orion said dreamily. "Not only does it make the room bathe in a buttery light, but I think it might make the room *smell* like butter besides."

From the opposite couch Dr. Vanderwide laughed a little. "You're right about that," he said.

"I see a teenage boy behind the popcorn stand," Orion went on. "He's filling up a bag that's as big as my head."

"Goodness gracious," Mother said. "I suppose I'll have to tell *him* that you're my children too. And what about that girl in the vest, standing in front of the theater entrance, taking tickets to make sure no one sneaks in?"

I closed my eyes even harder until I could see the girl, right down to her wavy brown hair, her paper cap, and her name badge that said KATIE. "I know what will happen next," I said. "She'll take our tickets and then I'll say, 'Did you know this is our mother?' She'll smile and say, 'Is she the best mother in the world?' And we'll say, 'Yes, she is.'"

"I think the girl is thrilled to see such a family as us."

"Can we go inside the theater now?" Orion asked.

"It's going to be very dark in there," Mother said. "I don't want you to be scared. There'll be shadowy figures when you first walk in, but you mustn't let them bother you—it's just the people who got there first and already took their seats."

All at once I felt the air in the room change, as if there'd been a clap of thunder. My eyes were closed, but I sensed it had grown even darker. It took me a few seconds to realize that Dr. Vanderwide had flicked the light switch off; opening my eyes to a squint, I saw his long shadow on the wall across from us. In that moment I loved him a little bit.

"Now, it's dark," Mother said, "but not *entirely* dark, for there are little rows of footlights—lights where the carpeting meets the walls, creating a reddish-yellow path. The shadowy figures will watch us as we make our way to the front, picking seats right up close to the screen."

"I think I hear the movie getting ready to start," Orion said. I couldn't resist peeking at him for a second. His eyes were closed—he had made his own darkness—and his eyelashes twitched against his cheekbones in a spirited little dance. "I see colors lashing out against the screen."

"And I hear sounds," Mother said. "Beautiful sounds that crash from one end of the theater to the other."

Across the room, someone cleared her throat, and the fluorescents buzzed before flooding with light.

"Next time," Betty said gently, her hand still on the switch.

"Next time what?" Orion wanted to know, opening his eyes.

"Next time you visit," she said, "we'll arrange for you to go to the theater in the town square. We'll have to plan it in advance."

But it didn't matter anymore. We pressed closer to Mother

and shut our eyes again until we were back in the theater, and the movie was starting. It would be a movie, I thought, about us—our complete family—restored to perfection.

I don't know how long we sat like that, but after a while Betty reminded us of the time. I'd written in my note that I'd be home by six, so we all got up reluctantly—except Dr. Vanderwide, who had slunk out of the room when Betty reappeared and was now meandering around the bookcase by the hall, pretending to look at the *Guinness Book of Records*. He rejoined us as we tracked Sandy down and bid her good-bye; she gave us our coats and said, "I hope we'll be seeing you again before too long."

"No question," Dr. Vanderwide said. "It was nice to meet you and Betty. And you too, Mrs. Hewitt. Children," he said, turning to us, "I'm going to wait outside for you while you say good night to your mother. Take your time."

Mother began walking us slowly to the door, an arm encircling each of us. "Do you have to stay here?" Orion asked.

"For now," Mother said. "But let's do this again. It meant so much having you here for a little while. We'll do it again *soon*. We'll make it happen, won't we?"

"Maybe tomorrow," Orion said.

"Maybe next week," Sandy revised.

My mother shot a look over her shoulder at Sandy and lowered her voice. "Next week, yes. We've got to make things happen. We mustn't reduce ourselves to being *mere witnesses*. Sometimes, here, I do feel like one—like someone who does nothing but *watch* things."

"That's where we come in," I said. "We'll do things with you."

"I would like that. So, so much."

My mother kissed Orion and me quickly, and Sandy held open the back door for us. "And remember what I said," Mother called out—to me, I felt certain—as Sandy put a hand on her shoulder and they watched us from the threshold. "About the girl with the flowers in her apron. Remember that!"

"Yes, Mother," I said. "We will."

The door seemed to vibrate behind us after it shut. It was only then that I realized we had been separated from Mother again—at least for the time being. But the doctor had called it *good night*—not good-bye—so maybe that's all it was: a good night, our first in a long while.

"Good night, Mother," I said, whispering to the door.

Orion and I didn't move from the stoop for a few seconds, watching the door to see if it might pop open again. When that didn't happen, we waited to hear footfalls on the other side— for any proof that Mother's life went on without us when we weren't there to witness it. We began to walk away, and I cast one last look over my shoulder. I caught sight of her shadow passing by the curtain with her chin tilted up in the pose she called REFLECTION. In the room she'd entered, a small light came on: the unmistakable light of a TV set, burning steadily in the window.

Then Orion and I remembered Dr. Vanderwide, who was at the foot of the hill, waiting for us.

He waved and started coming up to help us through the dark. "Let's reach him before he reaches us," Orion said, making it sound like a dare, so we quickened our pace. Halfway down was where we met each other. Then down the hill we went, the rest of the way, together.